THE
BOOK
of
AGNES

Pedretti, Michael 1942
–story of our stories: /pedretti

This book is sold subject to the condition that it shall not, by way of trade or otherwise be lent, hired out, re-sold, or otherwise circulated without the publisher's prior consent in any form of binding or cover other than that in which it is published and without a similar condition including this condition being imposed on the subsequent purchaser.

Written 1990 -1995
Copyright 2021

Print ISBN 978-1-7374165-0-0

I would like to first and foremost thank the mothers who time and time again planted seeds instead of discord; steering the sons away from war, violence and thievery. *The Book of Agnes* is dedicated to my mother whose life inspired these stories.

I thank Dennis Hamilton, Mary Ellen MacLaughlin, Christine Magnuson, Leo Pedretti, Susan Reindl-Thierman, and Nicole Waite-Sudhoff, who provided valuable feedback and multiple corrections on early drafts of this work. I would like to especially thank my wife, Nancy B. Hill, and daughter, Victoria Pedretti, who graciously allowed me the time to write and provided moral support when I needed it.

This is a work of fiction. Names, characters, business, events and incidents are the products of the author's imagination. Any resemblance to actual persons, living or dead, or actual events is purely coincidental

The cover photograph is from a vintage photograph collected by Berna Dean Howly and now a part of the Karen Woodhouse Historical Genoa Collection.

Busting Boundaries, Williamsburg, VA

MICHAEL PEDRETTI

THE
BOOK
of
AGNES

A novel about the extraordinary
life of an
extra ordinary mother

Book IX of a 12 part series titled

The Story of Our Stories

"As I read Michael Pedretti's book *The Book of Agnes* I wanted to laugh, cry, cringe and applaud. **This is a great book**. It stirs emotions and leaves you in awe of the advances made in the twentieth century. To me, Agnes was alive in my head and in my heart...This is a book I shall remember for years to come and I couldn't give it less than five stars."
Review by Lucinda E Clarke

"This book tells the tale of an extraordinary woman who is a mother above all else. The narrative was fast, the plot was interesting...The author kept the interest of readers alive, making them invest in Agnes' progress. You will make a connection with her, and you will feel like a part of The Book of Agnes!"
Review by Rabia Tanveer

"Michael's use of imagery is superb. He is truly a wordsmith. The story shows the life of a typical American rural family during the first part of the twentieth century. This is a fast-moving story of life. It seems as if time flies from the '20s until 1963. Heartbreak, financial struggles, emotional issues, illnesses, and more will draw you into the story as if you are there experiencing life yourself."
Review by Daniel D Staats

Contents

Preface vii

Introduction ix

Prelude 3

I: Water 9

II: Earth 85

III: Fire 137

IV: Air 203

Coda (2021) 251

Put what back in Christmas? 253

Appendix 261

Mary Caroline Nicolatti 262

Synopsis of *The Story of Our Stories* 270

I celebrate myself, and sing myself,

And what I assume you shall assume,
For every atom belonging to me as good belongs to you.

- Opening lines from "Song of Myself" by Walt Whitman

THE STORY OF OUR STORIES

Preface

It is possible that as many as 115 billion people were born before us. But you and I have each had more than one hundred billion ancestors since the first settlers arrived in the Valley of San Giacomo in Sondrio, Lombardy, Italy, around 840 AD. If you trace our ancestry back to the time of Caesar, each of us would have to identify more than 288 quadrillion grandparents or 288 million billion ancestors. If you would like to fill out your family chart dating back to the biblical Eve born around 4,004 BC, you would have to identify seven times as many people, or 1.6 to the 57th power. What if we go back to the year of Lucy?

You get the idea. There is no way, with that many ancestors, that you and I do not share a few billion of the same grandparents, making us not double cousins, not cousins tens of thousands of times, but cousins more than a billion times over. Our genes are so intertwined that we are closer than brothers, closer than sisters, maybe even as close as twins. Yes, you and I, we are cousins—we are of the genes of Mitochondrial Eve, and we share the same genes as billions of her children.

The Story of Our Stories is our story. These tales are as much your tales as they are mine. "We have lived them together, we are living them together, we will live them together." We are not only twins, you and I; we are joined at the heart. To quote Walt Whitman, "Every atom belonging to me as good belongs to you."

According to Adam Rutherford, a genetics expert and author of *A Brief History of Everyone Who Ever Lived,* "All Europeans are descended from exactly the same people. Everyone (living in Europe) alive in the tenth century who left descendants is the ancestor of every living European (including Americans of European descent) today."

- p 165

THE STORY OF OUR STORIES

Introduction

"I sing of arms and man"
—Virgil, The Aeneid

"I sing of kindness and woman"
—Pedretti, *The Story of Our Stories*

    The mandate for an epic is to identify and celebrate who the people are and what their potential is. In Homer's and Virgil's eras, the epic hero was a male warrior whose violent behavior led to victories that inspired loyalty, patriotism, and submission to the ruling class. "I sing of arms and man," is the opening line of Virgil's poem about a brutal warrior who begets a bellicose Rome and the ancestors of the combatant Caesar Augustus. His epic celebrated empire builders, encouraged retaliation, and downplayed the massive cost of lives, enforced slavery, and legalized classism.
    Should the modern epic celebrate dominance, war, and revenge? Will today's epic promote limitation, exclusion, and restriction? Is it not possible to put the historic, gentry-sponsored classism, war, violence, and tribalism into the past? Isn't today's hero the commoner, making things happen by mass commitment rather than individual supremacy—more interested in planting seeds than in accumulating power, in making advancements rather than blowing up people, tradition,

and peace—more willing to fight for fair treatment with words than domination by war—more concerned with kindness than control—capable of letting empathy replace revenge? Today's epic hero is a planter: one who plants and cultivates; one who plans and nourishes. Our hero has no power or desire to raid the work of others. Our hero cannot come from the privileged class—by definition a people who rely on other's plantings to harvest their successes. Our story is not the story—cannot be the story—of someone indulging in the unjust wealth born of another's labor. No, our story is hidden in the mothers, "who long since left the shores of craving, supremacy and war to explore generosity, affection, and creativity." Come; join me in play, kindness, and song:

> I sing of kindness and of woman
> Serf no more, never Lord
> And of the suffering they endured
> Trodden under the might of the Sons of Misogyny
> Those ministers of misery who maltreated our mothers
> Turning brother against sister, husband against wife,
> Parent against child, mother against mother.
> Tell me, reader, how it all began, why so much spite?
> What did our mothers do to deserve their vengeance?

In The Aeneid, Virgil celebrated the Roman conqueror; I celebrate the planter of seeds. Virgil celebrated war; I celebrate harmony. Virgil celebrated dominance; I celebrate parity. Virgil praised father Augustus; I praise mother Eve.

The Story of Our Stories is the story of Marianna and Petronella, Peter and John, Adelaide and Stefano, and Agnes and her children. It is about the individuals who populated the Mount of San Bernardo in Northern Italy and who turned the roughness of Badaxe, Wisconsin into the gentleness of Genoa; but first and foremost it is our story, the story of you and me. Our story is written as an epic composed of twelve books, each with a supportive appendix. Each book covers a different story. Some cover the life of a typical family member of a specific generation; others reflect many people of a generation; another traces the entire story from beginning to now; and one looks into a future predicated by the behavior of our mothers. Each volume tells a critical part of the story, is an integral part of the whole, and plays into the unfolding of the epic. While part of a whole, each book can be read independent of the rest.

The Story of Our Stories

An epic told in twelve volumes

1. *Time to Journey Home*—Read about the author's journey to discover an epic tale that defined who we are and that helps us find a moral compass.

2. *The Veneid*—Meet our mothers, going back to Mitochondrial Eve.

3. *Begetters of Children*—Track our epic family from 840 to 1951.

4. *Lost Book of Maria Prima della Morte*—Listen to a mother who was strong before her time (1758-1817).

5. *L'Ultima Preghiera*—Relive Teresa Cerletti's life (1805-1853) on the San Bernardo mountainside through her final prayer.

6. *Lettere d'Amore*—Join Stefano and Adelaide's love journey to the new world (1853-1855).

7. *The Diary of Giovanni Vener; An Immigrant's Journey to the Heart of America*—Discover an immigrant's life and insights by reading his private diary (1899).

8. *Peter, a Profile*—Meet the transitional master planter (1861-1951).

9. *The Book of Agnes*—Follow the deeds of one of Walt Whitman's "unknown heroes equal to the greatest heroes known!" (1922-1963).

10. *Hoe-ers*—Remember the good old days (1924-1995) told by thirteen siblings (1924-1995). (Thirteen may become the new lucky number.)

11. *Mick, Ponderings of a Planter*—Plan and plant with the author, from seeding cornfields and milking cows to making theater to producing international theater festivals to writing this epic.

12. *Il Lavoro di Artisti*—Delight in the visual imagination of the children of the children of Agnes.

THE BOOK *of* AGNES

"The man's body is sacred and the woman's body is sacred,
No matter who it is, it is sacred"
—Walt Whitman, "I Sing the Body Electric," Leaves of Grass

Walt Whitman had Agnes in mind when he paid homage to "the numberless unknown heroes equal to the greatest heroes known."

From *Song of Myself*:

With music strong I come, with my cornets and my drums,
I play not marches for accepted victors only, I play marches for conquer'd and slain persons.
Have you heard that it was good to gain the day?
I also say it is good to fall, battles are lost in the same spirit
In which they are won.
I beat and pound for the dead,
I blow through my embouchures my loudest and gayest for them.
Vivas to those who have fail'd!
And to those whose war-vessels sank in the sea!
And to those themselves who sank in the sea!
And to all generals that lost engagements, and all overcome heroes!
And the numberless unknown heroes equal to the greatest heroes known.

-Walt Whitman, "Song of Myself," Leaves of Grass

Prelude

It was an extraordinary forty years in the life of an extra ordinary woman. It all began on a rainy fall afternoon on September 29, 1923 when a spirited sperm struck pay dirt attaching to an ovulating egg at the homestead on Moundridge just outside of Badaxe, Wisconsin. It culminated forty years later, when Agnes' seventy-third offspring was carried up Zaboglio Hill Road to St. Francis' Church for a familial ritual of having an esteemed man of the community (robed in a black dress with a white blouse and a red, yellow and purple silk stole) pour a little specially-prepared water on "seventy-three's" quivering forehead while mumbling some words of which the witnesses could pick out only "baptize" "name" "the" "Son" and "Holy Ghost."

On that humid early summer afternoon when Agnes' ripe, ready, fertilizable egg successfully attracted William's lone and lonely but wildly lucky sperm, there were only a handful of folks who owned a car, and they often got stuck in muddy dirt roads; the first commercial flight across the Atlantic was more than fifteen years in the future, but not to worry—you could cross the Atlantic in only one month on a relatively newfangled steamship!

Indoor plumbing was a rarity in rural communities; Agnes and William would not get electricity installed in their house for another decade, but some folks in urban areas were already wired. William and four of his brothers, along with three neighbors, had started to save money to purchase the first gasoline engine tractor, a Hart-Parr, that they would have to crank-start for the next thirty-five years; thus slowly replacing the horse.

Badaxe's phone service was provided by a local company, but a recent deal with the monopolistic Wisconsin Telephone Company meant it was possible, although expensive, to place a call to most places in the state if you needed to communicate quickly outside the local phone district. William and Agnes, like most rural customers, shared a party line with eight neighboring households. In Badaxe City some folks only had four other households on their line. Few could afford to use the telegraph machine in Zaboglio's store, but it was there in case a really important emergency came up. Transatlantic phone calls were a thing for the future. Mail was the preferred way to send a message even to your neighbor. KDKA had the first public broadcast only three years prior and the first signal that would reach Badaxe was still a couple of years into the future. American farmers used about 20,000 horses to produce the power necessary to farm.

Forty years later, you could fly to any city in the world in a few hours, drive one of your two cars 65 to 90 miles an hour across America on super highways; enjoy indoor running water, toilets, showers; turn on with a flip of a switch electric lights, and most people had electric stoves, refrigerators, freezers, radios, TVs, and some even had air conditioners. You could hold a private phone call with nearly anyone in the world. The use of horses to farm had plummeted by more than 80%; farmers had two or more tractors, milk machines and a hay baler; the grain output per acre jumped from less than 10 bushels to well over 20 bushels, and the number of livestock in America more than doubled and has been holding steady since.

If I were to state that never has the world seen so much improvement in four decades, you could not accuse me of hyperbole. As you read about Agnes' fertile years, you would do well to occasionally envision these incredible changes taking place around her. You would also do well to fill in the voids and gaps in her story that we could not tell without writing a one hundred thousand page book.

Reader, I'm going to let Agnes tell her own stories—not in her own words but in her own activities—no added drama—no need for me to create conflict or suspense because her story is too powerful and too rich to enhance—too pure to tamper with. It was an extraordinary 40 years in the life of one woman's gentle manner, kindness, and fertility. Her story is our story and none of us want some itinerant storyteller making it up as he goes along.

My billion ancestors, I ask you to bear witness that I have simply described her days as she lived them.

Come; meet the archetypical person Walt Whitman had in mind when he called for a shout-out for an unknown hero "equal to the greatest heroes known!"

I

WATER

8 The Story of Our Stories

I: Water
(1924 -1933)

The Vow

She wanted to be a nun, to give in the beginning her life to Jesus Christ, to be celibate, to cover her body in black, to hold her head bowed in obedience, and to teach youth to love the Savior and to read and write.

But on November 15, 1922 Agnes came to the altar—not to wed her Lord, but to join in matrimony with William Genotti—the second oldest living son of the town patriarch, Peter Genotti. Her eyes fixed on the ray of sunlight cast on the chalice that held the Body of Jesus before her on the altar of St. Francis' Church when Father asked, "Agnes Marie Veneri, do you take William Charles Genotti to be your lawful wedded husband?"

She envisioned herself, her eyes shining, her cheeks rosy, saying goodbye to her mother who was in tears, her dad, dressed in his Sunday best, driving the team out of the yard, down Highway 56 and turning not left toward St. Francis, but right toward the convent in LaCrosse. Agnes had never been to LaCrosse, but she knew it was a big city more than fifteen miles away, and she knew you could reach it if you rode long enough.

"I think I had this dream before I can remember," Agnes thought as she watches her dad and herself ride along a vast stretch of the great Mississippi River in absolute silence. Her dad looks stern—upset, no doubt, at losing his oldest worker. The convent appears; the setting sun behind it gives a halo that assures Agnes that she is meant to give herself to Jesus and to strive for sainthood through a life of sacrifice.

The Mother Superior, seeing Agnes come, greets her with open arms—hugs her and leads her off to the dark, secret passages of the convent. She looks at her dad, wanting to kiss him, but he looks so stern, so disappointed, she cannot.

She walks through the sun-filled arch with a fullness of heart and a complete willingness to sleep on cement floors—eat bread and water—pray twenty hours a day and be silent for thirty days and thirty nights, if that is what preparing to be a nun requires. No girl longed more for her dream than Agnes.

"I do," she said.

Kiss Me Now

The wedding reception held in the basement of St. Francis was over. William and Agnes drove in their wedding carriage up Highway 56 toward the house which they were about to share with Peter and William's siblings. Agnes stared at the hoofs of the pair of horses that trotted ahead of them. She gazed to the left as they passed the only place she had ever called home as the road rose before them. She was glad William was silent as she had no doubt what he had on his mind, and she wanted nothing to do with it. As much as she prepared her mind and body for the moment, she prayed that some catastrophe would befall them to postpone the moment she would feel forced to be naked before a man. She had practiced several times over the past month. She undressed in the corner of her room with her back to the bed. She tested out getting in bed fully clothed and dared to imagine William would respect her and allow her to sleep. She undressed in the next bedroom and put on a robe and snuck into her own room to surprise William by unrobing—completely naked under her robe. She immediately felt dirty and thought William might think, "She is a slut." Or something worse; Agnes was not sure what was worse. Maybe William would gently undress her or better say let's wait a week. None felt right, and she played each scenario again through her head as William unannounced turned the team to the right and drove them down the now abandoned road that once led to where his grandparents had lived. Agnes froze. William called for the team to stop as they approached the creek near the now crumbling log cabin where William had been born.

"Agnes"

Silence.

"Agnes, I guess you are scared. I know I am." Longer silence. William extends his right hand to Agnes. She makes like she does not see him as she stares up the creek. Silence. William leaves his hand extended for what seems like an hour or two. Agnes cannot ignore him so she lays her palm in his. They often held hands so it felt familiar and comforting but it also felt wildly different for this touch was not leading to the same conclusion of any past touch.

I'd like to kiss my wife," William whispered as his hand squeezed hers a little harder. Agnes' glaze stayed fixated on the water flowing smoothly down the creek on its way to the Mississippi River. She felt William's eyes. "I want this, just as much as he does," she thought, but still her eyes and their home did not—maybe could not—turn to William's.

"Come on; let's take a walk down to the creek." Certainly it was William's voice. He steps out of the carriage and walks around the rear to her side. As he does, she turns to her right to await his hand to help her step down. They walk hand in hand the half dozen steps to the bubbling creek. Agnes has never heard the creek run so loud. William leads her one-half step ahead and wraps his arms about her waist. He waits for her to lean her head into his which she does in good time. Horse, buggy, creek, the wind, William and Agnes pause as if the moment needs more time. William slowly but firmly turns Agnes toward him so their eyes lock, then closes as their lips move softly toward each other. Both know this is Agnes' first kiss, but only William knows it is also his first. Agnes' fear melts in the tender hold and warm kiss that lasts longer than either meant. William terminates the kiss moving only his head away enough to look at his new wife. Agnes feels as if his stare is penetrating hers, and she discovers to her surprise that she likes it. As if on cue, they both beam a blush followed by a smile that gently turns into a titter. William kisses her again and again. Hand in hand, they walk back to the now impatient horse and William helps Agnes into the carriage.

That night, after William finished milking the cows, the family gathered in the living room. No one said much and after three minutes Peter told the rest of his children that it was time for bed. Agnes was not sure if they all left immediately because they were embarrassed, or they were scared not to do what her new father-in-law demanded. Peter waited until his children were gone, then he stood up and said "Good Night." Agnes thought he winked at William, but then decided she just imagined he had. William slid over and lifted his arm around Agnes and said, "Let's imagine that the creek is running by where that old carpet is." She smiles up to him and their lips pick up where they had left off. After a few more kisses,

William stands up, offers his hand to Agnes, and leads her to the back stairwell which will take them to the bedroom that he has prepared for the evening and that they will share until William can make the house on his newly acquired farm just over the ridge ready for them.

The Calling

Agnes' mother often told the story when Agnes was three years old she had dressed up in a black gown and told anyone who would listen that she was going to be a nun. Agnes was not sure if this story was true or just something her mother made up. What she did know is that she could not recollect when she first decided she wanted to be a nun—it dated before her memory. Even before she went to first grade, she had daydreams of teaching young people to love God and to learn to read and write.

Agnes, born in a farm brick house a stone's throw from Badaxe City in Badaxe County in Wisconsin, was the firstborn of Northern Italian parents whose parents had found the bluffs of western Wisconsin forbidding enough to remind them of the Alps of their youths. Shortly after arriving in Badaxe, both sets of her grandparents had cleared the hillsides and started dairy farms in places meant for other things. When Mary Margaret Veneri gave birth to her first child, she felt relieved it was a girl. She knew if it were a boy, her husband Thomas Bartholomew would never allow him to help in the house, garden, or with the chickens let alone to help raise the rest of the children. Mary Margaret had seen her Aunt Orsola give birth to four boys before she had a girl to help her. Now, barely thirty, she looked more like she was turning fifty. Mary Margaret knew how important it was for the eldest to be a girl, and she thanked God for sending her one. She christened her Agnes—for Agnes meant pure and chaste. Maybe she would stay a virgin long enough to help raise the dozen or so children Mary Margaret could expect to have. She needed help, and she looked at Agnes, only one week old, as her primary helper, and she hoped she'd stay pure and help out until she was in her mid-twenties, even thirty. To be so lucky.

It is fair to say that life in Badaxe Township in 1903 was very much like it was in 1853 which was very much like life had been for her Northern Italian ancestors for a thousand years before Grandpa Giovanni immigrated to Badaxe fifty years before Agnes was born. There were certainties that became part of her before she can remember—Jesus was God, women raised the children, cooked, raised a garden, gossiped and took care of the chickens, men took care of the animals, sin was bad and mortal sin could lead to burning in hell forever, girls became wives or nuns, boys were trouble, sex was bad, hay had to be made before the rain came, the world was divided into Catholics and non-Catholics and it was best if they never met, God made the world and man invented sin, rhythm was the only acceptable form of contraception, learning was good but too much learning was dangerous, lunch was dinner and dinner was supper, pride and vanity were to be avoided at all costs, wives should obey their husbands, husbands should love their wives, children were better seen than heard, barns were painted red, if the farm was prosperous the women in the family could get new Easter outfits, if not all should settle for a new "Easter bonnet."

In her most frequent daydream, Agnes saw herself in black—only her face seen by the world. Her hair, her ordinary body, hidden beneath the black robe of a nun. Only Jesus would see her when she took a bath or prepared for the day. She dreamed of waking to the quiet of a parish convent, kneeling in silence to Jesus—getting dressed—going to Mass before the priest—eating breakfast in silence. It was a life to dream about—not so much a life of sacrifice as a life of quiet and solitude for she was the oldest of nine children and the noise of her younger sisters and brothers was less than peaceful. She often wanted to spend a moment or two alone, but her brothers and sisters or mother were always there.

At age eight, Agnes had two sisters and three brothers to care for. She rose each morning at five o'clock, washed a load of clothes and made breakfast with her mother. Breakfast began with a prayer by her mother and was followed by Agnes and her mother washing the dishes followed by Agnes walking the mile to school that began promptly at eight. She walked home arriving at three and cleaned the kitchen from dinner, set the table for supper, helped her mother with the chickens, fed her brothers and sisters, washed the dishes and was in bed by nine.

Her father, who knew what a prize Agnes was, would remind her from time to time how she could do more and how lazy she was. "Daydreaming again, Agnes, you are so lazy. I don't know where you get it because your mother sure ain't lazy."

Still, she dreamed. No one could take away her dream. She saw herself going off to LaCrosse to study. Her eyes sparkling, her cheeks rosy. After a long ride to LaCrosse the convent appeared; the setting sun behind it. The Mother Superior, hearing Agnes come, greeted her with open arms—

hugged her and took her off to the dark secret passages of the convent. Even in her daydreams, Agnes could not conjure up a picture of the convent as no one was allowed in except those prepared to take the vows of chastity, obedience and poverty. The dream had many variations—but it always ended with her walking through the sun-filled arch.

Scary Egg

"Your dad is one scary egg—If he were my dad, I'd run away."

"Yea, where'd you go?"

"I don't know—he scares the bejesus out of me, I do not know how you get by."

Agnes was quiet, not because she did not know how she got by, but because she was not sure she wanted to say anything to Mary Ann, who was known to be unable to keep a confidence. Forty times Mary Ann, who was Agnes' best friend, challenged Agnes to run and thirty-nine times Agnes changed the subject. But today, she blurted it out. "I am going to the convent. Mom will get behind me—she really wants a nun in the family. I am doing it this week. I am telling Dad I am going to the convent—I'll ask him to drive me. Mom will be so happy. I think Dad will be proud. And I will be gone sooner than a bark whistles. That is how I survive—knowing my day is coming. I just have to wait for the right time. That is now. I talked to Father Kremer, and he promised to talk to Dad. I just finished helping Orsola with her baby and no one else has a new baby, so I can go. Mom will love it, I know she will. Father Kremer will be so proud to have one of his girls become a nun.

He will persuade Dad and if not he won't want to disappoint Mom."

Thomas Bartholomew had other ideas. He had no interest in being papa to a nun. Agnes should get married and make him a few grandchildren, and he had just the fellow in mind for Agnes—Peter Genotti's third child was ambitious and knew his onions. Peter's oldest was not interested in women and his second had drowned at sixteen, leaving the third the catch of the family, and what a catch he would be for Agnes. Peter had already announced publicly he was giving his homestead to William on the day he got married. Bartholomew did not think he had to do that—William was a handsome, hard-working boy and everyone knew he would be a catch. Peter throwing in a prize farm made his son the most sought after bachelor in Badaxe County. No one in Catholic Badaxe doubted Agnes was the catch of the century, and the fact that she wanted to be a nun made her all the more appealing. Thomas Bartholomew had no doubt he just needed to wait—it was inevitable they would find each other. After all there were not that many choices in Badaxe, and these two were meant for each other. No need to encourage Agnes and get her to resist.

Free Will

While there was supposed to be free will, the only choices for a Badaxe woman seemed to be what to gossip about and if you would wed or become a nun. Few became nuns so even that choice was restricted. For Agnes the calling was so strong she doubted there was free will even about wife or nun—the one choice that seemed real. She understood the Church's position on free will, still she would argue with herself—if all is God's will, how can I have free will; if all is set out in clear doctrine, how can I have free will; if nature is so clear in her demands, what's the use of free will. Not that her doubt of free will made her dream to be a nun fade one thousandth of a percent. "Some things are meant to be what they are meant to be—that in and of itself does not provide cause to doubt the theory of free will." "Or does it?"

Her will, free or stubborn, was to be challenged upon graduating from the eighth grade. Agnes knew from her priest that she could enter the convent right after finishing grade school. Early in the new year when she was in her last year at St. Francis, Father Kremer helped Agnes fill out the forms necessary to apply and mailed them to St. Rose Convent in LaCrosse. Agnes prayed daily for acceptance though Father Kremer told her she would be accepted. He also told her she would have to wait until the fall when the convent would take new postulants. For the month after Father Kremer mailed the application, Agnes eagerly awaited the arrival of Art Ristow, the mailman who arrived promptly between 9:15 and 9:20 every day. As he pulled away, Agnes casually sped to the mailbox—only to be disappointed. On April 17, 1917 the letter Agnes had anxiously awaited each day for what seemed like a year finally arrived. She read and then reread the return address. Mother Sister Mary Madeline, Franciscan Sisters of Perpetual Adoration, 901 Franciscan Way, LaCrosse, Wisconsin. She read and reread several times the name of the person the envelope was addressed to: Agnes Veneri, Badaxe, Wisconsin. "I better sit down," she said aloud to no one. She walked back toward her house, found the lower steps, sat, waited another ten minutes and only then hesitantly opened the envelope—everything she ever wanted was on the line—she was not sure if she could survive rejection. The fact that Father Kremer said there was no doubt she would be accepted, the fact she had the highest grades of anyone at her school in the past decade, the fact she received the only perfect score on her confirmation tests was not enough to overcome Agnes' doubt. She carefully peeled back the flap, gently removed the letter, and held it a long time before unfolding it to read:

"Congratulations, you have been accepted into the class of 1922." Agnes thought a watermelon landed in her stomach. Class of 1922? "Why am I waiting five years?"

"You need to plan to arrive at the Convent on September 4 between 10 a.m. and 2 p.m. If you have any questions, please ask Father Kremer or ask the operator to connect you to LAX-0500." Agnes sat confused for some minutes –then she realized Mother Superior was referring to the year the class would take their first vows to become nuns. "I am going to be a nun! I have been accepted!" She sprang off the step and ran as fast as she could the one mile to Father Kremer's rectory. Knocking on the door, she yelled before Father could answer, "I've been accepted. I am going to be a nun!"

Discussion Over

Both Father Kremer and Agnes were completely taken back when Agnes' dad absolutely refused to give his permission to Agnes to enroll at St. Rose. Thomas "Bart" Veneri was not one to use more words than necessary. "Talk to me after she reaches 18." Discussion over.

Agnes asked Father Kremer if she could repeat the 8th grade. If she finished nine years of schooling, she would qualify to be a teacher assistant at St. Francis, and Agnes felt the least Father Kremer could do after failing to talk her dad into letting her go to the convent was to hire her as a teaching assistant. She rationalized that this would let her teach, better prepare her for her life as a teaching-nun and get her out of the house she no longer thought of as home. St. Francis School was a two-room school so the eighth grade teacher also taught the fifth, sixth and seventh grades. When Sister Marie found Agnes was going to repeat the eighth grade, she met with Agnes and asked her if she would help with the fifth and sixth year classes. In order to teach four classes in one-room, Sister Marie joined the two lower and two upper classes for as many subjects as possible. Agnes was delighted to help with the fifth and sixth grade in effect becoming an unpaid teacher assistant. To make it look like Agnes was a student, Sister Marie did give Agnes some extra reading assignments and weekly Algebra problems. Agnes served as the upper class teacher assistant for the next three years. The day she turned 18, Father Kremer came to her house with a new letter of acceptance and presented it to Agnes' father.

"Get out!"

"Whoa, Bart, you promised."

"Get out."

"Bart, no going back on your word now—you promised Agnes that she could join the convent when she turned 18. That's today, in case you didn't notice."

"Get out, before I throw you out."

"I am not going anywhere. Agnes has been accepted as a novice at St. Rose's. She has accepted. She will be going to St.

Rose's in the fall, if not before. They have an early enrollment and I put in Agnes' name. She is likely to be accepted in which case she will start in a little over two months. She is going—it would be better for all if you gave her your blessing."

"Get out."

"Bart, Agnes is 18 and you cannot stop her from joining the convent. Do not do or say anything that you will regret. I will encourage Agnes to wait until the fall to enroll so you have time to accept what you know in your heart is the right thing for Agnes. You know Mary Margaret wants a nun for a daughter—I think you do too."

Father Kremer let himself out. At the door he turned, "Don't be late for mass on Sunday."

July 4, 1921

"Hi." Agnes looked up as William Genotti swung his left leg over the bench seat and sat down with a too full plate of baked chicken, risott, potatoes and gravy. "You make this?" he asked as he picked up a heaping spoonful of risott. Risott, (rhymes with begot) the local idiom for risotto, was to Northern Italians what spaghetti was to Southern Italians.

"Oh, I don't know—it all looks alike to me."

"I happen to know you made it. Everyone knows your risott is the best—so I made sure I saw which one was yours." William shoved a spoonful into his mouth and chewed as if he was savoring each kernel. "Definitely yours—best risott I ever tasted." Agnes blushed.

William kept talking—Agnes never had a boy pay so much attention or talk to her so much. She liked the way it made her feel even though his voice seemed far away and sounded more like gibberish than speech. "You want an ice cream cone?" Agnes nodded and William was back with two before she caught her breath.

Courtship

Some families sat in the same pew every Sunday. They did not rent the pew like parishioners did in the Presbyterian Church in Stoddard, but they "owned" it just the same. To be sure, most families sat wherever, but a few, including Bart Veneri's family had staked out their pew and everyone respected their claim.

When, on the Sunday following the picnic, William casually sat down next to Agnes in the fifth row pew on the center right side, there was nothing discreet about it. Everyone—except Agnes—but including Bart and Mary Margaret, took it as all but a proposal of marriage. Agnes did her best to act as if there was nothing out of the ordinary—still she prayed a little louder than she normally did and fidgeted with her dress.

"Hi Agnes," was the first and only words that came out of William's mouth as they left the church.

The next Sunday William sat with his own family near the back of the church. By the time the Veneri family exited the church, the Genotti family was driving away in Peter Genotti's new Tin Lizzie. "Hi Agnes," it was William who was waiting at the bottom of the church steps. "It is such a beautiful day, I told Dad I wanted to walk home. Would you like to walk with me till we get to your place?" William had to walk past the Veneri farm, which was about one mile up the road, to get to his home which was about three miles from town. Before she could say no, Agnes said, "sure."

They walked in silence down Zaboglio Hill, turned right up Main Street until they came to Highway 56 where they turned right. As they walked by the mailman's house, William said, "I didn't see Art in church this morning. I wonder if he is all right." Agnes replied "I hope so." They kept up the small talk for the next mile until they came to the Veneri farm. Agnes said, "Thanks. Goodbye." and walked briskly to her house.

One of Peter Genotti's farms bordered on the Veneri farm. Over the next month, William found reasons to work on the farm near where the two farms met and eventually his diligence paid off as he spotted Agnes coming to get the cows that were grazing nearby. He waved, and then jumped the fence that separated the two pastures.

"You gettin' the cows?"

"Yes"

"You gotta few minutes."

"Sure"

This exchange was followed by an awkward moment as William fished for something else to say. "Think your dad would sell that horse?"

"Nelly? No way—he loves Nelly, and he knows I love her too."

"Yea, she is one fine horse. I can see why he wouldn't want to sell her."

The awkward conversation continued a couple more minutes until Agnes said, "I gotta get the cows home so Dad can milk them."

As the summer progressed, Agnes and William often found themselves at the same time in that corner where their farms met.

William Genotti

Peter Genotti was the wealthiest and most respected man in Badaxe. He had been born on the poorest farm in a log room buried in the valley overlooking the most worn land. Peter's father had emigrated from high in the Alps from a place called St. Bernard. With his new wife, he wanted to be on the edge of the frontier. They chose to head west to the newest state in the Union. It would give them the privacy they wanted, but not put them into Indian Territory. When they came to Wisconsin, the land was too flat. Every time they saw a piece of land they could claim, they could not imagine living on such flat land with neighbors you could see off on the horizon. "Could have moved to Milano if we wanted neighbors so close."

They settled on the backside of the biggest bluff they could find on the Mississippi River. When they first climbed that hill, Stefano and Barbara Genotti looked at each other and knew they had found home. Stefano marked a spot to build near a creek that ran down the east side of the hill and the land was too steep even for him to furrow. They climbed the rest of the hill and when they came to the top they could see a sea of trees that opened into a view of the widening Mississippi River. Barbara looked up at Stefano and took his hand to say, "This was worth the trip."

Stefano never worked the top of that bluff without longing for his homeland high up in the Alps overlooking

Chiavenna while expressing thanks for the richer fields and easier days he had found in this virgin land.

Peter was born in 1861 in the log cabin Stefano had built on that land. Peter made that farm more productive after he took it over from his father. Eventually he purchased almost half of the township. But misfortune struck. First his second son drowned in a suspicious Mississippi River accident. Then his wife—thirteen years his youth—died in childbirth. His oldest son left home. His third son, William, a somewhat worthless boy—but well-intentioned—needed a wife, and Peter needed a woman to care for his young children. Peter mourned his beautiful wife and knew he could never take another. The right thing to do was to marry William to a woman ready to care for his younger children. No one was more prepared to do this than Agnes Veneri.

Fate

There was no magic moment when Agnes was swept off her feet by William. They enjoyed each other's company. As their friends and family saw them together more and more, many began to see them as a couple though they had never gone on a date or publically demonstrated any feelings of intimacy. They met more and more often at the crossing and William began to sit in Agnes' pew most Sundays. One day as they were sitting on the same clearing William's grandparents had so admired, at the peak of the hill just up from where the Genotti and Veneri farms met and staring in silence past the sea of trees that opened into a view of the Mississippi River, William rather offhandedly said, "Will you marry me?" Agnes surprised herself as much as she surprised William when she answered, "Yes"

Conception

The forty years of our story begins with the conception of Agnes' firstborn. Agnes had not noticed that she'd missed her period the first two months. Then she began to worry about it. She had been regular—every twenty-eight days like clockwork. She wondered if living with William's family and caring for the children under the scrutinizing eye of William's father, Peter, was too much for her. She seemed tired most of the time and very weak in the morning. The next Sunday while visiting her family, she took her mother aside to ask her about being so sick in the morning. Her mother asked if she'd had her period lately. Agnes told her she didn't think she'd had one since September—maybe August. Mary Veneri got a big smile on her face and told her daughter if she missed the next period she'd know for sure she was three months pregnant. "You mean I won't get my period while I'm pregnant?" Mary wasn't surprised when she realized Agnes didn't already know this because she remembered asking her friends what was wrong when she'd first missed her period.

Agnes went back to the Genotti farm with renewed faith in her health and her ability to meet both Peter and William's expectations. She knew about morning sickness and that some women couldn't even cook during those first few months. She felt strong, and she would cope now that she knew what was causing her fatigue.

She kept her little secret for the next two weeks. Sometimes she thought she felt something move in her womb. But then she'd listen carefully and try to feel any movement and there was nothing. Then December 19 came, December 20, 21, 22 and still no blood. Better tell William. He'd be proud and he'd know that it was time to move out to the farm he'd bought from Peter. William would know that Agnes couldn't take care of Peter's children and her own baby.

On the morning of Christmas, before Agnes and William headed to Badaxe for church Agnes touched William's arm and said quietly, "I'm pregnant." William didn't say anything but all day he carried himself a little higher with his shoulders back a bit too far. Agnes was glad he was so proud.

That night William told Peter. His dad just said, "Already?"

Agnes began to watch her belly daily. Was it getting any bigger? There was a light that seemed to emanate from women big in the belly with child and Agnes had always been attracted to a certain spiritual look that she detected. She wanted her baby to show. She wanted her friends to notice that she was with child and that she was soon going to be a mother.

Day after day, she woke wanting to show. But she could detect no change. One Sunday her Aunt Orsola looked at Agnes and asked, "When is it due?"

"How did you know?"

"Well, it is pretty easy to see."

Agnes looked down at her belly and noticed for the first time that her belly might be pushing out a little on her dress. A smile spread across her face as she said, "In June."

"Congratulations."

Agnes could not wait to get home. She wanted to look in the mirror when she changed from her Sunday dress to a house dress to make dinner. She had looked at her belly this morning but it had looked like it did the day before. But it was showing enough for Aunt Orsola to see it. She wanted to stand in front of her mirror with no clothes on and look at her growing belly.

She looked and she wondered how Orsola could see it. It still looked the same. She turned sideways in front of the mirror and imagined a small protrusion. She placed her left hand over her belly and moved it slowly up and down side to side and around. Yes, she could feel a slight enlargement. She thought her belly felt warmer—full of life. She closed her eyes and put both hands on her belly. She felt lightness in her arms and spiritual energy enter her body. Jesus was coming to help her give life to the thing inside her. She could feel him running lightly throughout her bloodstream.

She picked up her work dress, slipped it over her head and buttoned it up. She went out into the kitchen to make dinner for William. William looked at her and asked, "Are you all right? You look pale. Are you okay?"

"Yes, I'm fine, I'm just fine." She took the large black frying pan, placed it on the wood stove, put in a heaping tablespoon of lard, took the chicken out of the ice box and began to make dinner.

By April Agnes was big. She began to wonder when she and William could move out of Peter's house into their own home. William's new farm had a big house. There would be plenty of room to raise their family. It had been empty since Peter bought the farm to resell to William. William walked to the farm every day and came back every night. Agnes spent the day caring for William's brothers and sisters and cooking meals for the Genotti brood.

Agnes knew it wasn't her place to suggest to William that they move. But she couldn't wait much longer. She'd finally decided if William didn't arrange the move by the end of the month, she'd just have to tell him that they had to move. She couldn't wait until the ninth month to move, and she was not going to give birth to their baby in Peter's house.

The next week Agnes stepped out of the house to get some fresh air after cleaning the kitchen after dinner. None of Peter's children wanted to help her, and she'd tired of asking them, so she washed all the dishes and cleaned up the kitchen and dining room herself. For a mid-April day it was uncannily cold. She remembered when she dreamed of becoming a nun and telling her friends, "It'll freeze over in hell before I get married and have children." The thought made her laugh.

As she came out the door she heard Peter say "When are you going to get into your own home?"

"Eh, ugh, well, I hadn't really thought about it. Don't you need her? Who'd look after Adley? I mean, gosh, I hadn't thought about moving."

"William, a man's got to make his own home. Agnes is pregnant and she can't be making you a family while you live here. I can always get a girl to come in to take care of the children. Agnes' sisters Sara and Stella would do. They're pretty big now. We can take care of ourselves. You got to take care of Agnes."

William didn't say anything to Agnes. Easter came and she cooked up a holy day dinner for everyone. After dinner, William came out to help her clean up the dishes. He was pretty awkward with a dish towel, but he looked so cute Agnes couldn't help but want to kiss him. But she didn't. It wouldn't be right in Peter's home.

William was uncommonly quiet while he helped. The dishes were all washed, dried and put away. As they scrubbed up the counter, William said, "Agnes, I think it's time to move to our own home. Uncle Steve and John are going to come over Sunday to help me and Dad move our things to the new place. Dad's going to give us this table and the rocker, and the two gray chairs in the living room. He is also going to let us take the bed and chest from our room. It'll be a little bare but it'll be our place."

William looked as if he thought Agnes might not want to strike out on her own with so little. She smiled at William and leaned over to kiss his cheek; she said simply "Thank you" and William broke a smile of relief.

The men moved things and wouldn't let Agnes lift even a pot. As if she hadn't lifted a lot more over the last months and wouldn't continue the next day as she made the house a home for William and their baby.

The house seemed so big. It wasn't as big as Peter's, but with just two of them instead of Peter's nine children, the place seemed twice as big. Agnes picked one of the rooms for her baby and set up the crib that Uncle Steve had brought along when he came to move. She got out the sewing machine and then cut and sewed the blue cloth that she had purchased into curtains for the windows.

She came downstairs and sat on the rocker and rocked trying to hold in her arms the baby that she would soon give birth to. She was waiting for William to come in from the evening milking. He had already built his herd up to eighteen cows. This had taken every penny of their earnings. Agnes knew how important it was for their future family for them to build up the herd. Each month, when the milk check came in, William paid his father for the farm first. Then they kept out some money for the church and groceries. The rest went to buy more cows. William had figured the land was big and rich enough to feed twenty-eight milking cows along with a few calves, a bull and some heifers.

It took William an hour to milk 12 cows, so he knew he could milk twenty-eight in a little over two hours. If he got himself in the barn by 5:30 a.m. he could have the cows milked, clean up and eat breakfast by 8:15-8:30. That would give him more than eight hours in the fields plus a half hour each for dinner and supper before he had to be back milking the cows around 5:45 p.m. By 8:30 he'd be finished and have time to make love to Agnes before he fell asleep around 9:30. Not a bad life at all. If he worked every day, six days a week, he figured he could keep up to the farm. Sundays, he'd milk the cows, go to church and then have the afternoon to hunt, fish, visit his dad, or just snuggle up with Agnes. Of course when it rained, he might take part of the day off. Couldn't do much in the rain.

William had things to do in the barn and work shed on rainy days, and he'd spend most of those days fixing things. But he liked to sneak off for an hour or two late in the morning or in the mid-afternoon and quietly come up behind Agnes and press his hand to her breast. Agnes liked it. Not so much because her breast responded to his touch, because in fact it felt more icky than pleasurable, but because William would take a break from his work. He worked so hard and so long. If he had to make love to her to justify a break, then she would make love.

William would pull her around—a little too roughly and kiss her with a warm wet kiss that would make Agnes want to please him. He did know how to kiss. But Agnes found little pleasure in sex. William didn't seem to have the patience to get her prepared before he entered her—and it never entered her head to ask him to fondle her longer. She thought it natural that a man should set the pace and that his thing would scrape along her vagina walls.

The pain was there to remind her, and all women she supposed, of her role in the family. She should suffer to give joy to her husband and to give birth to her children. It was the way of things and must be meant to train her for a life of sacrifice to be a good mother and wife. William preferred rainy day love sessions. He became more aroused while at the same time gentler than in their regular night sessions. He touched and kissed her longer and she liked it. Sometimes it would not even hurt much when he entered her.

On those occasions Agnes felt a stirring inside her loin that made her want to clasp her legs around William and pull him into her. Maybe hold him still with the strength of her legs so she could feel the power of his pecker without all the thrusting. By the time she would have these feelings, William would already be wild, and he would whisper into her ear that he wanted to plow her furrow. She'd smile to let him know it was fine, and he'd' thrust her with a force that made her fear he would tear open her vagina. She bared the pain for she saw that it pleased her husband.

William never "plowed" her at night—but he also never kissed her so tenderly—so she preferred the rainy day sessions the most. It must have been one of those sessions that gave her the baby now inside her belly.

Expecting

A few months earlier she had felt a kick. She wanted to tell William; to have him hold her belly until a second kick came, so he too could feel the life. But William was in the back forty. It was just as well because the baby didn't kick again for three days. Agnes laughed to herself the next day about William holding her until the baby kicked again. "Guess his hand would get tired, and who'd milk the cows?" She laughed out loud.

But the baby began to kick more often and William often held her belly while she was cooking him breakfast in hopes of feeling the kick. When they went to bed he held her spoon style with her back to his belly and his hand on her belly. William sometimes asked, "Was that it? I felt it—did he kick you?" The first three times he asked she had to say "No." She felt her body growing one with William when he held her like this. "That's it, yes I really felt it that time," William said as he held her one morning. Agnes turned around and gave William a big kiss. "Yes," she said, "it kicked this time."

Agnes got bigger and bigger. William still held Agnes waiting for a kick now and then but Agnes missed the attention he had given waiting for the first kick he would feel. One Sunday morning she leaned over to tie her shoes, and she could not reach them. "William, would you tie my shoes?"

"What?"

"I can't seem to reach over enough to tie my shoes, would you tie them?"

William knelt in front of her and began to tie her shoes. Deeply touched, Agnes ran her hand through his hair. He slowed down; tying her shoe more deliberately. He looked up at her directly into her eyes and tilted his head and laid it on her belly. Agnes slowly ran her hands across his face and down over his shoulders. He slipped his hands around her backside and rolled both hands across her butt. Agnes pulled her hands back across William's face and touched his lips with her fingers. She pulled her fingers across his cheeks and rolled her finger under his ears and began to massage his hair.

Bop, she felt a kick in her stomach. William jerked away from her belly and began to laugh. He looked at Agnes and she joined him in laughter. They held hands and laughed at the thought of the baby kicking William in the face through Agnes' belly.

Day by day Agnes felt riper. She liked that word, "ripe." I wonder if the apple tree gets this feeling of fullness when it ripens. She had noticed before that a ripe watermelon, apple, blackberry looked like they might burst. Tonight Agnes felt like she might burst. The image of her baby erupting from her belly and flying off to the crib made her smile and think of Athena flying out of Zeus' head. As she rocked the chair, she tried to think back to a rainy day nine months earlier. But somehow no rainy day stood out, and she was not able to distinguish one from another.

The clock chimed 9:00 p.m. Agnes wondered where William was. He was always in the house by now and often in bed by nine. Where was he tonight—when she was so ripe and desirous of having his rough hands rove over her very pregnant belly? She loved being pregnant most when he did that. It was not a pleasure she had expected for she had never seen her father touch her mother's belly when she was pregnant. William seemed fascinated by the growth in her stomach, and he rubbed his strong hands over her belly several times a day—she liked it when he came in for dinner and reached around her to hold her enlargement while she was bent over the stove.

Even more she liked it when he came in after milking the cows at night. Sometimes he'd lay his head on her womb as if trying to hear the baby, and he'd kneel in front of her and move his hands under her belly and just hold it.

She wanted him there that moment to do that—to put his head on the baby and to hold her from bursting open. Where was he?

William came in a few minutes later. He looked more tired than usual. He'd been in the hayfields all day and Agnes knew this was the hardest work of the year and that William was exhausted. She wanted him to touch her belly for she knew that would make this tired man happy.

William pumped some water into the wash basin—wet his hands—took the soap and lathered it enough to wash the chaff off his arms and face. He left nearly as much on as he washed off, took the towel and wiped some more off and without looking at Agnes said, "I'm going to bed."

She watched him drag himself to the bedroom. She wanted to call him back—to tell him she was ready—to share the moment—but her mouth did not open.

Agnes' expectation transformed to loneliness. She sat for a few moments feeling sadness steal her moment and then condemning herself for failing to understand how tired William Charles was.

She got up, went to the outhouse and then carried herself off to bed. As she entered the bedroom she could hear William's heavy breath and light snore.

Agnes rested on the bed looking out at the stars for what seemed an eternity. She wondered if she made a mistake to conceive this driven man's baby. Was he ready to have a child? Would William treat the child with love? What if it died in childbirth? She couldn't handle that. I think I would die too, she thought.

She wanted to sleep. She had worked a long day—cooking meals over the wood stove—working in the garden for over three hours in the morning—sewing some rags into diapers for the baby in the afternoon.

Yes, William milked the cows twice a day, but she had this big house to clean, and she cleaned it every night after supper. The day's dishes were washed and the kitchen cleaned. It was all she could do now that the baby was so close.

Agnes felt a piercing pain from deep inside herself. The pain shot through her body, tightening every muscle. She screamed into the night—so loud she thought that the neighbors must have heard her. She reached for William—but stopped as the pain subsided and William snored a little louder.

She wondered how William could sleep through her scream. He must really be dog-tired. She looked out the window for the stars to see that the sky was beginning to lighten. She looked to see the time and surprised herself to see it was 4:00 in the morning. I must have slept some—I thought I was awake all night—I'm glad I slept because I need sleep for this baby is coming today.

The pain came again and Agnes grabbed the bedpost and squeezed so hard the blood stayed in her hand. She wanted to scream but she held it so she would not wake William. As the pain released, she felt the sweat pour out of her skin. She lay back, breathed deep and enjoyed the coolness of the air circulating over her wet body.

Again the pain. It was strong, but she now had control of the impulse to scream. William would want to share this moment—she should wake him no matter how tired he is.

Agnes sat up on the bed and looked at William. He looked more like a little boy curled up with a slight mischievous grin than a man running his own farm, building a large herd with twenty-eight milk cows and about to become a father.

Agnes looked at this boy lying there so quietly in the pre-morning light. She wanted to lean over and kiss him to life. As she reached her lips toward his cheeks a pain reached her deeper than the others, she grabbed William's arm and squeezed so hard William jumped clear out of bed. Agnes hung on and William quickly realized she was in labor. "My God, oh my God, What do I do now? Oh my God."

Agnes' contraction finished, and she looked at William and smiled. She had never seen him scared before. This big man of hers was afraid of birth. Even when Leonardo, their rather vicious bull, took after William, he had stood right up to him and forced the bull to back down. She smiled to see him panic over something as natural as childbirth. Agnes had helped her mother through childbirth twice, so she had a good idea of what needed to be done. She could have talked William through the birth, but she decided he was too nervous to be of much use and besides she really wanted her mom to be there.

"It's okay William. The baby won't come for a while. Maybe not even today. But I hope it comes today—I sure don't want to be in labor for days. She laughed a little. Call Mom and ask her to come. Dad won't want to get up to bring her here—but better to do it now than when he and you need to be milking the cows. He'll just have time to get Mom here and get back to his cows."

William picked up the phone and rang two shorts and a long. There were nine other families on the line and William knew every one of them would pick up the phone to see who was calling so early. One by one he could hear the receivers being lifted. Then he heard Mary Veneri's voice, "Hello." William was thankful that it wasn't Bart on the line for he might be yelling, "Take care of her yourself, boy." William told Mary that Agnes was having a baby. "Tell her to wait'll I get there." Click.

Forty-five minutes later Mary and Bart drove up to William's house in their buggy. Mary got out and headed right for the bedroom. Bart asked, "How's she doing?'

"Fine, she's doing fine."

"Well, I better get back to the cows. They won't wait." He turned the team around and headed out the yard. William wondered why Bart didn't get an automobile. He could afford it. Everyone was getting one. William thought, "I'd get one if I had the money."

William headed out to milk his cows. When he came back in, he half expected to see a baby boy. But what he heard was another scream from Agnes and Mary telling her, "Relax, take it easy, just relax, breathe, let it happen." Agnes screamed when the pain was too much, but she was suffering with dignity. She knew pain was part of childbirth, part of life and her job was to accept it. God must have designed this birth pain to help mothers love their children more. If giving birth was so painful, the rest of raising children could be more bearable. Agnes knew some of the trials of raising children, but all that paled in face of the pre-birth pain. Now she understood how her mother could be so patient.

Noon came and went. The afternoon passed too slowly. William went back to the barn to milk the cows. The sun set. William came back in and held Agnes' hand. Mary had helped Agnes change her clothes three times and kept a cool towel handy for Mary to wipe off the perspiration.

The contractions got closer. The pain became more bearable even if the contractions got stronger and quicker. At 10:30 in the evening Mary began to move about. "William, boil some water, get me a clean sheet. Boil Agnes' best scissors."

Agnes did not feel any different. But she could see in her mother's eyes that the baby was coming. Her mother stared between her legs, "It's coming, it's coming, push, push."

The pain overwhelmed Agnes. The next thing she knew, the baby was being held upside down by her mother who was patting the baby on the butt.

"It's a girl, Agnes—she'll help you out with the rest. It's a girl—you're lucky."

Mary cleaned off the baby, took the scissors and cut the cord, and gave the baby girl to Agnes.

Though she would give birth to fourteen more children—this moment would stay upper-most in Agnes memory for the rest of her life. The pain of her body rushed toward pleasure, and she felt her blood change from battle to play. Her skin prickled, her muscles felt like strawberry jello, and every nerve ending was alive to receive the touch of her child. The softness and newness of life rushed to her cheeks and the red contrasted to the brilliant shine of the white in her eyes.

Agnes had dreamed of becoming a mother. No dream, except the dream to become a nun and to offer her chastity to Jesus, had been so strong. Yet her greatest imagination did not predict the lusciousness and the joy of this moment. At no time in her life had the present loomed so directly before her.

Agnes—the baby—her bedroom—her mother—the future—the past—it was all time mashed into the present moment. As if all time was made for this moment of birth.

Agnes picked up the baby—kissed her ever so gently—whispered just loudly enough for Mary to hear, "Giuseppina, Pina."

Gotta get the Hay in Before it Rains

Agnes looked across the table and wondered, "Who is that man eating with me?" He was a stranger, bent over his food, slapping it into his mouth, dirt on his arms and forehead that had been only partially washed off. Whoever this man was he had not acknowledged her existence since coming into her kitchen. He looked like the man she had married and who had fathered their three children, but he could not be! Agnes' mind wandered back five years earlier when William Genotti, of the Peter Genotti family, had sat next to her at the Church picnic and later came to call on her. She had been so surprised. Peter Genotti was the patriarch of the community, the biggest supporter of the Church and maybe the richest man in Badaxe. Agnes had been pleased with the attention that she received from Peter's third son and one thing had led to another to the altar, pregnancy, one, two, three children. She had thought that in the process she had gotten to know this man and to like him. No, more than like him, she had thought she was falling in love with him.

But now she looked across the table and saw a man that aroused little in her. He had never held or kissed one of their children. Oh sure, he carried them to the car and now and then to bed, but she had never seen him actually hold one of the children with affection. He seemed more interested in getting the hay in on time than what Pina, Hannah or Alexandra had done that morning—could eat an entire meal and never say a word or look at her. Suddenly she noticed that some times she would talk to William the entire meal about the children, the garden, the blooming peonies, and that he never responded, maybe never heard a word. Where was he? Who was he? How had he changed? What happened?

William finished eating, got up, and headed out the door. "Gotta get the hay in before it rains."

Was it an apology for rushing out, for not saying a word, for ignoring the children, for taking her for granted?

Agnes helped Pina and Hannah finish eating, cleaned up the messes left by them and William, did the dishes, put Pina and Hannah down for their naps before she picked up the baby, sat on the rocker, unhooked her bra and fed Alexandra. All of this without a thought of what she was doing or about the predicament she was in. It was as if her mind needed some time without thought.

Alexandra suckled on Agnes' breast which pulled her mind back to thought. She wondered again why and how William had changed. She started to relive the past five years. She saw them eyeing each other, William trying to get her alone, asking her father for her hand, trying to kiss her before they were married, the wedding, the fear she had of that first night, William's roughness that seemed touching while also frightening, the pride he had when she first said, "I think I'm pregnant,"—the first baby. All these memories made Agnes smile and take pleasure in having shared them with William. Yes, this was the man she would share things with and with whom she would find love, pleasure and meaning in life. A feeling of closeness wailed up in her chest and rushed to her breast that Alexandra was sucking. She realized that it was empty, so she moved Alex to the other breast. The image of the stranger came back. It did not make sense with the image of the man she had just remembered. The past was replayed again, this time in slow motion. As the images passed through her mind, she began to watch William instead of herself. She watched as William tried to get her attention. She saw how timid he was and how discreet and she liked it. But wait, what is that other look on his face, the look of the conqueror, the hunter after his prey. Does he want me or does he want victory. He smiles at her, she smiles back. He blushes—she had thought out of embarrassment—but she now sees a look she has seen after he has broken a horse—William leaves, wait, he's meeting up with his brothers, he's telling them something, clearly he is bragging, they are laughing—is he telling them he got me to smile? Why is it funny? Her mind goes to the moment she tells him that she is pregnant—again she sees his pride, she keeps looking—what is it that is in his eyes? Something else. And the birth of Pina—she is looking at him, wanting to fall in love, they have given birth to a new soul,—they are now really man and wife. Agnes sees that she is ready to fall in love, what stopped her? She looks at William, she holds Giuseppina out for him to hold—he tightens up, pulls back a little, she holds Giuseppina closer, he must be afraid he'll break her, but Agnes knows he'll hold Giuseppina correctly—so she insists, William takes her, but he is stiff. Agnes smiles, it's really cute that this farmer who cuddles the calves and handles tiny baby pigs with care is afraid to handle his own baby. She sees that there is more than fear in this man's eyes. The three years and two more babies flash through Agnes' mind in a moment, and she sees William avoiding contact with the children at all costs. My God, My God, does he not like children? Why did he marry me? Why does he bed me? God made marriage for children. William knows that—he is a good Catholic. Why did he marry me if he has an aversion to children? More images thrust their way into Agnes' head. They wouldn't leave her alone now. She sees herself talking to William, telling him about the children, about the garden, about church—he's not listening. Where is he? She can't tell. Then he grabs her, pulls her toward the bedroom, kisses her, fondles her, throws her on the bed, enters her, thrusts her too vigorously and comes a minute later. He rolls over and goes to sleep. She recognizes the scene for they play it daily. It is the one time he pays attention to her.

Alex finishes feeding. Agnes gets up from the rocker, puts Alex in the crib, hooks up her bra, goes to the front porch, and looks at the sky. "No," she whispers. She takes the hoe off the porch, walks slowly to her garden and begins to cut the weeds out that threaten to take over the sweetcorn patch.

Weeds

It was one of those hot muggy Mississippi Valley Wisconsin days. There were a dozen of them a summer. Temperature hit 100 at midday and the humidity must have been 90% plus. Agnes did not mind these days. She'd go on as usual though she did notice that everything took just a little longer to do. Still, no sense sitting in the shade refusing to work. She knew that some doctors recommended that, and some claimed one could get a stroke working on days like this. There were things to do. The times she did sit in the shade, she was more aware of the heat. Sitting there with nothing to do, all her thoughts were on the heat and humidity. Even though she knew it had to be cooler in the shade, the heat became overbearing. As long as she was working, the need to concentrate on the task kept the heat in the background and it did not seem so unbearable.

Agnes was hoeing the garden and pulling weeds where the hoe was to wide to use. She stopped for a moment, looked up toward the sun, felt the sweat roll down her face and listened to her own heart. She wanted to notice if there was anything wrong—maybe she could feel that stroke coming and get out of the sun in time if she paid attention. She didn't feel anything, but she did notice how thirsty she was. She stepped over to the corn patch and picked up the Kool-Aid jar that she had put there in the shade so the ice wouldn't melt too fast. She unscrewed the lid and lifted the jar to her lips. The jar was a two quart mason jar and Agnes had mixed a package of new Kool-Aid with a cup of sugar and a jar full of water and ice earlier. The ice was gone now, but the Kool-Aid was still cold enough to feel good on her tongue. She liked cherry the best of the six Kool-Aid flavors. William liked strawberry the best so she usually drank strawberry. But today she had made the drink just for herself so she made cherry. It tasted delicious.

Agnes took the end of her right sleeve into her left hand and ran it across her brow wiping off the sweat and dirt. She noticed—but just barely noticed—how dirty the sweat was. It was that kind of day.

She went back out into the sun and bent over to pull the weeds out that had managed to grow between the vines of her tomatoes. The vines were so thick she always wondered how the weeds could get growing. She wanted to be careful that she did not damage any of the young tomatoes or the buds that were still coming. She slid her hand down the stem of the weeds and gave them a firm but gentle pull. Then she threw the weeds flat on the ground allowing them to become fertilizer for the plants.

She began to wonder about the weeds. Where did they come from? How could they grow when her plants were so thick? Where did they come from week after week? She'd pull them all out one week and the next week some stood one or two feet tall. She did not have any plants that grew that fast unless it was the corn. Even corn took all summer to grow tall. What made weeds so hardy and persistent? Why did the plants she had sown take so much care to grow? If she didn't water them, keep the dirt loose and built up, keep the weeds out, her plants wouldn't grow at all. Why did the weeds get the preference?

Agnes began to wonder how that related to human life. The good people always seemed to have to struggle while the evil people popped up all over the place and flourished. She didn't know so many evil people, but she had heard about those people who lived in cities or in some villages where sin ran rampant. In Badaxe, I guess things were better. Father Duffy kept the weeds out and kept the good plants fertilized with his sermons, picnics, rosaries, and Stations of the Cross. She was lucky to have been born in so fertile a field where the gardener was good at what he did. St. Francis had always had a good priest. Monsignor Kremer had founded the church and was still the priest when Agnes was growing up. She remembered his funeral. Everyone loved Father Kremer and he had been in Badaxe for so long no one could remember before that time. The whole congregation had wondered if it was possible to have a church or even a town without Father Kremer. Then Father Beck came and everyone was pleased. He was a generous man, quiet but a strong speaker. He wasn't Father Kremer but the people learned to admire him, and they often said, "Sure glad Beck is here, we could have gotten a lot worse." Beck stayed on for about fifteen months before the bishop called him to work at the archdiocese office. Father Duffy came and on the very first Sunday Agnes fell in love with him. He was outgoing, friendly, caring, and he could shout from the podium as no one she had ever heard. Father Duffy became everyone's friend and going to church was always to be looked forward to because you knew that you were in for a great sermon. Duffy had been at St. Francis for five years, and he was a gardener of all gardeners. Keeping the weeds under control and letting the good plants flourish in this town. Agnes thought she was living in the best place in the world. When Fr. Duffy got going with one of his greatest sermons, she wondered if Badaxe wasn't the center of the world. Why else would so brilliant a man come here to be with them?

But cities—they were different. From everything she heard, she knew they were weed patches. They were the place where the good were suffocated by weeds.

Tin Lizzie

William never saw a car he did not want. The first car in Badaxe was purchased by Leaflad the banker. No one was surprised at that—for everyone knew he was the richest man in town. Peter Genotti had worked harder than anyone and he was well-to-do, but the banker who had nothing to do but count Peter's and the rest of the Badaxe farmers' money, had become the richest of them all.

But soon others bought cars. William's uncle Joseph Genotti had his own car when William was still in grade school. William's dad got quite upset saying, "I can't believe that dumb-ass Joseph bought a car. What the hell does a farmer from Badaxe need a car for? Can't make hay or plow a field with a car. Where does he think he is going? How can he afford a crate, anyhows? Make ole fancy pants Ford rich I guess. Maybe Joseph ought to take care of his family instead of getting a damn new fangled car and spending all his money and time on it."

William noticed his dad staring at Joseph's car on Sundays when he drove it to church. William did not remember how long it was before his dad bought a car—but there were not too many Sundays that passed before they all piled into Dad's Model-T and drove off to church.

Now that he was married and had a farm, William wanted his own car. Even Agnes' dad had finally purchased a car. William thought he could count on one hand the number of married fellows who drove their wives and children to church in a horse and buggy. He did not want to be the last one to buy a car.

Every Sunday on the way home, he'd say to Agnes, "Think I should go look at cars this week. Maybe Dad could drive me to LaCrosse to buy one." Agnes was concerned where William would get the money for a car the first time he mentioned it. But he did not go to LaCrosse with Peter. Still, every Sunday, week after week, William said, "I think I should get Pa to take me to LaCrosse this week. Should get a car before winter. No sense freezing you and the kids to get you to church on Sunday."

One Thursday, William got up early and milked the cows a half hour before usual. After breakfast, he said, "Got to go help Pa today." Agnes did not think anything unusual as William would help his dad out every once in a while.

That afternoon, about 4:00 p.m., Agnes jumped at the sound of a car horn just outside her window. She looked out and saw William, as proud as she had ever seen, driving a brand new Model-T with Peter sitting next to him. "Agnes come on out and see what I got." He honked the horn again. Too long and too loud.

"Where did you get this? Grandpa, did you buy a new car?"

"No, Agnes, it's ours. Dad took me to LaCrosse and I bought it." William was beaming from ear to ear. Agnes had never seen him so happy. She wanted to say "How could you? We don't have the money to buy Hannah a pair of shoes. She has to wear Pina's hand-me-downs. How could you go buy a car? We have a horse and buggy. We get along just fine without a car. How are you going to pay for it? Who gave you credit anyway? Does this mean we got to pay Peter more money every month? You must have borrowed the money from him; the bank certainly would not lend money to buy a car. What happened with your saying that we should not buy anything we cannot pay for?"

She knew the right thing to say was, "It is a beauty, William."

But she said: "Where did you get it?"

"I bought it at Gunderson's—you know where they are—we stopped there last time we went to LaCrosse to look at the new cars. He made me a real good deal. Got it for just $249. Good price. I been checking them out and this was a good price. Dad was surprised I got so good a price. Look at this gasoline engine." He jumped out of the car and showed Agnes the engine. "To start it you just get out this crank and turn it and off it goes. Don't have to harness it up or nothing and you can ride with me to church. No more freezing in the buggy. The heat from the engine will keep us warm. What do you think?"

"It's nice, it's real nice." But Agnes could not say it with the enthusiasm she knew she should have. How could he just go off and spend all this money on a car? And not ask her? Sure he had said he was going to buy a car, but he had been saying that since she was pregnant with Pina. She thought he was only talking.

She heard William say: "I got to take Dad home; I'll be back in a few minutes. Take no time at all to give Dad a ride home and get back with this beaut."

He gave the car a crank and it sputtered into rhythm. William ran around to the driver's side and shifted into reverse and backed the car around the big tree, shifted into first and with a "Hiya" drove out the front yard and headed down the road toward Peter's place.

Agnes went back to her kitchen and continued to make supper. In a few minutes William drove back into the yard, honked the horn and shut off the engine. He honked some more. All the children ran out to see the car and climb into it. William honked again and the children broke out in applause and let out a hoot or two.

Finally, William came into the house. "Don't you want to come out and see the car? Maybe go for a ride."

"How could you? How could you buy this car? Who did you borrow the money from? How we gonna pay it back?

William looked at her with sheepish pride. "I paid for it. Cash! I saved the money. I been putting eight dollars away every month from the milk check. I saved the money. I knew they wanted $290 for a runabout. When I got to $260 I said to myself, I'll just tell them it's all I got. One hundred percent or nothing, and they'd have to take it. Or at least I could not pay more, so they'd have to sell to me or I'd have to wait. Well I showed him $240 and said it's all I got. My last penny. He said, 'Maybe your dad could throw in a little.'—Dad took out his wallet and counted out $9.00. He took it. $249—He even filled the tank with gas. Said if it is your last penny guess you won't have any money to buy gas—I better fill it up so you can get home. Which he did. I hadn't thought about gas. I led the way home with Dad following me. We stopped at his place, and he jumped in so we could bring it over for you to ride in. Quite Spiffy, ain't it?"

Agnes did not know what to say. She was proud of William for saving so much money. It must have been hard. But did he have to take the money for Hannah's shoes to buy a car? She never wanted her children to wear hand-me down shoes because she had been told plenty that it was a way to destroy the child's feet. William bought a car and Hannah might have bad feet for the rest of her life.

"Let's go for a ride." She climbed into the car like she had seen her mother climb into her dad's new car. William cranked it up, and they drove up the road toward Vito's where William could show his younger brother that he had a brand-new car.

William drove out of the driveway a little too fast. He wanted to show Agnes how well he could drive, but it was also obvious that he had not had much experience driving a car. Peter had purchased a car six years before but William had few opportunities to drive it.

They drove down the road more designed for horses than cars but William did not seem to mind. He was driving his own car and it gave him a feeling for manhood that he had never before experienced. Agnes felt William's pluck and it both pleased her and frightened her.

She began to enjoy the ride, the wind blowing across her face and the fields speeding by. In no time they were driving into Vito's front yard. Vito and Arlene and their children had heard the car coming, and they had all gathered in the front yard to see who was driving in to see them. Cars were still scarce enough in Badaxe that only Grandpa Genotti had ever driven a car into their yard. They knew Grandpa would not be visiting them on a Thursday afternoon, so they wondered who it was.

"It's William and Agnes," Vito said in total amazement. William pulled up short and shut the car off.

"William, whose car you driving? It's real swanky."

William smiled and after a long pause said, "It's mine,"

Vito's children whooped and hollered. "Uncle William's got a car. Uncle William's got a car."

"Want to go for a ride? William asked Vito.

"Is the Pope Italian?"

Agnes stepped down and Vito got in the car. Vito's oldest asked "Can I come?" "Sure," Vito said and pulled Jim up onto his lap. William got out and gave the car a good crank. He turned the engine over with such sureness and strength that it kicked in with one crank.

William got behind the wheel, stepped on the clutch, shifted into reverse and began to back out of Vito's yard.

Calvin's Calamity

Agnes wished William did not have to work so hard and that he was more affectionate with her and the children. He was a good man, went to church, did not drink or swear very much and was a hard worker. Agnes could have it a lot worse. The children were doing well. Giuseppina was already in the second grade and Hannah who had started school a few months too young was also in the second grade. She was very smart and was doing better in school than Pina. Alex was only five, but she was already helping William with the chores. She went to the barn every night and washed the cows' teats and carried milk to the milk tank. William seemed to enjoy having her help. Matthew helped now and then. He was a very strong boy at three and very independent. The baby was hearty and starting to walk. Yes life was good.

Life in America was good. Maybe too good for Agnes heard about how some people in the cities partied all night and the girls wore clothes too high on their legs. She thought they were called flappers. Once in a while Father Sheen, who preached on the radio during Lent—Agnes never missed his broadcast—railed about how the country was going to pot with speakeasies and bootleg booze and skirts too flimsy for a woman to be seen in public. Agnes thought this shameful life was probably due to all the prosperity in the country. There was just too much money and people did not have to work hard enough to make a living. It wasn't good. She was more determined than ever if William made a lot of money, she would give ever more to the church to keep from getting lazy themselves. She wanted William to save for old age and to have enough to buy the things he needed to run the farm. But she did not want any fancy clothes to spoil herself, and she did not want her children spoiled by too much money.

In year seven of their marriage, the herd grew by three and in year eight another three. The herd was up to twenty - seven and for the first time, with the proceeds from the milk and the sale of the steers and old cows, the Genotti's put three hundred dollars in the bank. In one year they more than doubled the entire savings they had struggled so hard to build during the first seven years of their marriage. Agnes was pleased for William because she knew how important it was for him to have saved some money. William had purchased a gallon of wine the day their deposit in the bank reached five hundred dollars, and he and Agnes had celebrated with a quiet toast after the children were in bed. It was a wonderful year.

Then Black Tuesday hit. It did not hit Agnes or William on Black Tuesday or Wednesday or Thursday for that matter. They did not hear about it until Sunday when they went to mass. Everyone seemed to be talking about the crash and wondering what it meant to them. Uncle Stephen, who was still single, had invested a lot of his money in the stock market, and he knew what it meant to him. He'd lost 90% of his investment. He did not say how much, but William had said he thought Stephen was worth more than $10,000. Enough to pay outright for William's farm and then some. Agnes did not think he was worth that much, but if he had half that in the stock market, it would be a huge loss. People were saying that some people lost so much money they jumped to their deaths. Committed suicide over money? Agnes found that impossible to believe. No money could justify taking one's life. How could it be so bad?

Vito and Angelo were talking about taking their money out of the bank. They laughed that they did not have so much, but what they had was 100% of what they had, and they said they were going to be at the bank first thing Monday to take it out. "Maybe, we'll sew it in the mattress." They laughed—but the laugh died fast.

William and Agnes had no money in the stock market. In fact Agnes did not have much idea what the stock market was except it was where rich people bought and sold stocks. She did not know what a stock was or why one would buy one. She did know that it was considered a risky way to spend money and that she and William would keep their money in the bank—where it was safe. But now they were talking about the banks folding too. It would be necessary to get one's money out of the bank to keep it safe. What was happening to the country?

She wondered if Al Smith had been elected president if this would have happened. People at church were saying that the country was blaming Hoover. She had voted for Al Smith. He was the first Catholic to run for President and Father Sheen had made it pretty clear in his sermons before the election that a vote for Hoover was a vote for the devil. When the votes in Badaxe were counted Al Smith had received one hundred and twenty-six votes and Hoover three.

On the way home, Agnes asked William if he was going to take their money out of the bank on Monday. William did not answer her right away. "No," he said, "If it is not safe in the bank, where is it safe?"

"William, what do you think this will mean to us?" Everyone had been so worried at church. Most of them had heard about the crash before coming to church and had time to think about it. There was a nervous concern for the future that Agnes had never before witnessed. It seemed bad, but it was impossible to think about what it meant.

"I don't know Agnes, I just don't know. We don't have any money in the market. So we haven't lost anything yet. I can't believe that the bank will close. Old Leaflad is a smart cookie. I think he'll know what to do. He was awfully quiet today. I wonder how much he lost on the stock market. He must have had a lot of his own money in the market. But our money is safe in the bank. I don't think we should pull it out. Where would we put it? Besides, we are making some interest on it. I guess it will keep making interest. People got to eat, so they will have to keep buying milk and eating butter and cheeses and meat. As long as they drink milk and eat meat, we should be able to sell our milk to the creamery and the steer to the butchers."

But William and Agnes discovered at the end of the month when they got their milk check what Black Tuesday meant to them. The check was 15% lower than the month before. William thought Fred Beratti had made a mistake when he wrote his check, so he asked him about it the next day when he came to pick up the milk.

Fred said, "William you're lucky you got that much. The price of milk has fallen so bad; I had to stretch things to keep the milk checks as high as they were. If things keep going the way they are, it is going to get smaller. I can hardly get rid of the butter and cheese we are making at any price. People are losing their jobs right and left, and they just can't buy as much milk, butter or cheese as they did. But you're still making as much so there is a lot of extra cheese. I got to undersell the other guy in order to get the stores to buy any, and it is getting worse every day. Let's just hope we can keep selling the cheeses and butter we make, or we wouldn't be able to pay you anything."

William saw his checks get smaller and smaller. He told Agnes they could not spend money on anything. There wasn't enough money coming in to make the farm payments at the end of the year. William had to pay his dad $575 a year for the farm, but the milk check was only averaging $42.00 per month. How could he pay his dad? At the end of 1930, he had to draw down his life savings by $100 to make the farm payment. By 1931, he would have had to draw $200 but Peter said with the depression and all, he'd only ask for $500 so William took the $350 he'd saved up that year and added $150 from what he had hoped was their nest egg to pay. Things did not get any worse or better in 1932.

Franklin Roosevelt announced he would run for President. Agnes had hoped Al Smith would run again. What this country needed was a Catholic president. Someone who could talk to God and get him to help us out of the depression. Clearly the depression was more than a mere mortal could deal with. The government had had three years to get the country back on its feet and nothing was getting better. In fact things were worse. The price of milk had never been so low. The extra dollar for a steer hardly seemed much improvement when you consider William sold steers for two and one-half times as much three years ago. No, man could not do this by himself. He needed God and the best way to get God to help was to elect Al

Smith or some other Catholic. With all the Catholics in America there must be a way to get one elected that could get this country back on its feet.

But if the country wasn't ready for a Catholic, Roosevelt might be the next best thing. Agnes knew that he had worked for Al Smith. In fact, she thought Roosevelt had nominated Smith for President at the last convention. He had to be a good man. He spoke with passion and belief. He could get this country out of the depression. It just took some faith and some action. This made sense to Agnes, so she decided early to vote for Roosevelt. The radio was saying Roosevelt would win. Things would get better. She just wished that William would have more faith—it's what Roosevelt was saying we all needed to get past this.

By 1933, milk checks dribbled to $36 a month and William had to sell five of his best steers for $25 each. The old cows were selling for less than $5.00. Agnes raised a bigger garden, William butchered all their meat. Agnes sewed and mended all their clothes, but they still had to buy sugar, salt, spices, clothes and replace some tools. William had to pay Jamboys to repair some of his machinery that he could not fix himself. Agnes insisted they give some money to the church if it was only ten cents a week. Even when they watched every penny, they needed a dollar a week to get by. William was able to sell enough calves, heifers and cows to bring in a little over $100 and the milk brought in a little over $400. He had to draw his account down another $200. William and Agnes only had $100 left in their nest egg, and they worried daily how they would be able to make the payments the next year. They cut down on the sugar they used and Agnes told the Watkins man that she could not buy anything this year. She felt sorry for him, because she knew he was being told this by everyone, and he had a family to feed too, but she could not do anything about it. William only drove their car to go to church on Sunday to save on gas. Agnes lowered their contributions to the church to five cents a week. The milk checks stayed the same and the price of cows edged up about a dollar. But they weren't making enough to make the farm payment.

Agnes asked William, "Will you ask Grandpa if we can pay less this year? Maybe he'll take three hundred dollars and be satisfied."

"How we gonna pay him back later? We been in this depression over three years now and it ain't getting any better. If we pay Dad $300, we'll owe him another $200. When will we ever get that much money to pay him back?"

"The depression can't last forever. Besides what can we do? Your dad has plenty of money. You know Andrew and Vito aren't paying your dad the full amount. I'd like to pay the full amount. But we did not make the depression. We didn't vote for Hoover. What can we do? We don't have enough money. Even if we did not spend a cent, you are making at most $500 a year even with selling cows. How can we pay Grandpa $600?"

William mumbled something about a road job and shuffled out of the kitchen. Agnes found it more and more difficult to talk to William about money. She understood that he wanted to make those farm payments, and he wanted a nest egg. So did Agnes. Their family was growing, and they were getting older. Not so old yet, but things being what they were, they'd be lucky not to end their lives in a poor house—living off the county. She knew it would kill William to live off the county. He scoffed at her Uncle Rocco who spent his winters in Viroqua at the poor house. William had said, "I'd rather freeze in the woods" and she figured he meant it. Agnes did not want to spend her old age in the poor house either. But she also knew they could not make the farm payments. "Why doesn't William ask Peter to lower the rates or at least take less for now? Couldn't he add a year or two to the payments? The depression cannot last forever. If it does, everyone will go broke and soon starve to death because no one will be able to afford to raise crops let alone own their farm; things have to get better."

Nick

Things had lightened up a lot since Nick came to work. He just wanted a place to sleep and three meals a day. In these times it was all any single man without property could expect. He was quiet. He never said there was too much work to do— he did his work, ate and slept. He never complained about the depression. Once she had asked him if he would mind wearing a shirt when he ate. He said "Wearing a shirt would be like asking William to wear a jacket. If it bothers you, I'll eat on the porch. I wouldn't mind, but I can't wear a shirt to eat. It'd be no problem."

"No, it's fine, you eat with the rest of the family."

Except for that, Agnes could not remember a time that Nick had not immediately agreed to whatever was requested and gone about doing it. It didn't seem to make any difference if she or William asked. Nick did it. Though he was so quiet that there were days when she did not hear him speak one word, she found herself enjoying his company. He was strong and gentle at the same time. While he seldom looked at her, he always seemed aware of her presence and attentive to her needs.

When he came into the kitchen, and she was juggling five things, he would know which two to do for her. He'd finish them and sit down to eat and never say a word. William never noticed what needed to be done and so Agnes had to ask him to help, and he would let her know how much he had put himself out after a tough day in the fields.

    William was making $2.50 a day working on the highway for the county. They needed that money to make the payments on the farm and to pay the property taxes so William had asked Carl Pemchi for a job working on the road for Badaxe County the summer of 1931. Agnes and William had not spent any cash since Christmas of 1929 for even food or clothes. Everything they ate came off the farm and anything else they needed they went without or traded to get. The depression had hit everyone hard. William and Agnes never felt like things were any worse for them because they saw how everyone suffered. They were thankful that they had their land and always had a good meal on the table; William paid his taxes on time and never missed a payment on his land. Everyone had to work hard. The oldest children were barely in school but they worked around the farm and did all the day to day chores for William was working on the road from dawn to dusk. It was his "cash crop" he liked to say. So, Agnes found herself hoeing the corn and helping make hay as well as raising seven children, fifty chickens and an acre and one-half of garden. Matthew and Alex were in the barn between 5:30-8:00 every morning and night milking the cows. In between they were either in school or taking care of things around the farm. Pina and Hannah helped around the house, cleaned, did the dishes and assisted with the care of the smallest three children.

The first summer William worked on the road, he had been able to come home each evening. For the past six weeks they had been working on the other side of the county and William and the rest of the men were sleeping in abandoned houses during the week. William came home Saturday night and had to be back on the way to work by 4:00 on Monday morning. There was so much to get done while he was home. He went over the work that needed to be done that week with Alex. He repaired any tools or machines that might have broken down during the week. He then did whatever work might take a grown man to do. If one of the children needed special discipline, Agnes asked William to take care of that. The only time to relax was at Sunday Mass. Lately William seemed to be sleeping through most of the service. Agnes used to get embarrassed when William fell asleep during Mass. But he was working so hard now, she was sure that God understood; besides she was so proud of him she didn't really care what the neighbors thought.

Agnes hadn't always been proud of him. In fact, she had thought he was rather lazy. All of her brothers were bigger and stronger than William, and they were hard workers and hard drinkers. She was glad that William didn't drink, but she wished he were stronger and more ambitious. It seemed that the beautiful farm they had bought was already beginning to fall apart. William just wouldn't fix things up. Oh, he tilled the fields, planted, cared for and harvested the crops, and he milked a full herd of cows every morning and night. But he did not have that little extra pride and ambition that it took to keep things fixed. Sometimes she thought she was too hard on William. He worked long days and every day. But if he were a little stronger and faster, he'd have time to keep things fixed up too.

As the depression set in Agnes remembered the old saying, "Hard times bring out the best and the worst in people." Agnes' brothers' response to the thirties was to turn more and more to the bottle. They had found ways to brew their own and their farms had deteriorated rapidly. They too had purchased their farms from their father and Agnes knew for a fact that they were not making payments. She suspected that her dad was paying their taxes for them.

William said, "Agnes, the country will bounce out of this, and when it does I don't want to be indebted for the rest of my life for the payments I missed." So he got a job on the road. He put the children to work in the fields and taught them how to milk the cows. Alex and Matthew were only eight and six when they first had to milk the cows by themselves. Before that, they had helped William with the chores, washing the cow's teats, carrying the milk to the milk shed and occasionally milking a cow. So when William began to work for the road, the children knew what to do. William got the crops in on time, kept the weeds at bay and harvested the crops before winter took over. William had jumped at the chance to hire Nick whom he had met working on the road. Nick had been working for the county for years when William joined the crew. Nick was the hardest worker. Everyone looked up to him because he just kept repairing roads no matter how hot or cold. Sometimes he'd say, "We gotta give the taxpayers their money's worth." Other than that he didn't talk much. All the guys would complain that the work was too hard and the pay was terrible. Nick never said anything.

One night after a long day, William and Nick decided they'd just sleep under the stars. They were too tired to go back to the shack the county called home for them. William lay on the ground. He was so tired he thought he'd fall asleep instantly. But he was too tired to fall asleep and his mind raced with pictures of his farm, his cattle, wife, children and all the work that the farm needed. He resented working on the road when he knew he should be working his farm, but he also knew he had to get the cash from working on the road to keep his farm. He had seen many farmers go under. The banks would foreclose instantly if the payments weren't made and the government had put up places for sale when the owners had failed to pay their taxes. "They're not going to get me," William thought.

The images kept racing through his head until finally he had to talk about them. There was only Nick, and he might listen and if he didn't, William had to talk to somebody. William began to tell Nick about his farm and wife and children. He talked to Nick about the day he realized Agnes was the woman he wanted, courting her, getting married, buying the farm from his dad, finding out Agnes was pregnant on Christmas, moving to their own place, the birth of Giuseppina, and the births of Hannah, Alex, Matthew, Marie, Mark and Emma. Emma was the baby, and William said, "You can already tell she's going to be a pistol. Hardly six months old, and I can tell she's a tomboy." Nick could tell that William was not disappointed that Emma might be a tomboy. But mostly William talked about his farm. He talked about plowing fields, not just any fields but his own fields. He talked about his horses that worked so hard next to him. "They're more like my brothers than my brothers." He talked about the sweet smell of fresh cut hay and the difference he felt when he finished making hay all day and digging ditches for the road. "I suppose there's not so much difference in the work. But after making hay all day—sure my muscles are sore—but I go to bed and I know I'm going to sleep and the next day be ready for another day. Here, my muscles are not as sore, but I just lie awake and the next day is a dread. Making hay, that's a man's work. This work is for—I don't know—maybe no one."

William talked about milking cows and talking to the milkman when he came every morning, and the pride he felt when that first milk check came in. "These days, it isn't enough to pay for the mortgage on the farm, but it's my check from my cows and I still get a kick every month when the milkman delivers the milk check. No, of course it's not like it was when the check paid the mortgage, provided a dollar a week for the church and a little money to pick up some store bought things. That was when times were good. Before that son-of-a-bitch Hoover fucked up the country. Never vote for a Republican again. But that check is from my farm, my work, my cows. No check, no matter how big, from the county can ever have the same feel. Fuck, I wish I didn't have to work for the damn county. But how else can I keep my farm.

"But you know the hardest thing working for the county isn't the hard work or the sore muscles or even working for someone else. It's that I can't keep my farm up. The weeds are winning. The buildings are falling apart. The machinery needs fixing. The children don't milk the cows right."

During this whole time Nick said nothing. William wasn't sure if he was listening, but as he told the story William felt a heaviness lift, so he didn't care if Nick was listening—he was telling him anyway.

William finished—a long silence followed. "You're lucky—I'd give anything to work the land. I hate this job," Nick said. There was another long silence. Five minutes and neither person said a word. Nick was thinking back to his youth when he grew up on a farm in Virginia. He'd worked hard but he'd felt one with the land—for Nick it was that feeling that life was about. "Workin' for the highway, the land is taken out of production. It's not right, I hate working on the road gang," he said.

William began to think, "Nick is single. He doesn't seem to have many needs. He works harder than any of us, but he barely makes enough money to buy food. Nick may have to spend all his money on food. Now that I think about it, he must not have a place to live. The only home he has must be the tent or shacks we sleep in during the week." William had been too focused on his own need to make some cash to meet the taxes and payments on his farm to realize someone just working on the road probably couldn't do more than get by. "If Nick really wants to work the land," William thought, "hell, I can offer him food and a house to sleep in. That wouldn't cost me a penny. Another mouth to feed would not take any cash. If Nick worked the farm it would take a lot of pressure off me and the kids. Hell, if he did a good job it might mean a little extra income." William wondered if Nick would work for room and board. "Shit, why not, it's as much as he is getting here."

"Nick, you mean you'd rather work on a farm than work here? You know there is no money to be made on a farm. That's why I got to work my farm and work here too."

Nick replied, "I don't work here for money. I got to eat and I barely make enough here to do that. Maybe I get a couple of drinks on Saturday night and then it's gone. Who needs it?"

"Nick, you know I could use some help on the farm. Now mind you, I couldn't pay you nothing. But I got an extra room in our house and Agnes is the best cook in Vernon County."

Nick had wanted to ask William if he would take him on for room and board, but he had been too timid to ask. "You mean you'd give me room and board free if I worked for you? I'd work hard, and I know farming. You wouldn't be sorry. I don't need much, a little room, I don't need a bed, I'd sleep on the floor, and I'd eat whatever was left over. I wouldn't eat till after the children are done. I'd eat on the porch. I won't be a problem."

William was stunned. Stunned as much by Nick talking so much at one time as by his offer. Nick's offer sunk in. He'd work for room and board. He'd work for less. Room and board was no problem. William's spare room had a bed, and with Agnes' garden, the milk from the cows and the butchering, the Genotti family always had food. As hard as the times were, they had plenty to eat and they had plenty of room. William's problem was to get some cash to make the farm payments, pay the taxes and maybe buy some shoes for the children, so he had gone to work on the road. Now he was so tired he couldn't keep up the farm even with Alex and Matthew working like grownups. If Nick would become his hired hand—"naw, it can't happen."

"It's a deal. When you want to start?"

"Now"

After work on Saturday, Nick told the foreman he was quitting, packed his things in a nap bag and headed west up Highway 56 with William. Agnes saw William and a tall dark strong man with no shirt on walking toward the house. William would bring home a friend from the road crew now and then.

Agnes didn't mind much if they helped William around the farm. She missed the chance to be alone with her husband, but with the children and all the work they rarely had a moment together anyway. She waved to them and William and the shirtless man waved back. William came right to the garden with his friend. Usually he went to the barn to see how the cows were doing and if the children were taking care of the chores. "Hi, Agnes, this is Nick. He's going to be our hired hand. He can stay in the North bedroom on the second floor. Take his things to the room. Come on, Nick, let's go to the barn. Matthew's probably still milking the cows. He can show you what he does and tomorrow you can take over. I'm sure Matthew will like that." William and the stranger headed off to the barn.

Agnes picked up Nick's sack and headed off to the house. She stopped in the kitchen and tossed another piece of wood in the stove. William and Nick would be hungry when they came in for the night so she would heat them some goulash. She grabbed the dust mop and headed for the North room. She was using it for a sewing room, so she'd have to move some things out and clean it up. She called for Giuseppina and Hannah to help. They hauled the sewing machine down the steps and set it up in the front room. Back up the stairs to haul most of the boxes to the attic or basement. Agnes decided to store some in her bedroom. She did not want the clothes she'd stored for the next baby to go to the attic or basement. Then they dusted, mopped and scrubbed the room to get it ready for Nick.

"Better finish your studies."

Agnes went back to the kitchen, took the leftover meat, potatoes, gravy and vegetables from dinner, dumped it all into a pot and heated it over the wood stove. Just as it came to a boil,

William, Matthew, Alex and the new man came into the house. William showed Nick where he could wash up in the sink. Nick splashed some water over his hands, took the nearest towel and dried his hands. Agnes noticed that he didn't wash around his mouth. William and most of the farmers around there also always tossed some water over their mouths. Agnes was never sure why they did. She'd noticed that William often left dirt and grease on his face as did most of the thrashers. It was more a ritual than a cleaning, but Nick did not bother to feign that he was cleaning his face before eating. William sat at the head of the table and Nick sat right down at the other plate—bare chested. Agnes was used to seeing men without shirts, so she barely noticed Nick had not been wearing a shirt when he came home with William. Agnes figured that he had his shirts in the sack she had put up in his room, and he was too shy to ask where she had put it. "Nick, let me show you where your room is."

"Sure, but why don't we eat first? I'll probably just go to bed after supper." Nick poured a big helping of goulash onto his plate and began to gulp it down. It was clear he hadn't had a hot meal in some time. Agnes just stared at Nick. Alex, who had hung around the kitchen to help, also stared. Nick suddenly realized that they were looking at him. "Oh, I hope you don't mind. I just can't eat with a shirt on. I'm just not used to wearing one. I feel all bound up in a shirt. I hope you don't mind. I can't eat with a shirt on."

Agnes and William both said, "Oh it's fine." Agnes did not like it, but he was a guest and guests should be allowed to be at home and that meant being comfortable. If Nick felt uncomfortable with a shirt on at the table, then he should be allowed to eat without one. It was clear that Alex didn't mind.

She was staring at Nick and his chest with a crush so obvious that Agnes wondered why Nick wasn't embarrassed. But he seemed oblivious of Alex. He was eating the goulash like it was a Sunday dinner. After supper Agnes showed Nick his room. He thanked her, closed the door and went to sleep.

William looked very happy when Agnes came back into the kitchen. "What a lucky break. Nick is a great worker. Best man on the road crew. He wants to work for room and board. We don't have to pay him a nickel. We can keep the farm together and I can keep working on the road, so we can make our payments. I never felt so lucky." William grabbed Agnes' butt and squeezed it. He went off to the bathroom and shut off the tub water, crawled in and took a bath. Agnes was glad that he was taking a bath. Sometimes he'd come home from working on the road all week, say he was too tired to take a bath, come to bed all dirty and want her to make love. She knew that she'd have to make love to him tonight, but at least he'd be clean.

Nick caught on immediately. William and Matthew showed him how to do the chores around the barn on Sunday morning. Sunday night Nick told William he'd prefer to milk the cows himself. He didn't want little kids getting in his way and William should spend the time with his nice wife. During the day, William went over with Nick the things that needed to be done around the farm for the week. The corn needed cultivating, the barn had a few boards that needed to be repaired, one of the corn fields needed the rocks removed from it and Agnes needed a part of the west hayfield plowed because she wanted to plant some late sweet corn. Nick said no problem. He pointed out that the weeds were taking over the corn field. "Maybe I should hoe the corn fields too?"

"Matthew and Alex can do that," William said. "They should have time now if you do all the milking and the other work."

Monday morning, Nick was up reorganizing the barn to his own needs before William was up to get to Viroqua to work on the road. When William left at 5:00 a.m., Matthew was chasing the cows into the barn. William overheard Nick say, "Thanks, Boss. Why don't you start hoeing the corn field behind the garden? I can milk the cows myself. That way we won't be wasting each other's time." Matthew skipped off to the garage, grabbed a hoe and headed for the corn field. He didn't like hoeing much, but it sure beat having to milk the cows.

William saw that his farm was in good hands as he rode his horse over Moundridge and headed toward Romance where he would be working on the county road this week making $4.00 a day that he would turn over to his father to pay for the farm.

Nick got up early, milked the cows, ate breakfast with the family, worked in the fields all day except for a short noon dinner, ate supper, milked the cows again and went to sleep. Only on Sunday's was it apparent he wasn't just another Genotti. He did not go to church on Sunday morning and after Sunday dinner he would go into the woods to be by himself. He always said he needed some time alone. Agnes knew that he spent most of the day alone working in the fields. She figured that he wanted to leave her and William alone with their family. She did not think that was necessary, but she appreciated his thoughtfulness and never once suggested to him that he did not need to go away.

Agnes had never seen anyone as strong as Nick, or anyone who could work so long. He was at work before 5:00

every morning and worked straight through to after 8:00 every evening. On Sundays, he'd milk the cows in the morning and evening. Chores took over two hours each time. Nick didn't take off for holidays except for Christmas. He said, "The weeds don't take off holidays, so I guess I can't either." The corn fields stayed cultivated and hoed. The manure was spread evenly throughout the fields. The corn and oats were planted at the best times and the harvests got bigger each year. The cows gave more milk and William got a little raise at work. Over time the number of milk cows increased because William didn't have to sell as many to pay the taxes and Nick was there to milk more cows.

At first Agnes was afraid Nick might do all the work and her children would grow lazy, but she had nothing to fear. Nick didn't like having the kids under his feet, but he knew that it was important for them to work if they were to grow up and be more than no-goods. So he always had plenty of work for them to do, and he always made sure they did it. He would have them working in his eyesight if at some distance from his own work. Nick inspired the children to work hard. Matthew and Mark looked up to Nick and wanted to be strong like him, and they knew they would only get that way if they worked hard like Nick did. Alex maintained a crush on Nick, so she wanted to please him. Agnes was glad that Nick failed to notice not only that she had a crush on him but that she was a girl. Nick treated Alex just like Matthew and Mark, and he expected her to work just as hard. With Nick keeping the three farm workers busy, Agnes found she had more time to do her own work and that Giuseppina, Hannah and Marie were more helpful around the house and with the babies.

The first summer with Nick went by quickly. The weeds disappeared and little by little things around the farm got fixed. One day Agnes discovered that the hinge was fixed on the cellar door and that the window that had been painted shut two years earlier was open. It was great to have a handy man around. Before it seemed possible, harvest time came. William had had to take days off from working on the road to handle the harvest the year before and for the first time they had gotten behind making payments to William's father for the farm. William had sold one of their very best milk cows to catch up on the payment. But this year, Nick told William to keep working on the road. If he got behind, William could take off. Nick never got behind and the harvest was finished before most of the neighbors and well before the first snow. Agnes thought Nick would hang around the house more in the winter, or he would take up fox hunting and ice fishing, but Nick used the winter to fix up the buildings around the farm and to repair the machinery. His days were as long through the first winter as they had been all summer.

During the winter, Nick suggested to William that he let him raise some tobacco. "Give me something to do in the winter—this winter I can build a wagon and turn the top of the machine shed into a place to cure the tobacco. Next winter I'll have something to do—to cure it and strip it and get it off to market." William had never raised tobacco but he knew it was a good cash crop and with the Depression, tobacco was one of the few things that still bought a good price.

"I guess people got to smoke, Depression or not." William told Nick he never raised tobacco wouldn't know how to tell him to raise it. Nick said simply, "I was raised on a tobacco farm. My folks worked the tobacco fields for generations." Nick spent the winter sawing lathes, building a second story in the machine shed and stringing poles to hang tobacco on and building a wagon frame to haul tobacco. When spring came he prepared a tobacco hotbed, planted the seeds, grew the seedlings, transplanted the tobacco sets and watered them with care. The tobacco grew better than even Nick expected. He taught the children how to pull off the tobacco worms and to sucker and top the tobacco plants. Nick cut the stalks himself, speared them onto lathes and hauled them off in the special tobacco wagon he had built to be stored in the room he had prepared above the machine shed. That winter the tobacco sold for a good price. William made enough he still had some money left after he paid the taxes and farm payments. He decided it would be fairest to split what was leftover with Nick. Nick refused the money saying, "What I gonna do with money—I got everything I need right here." William said, "Nick, I'll start an account for you at the bank so when you leave here you will have some money to start over. It was the first time since the Depression began that William had enough money to have a bank account. He was able to save all of his income from the next summer to increase his savings. William vowed then that he would never live without some money saved. He never wanted to have to work just to pay his bills. Agnes agreed. She did not like being without some cash. Neither William nor Agnes could accept the idea of buying something now and paying later. Even when credit became easily available many years later, they would not use it. One had to buy one's farm on credit. Everything else, including the retirement house they would live in, should be paid for with cash. Agnes wanted some of the money they had saved to be put away in the mattress. FDR had told the people that they should put their money in the bank and FDR was a great leader. William trusted him completely, but he put 25% of his savings in the mattress all the same. He knew too many people the banks had ruined in the first years of the depression.

Agnes found herself feeling more and more comfortable around Nick. It stopped bothering her that he didn't wear a shirt at the table. Even in the winter, he'd sit at the table bare chested. Only on Sunday would he grace the table wearing a shirt. Agnes noted that the long silences began to feel good. William didn't talk much either, but Agnes always felt a need to make conversation with him. With Nick, she was able to enjoy his presence without talking.

The county always stopped new construction on roads on Thanksgiving so William was home during Nick's first winter as Genotti's hired hand. William was used to taking things easy during the winter. He'd do a lot of fox hunting, deer hunting and ice fishing. On freezing days he'd stay in the house, and usually approach Agnes right after dinner to take a nap. Of course, she knew he didn't mean nap, but she also knew that she would get a nap after William would please himself in her body. She didn't mind so much, because she too liked to curl into the bed on cold winter days. But this winter William did less hunting and fishing, because Nick always had a job going. Now William didn't have to work just because Nick was, but he felt guilty and would wind up helping Nick. But there was no way that William was going to work outside on those cold days when the thermostat would refuse to climb to -20 degrees so Agnes and William had a few cozy afternoons—but not so many as earlier years.

Spring came and William went back to work on the county roads. Agnes became more aware of Nick's presence.

She could smell him when he came in from the fields for dinner and supper. It was a smell she liked, and she began to notice that her eyes would fall pleasingly on his bare chest. As the spring warmed up and Nick's smell grew more pleasant—by 11:30 she would start wishing for him to come early. But he always came right at noon as if he were the cuckoo clock announcing mid-day. Agnes wondered how he could always be so prompt. William always came to dinner right around noon, but if he had a job to finish he might come at 12: 10 or even 12:15. She ran things through her mind as she waited anxiously for Nick to come into eat. Maybe she'd tell him about what she had been doing all morning. Or ask him what he was doing. Some days she'd relive the dreams she'd had and dream about telling Nick about her dreams. Maybe he'd tell her about his dreams. Maybe if she told him about her dreams he'd see how much she liked being with him.

Every day Nick walked in the door as the clock pointed to 12:00. He didn't even own a watch. He would wash his hands; sit at the table in his bare chest, and more often than not eat in silence. She had never noticed a man's special smell before, and she found that she liked it.

Day after day went by, with Agnes getting more and more anxious to be in Nick's presence. She began to feel like a schoolgirl. She wondered if she looked as foolish as Alex had the summer before when she looked at Nick with the biggest crush Agnes had ever seen. Now she found herself looking at Nick with that same feeling—not able to take her eyes off this man or her nose off that sweet smell he sent her way. It was a smell aroused from his work naked in the sun. He emitted sweat, muscles, strength. She drank them fully.

She'd ask how his day was. What had he done? Or she'd start to tell him of her dreams. Or even how much she liked his smell and how glad she was that he did not wear a shirt to the table. But nothing came out of her mouth. For the very first time in her life she was tongue-tied. Nick said nothing. He'd just eat his dinner or supper and say nothing. Fifteen minutes and he'd finish, get up, wash his hands and head back to the fields or out to the barn. He seemed as oblivious of her as he had of Alex the summer before. For that Agnes was thankful. Would he leave the farm if he knew she was attracted to him? He was a decent man and William's friend. He would be so embarrassed if he knew she wanted him that he would leave, and then they would all go back to the old days when everyone had too much work to do and the farm fell apart at the same time.

Two weeks passed with Agnes torturing herself at every meal. She had fallen for this man, and she wanted him—today, she had dreamed of him grabbing her and throwing her on the bed. Touching her with his strong hands, unzipping her dress, looking at her with lust in his eyes, touching her so gently and yet so strongly. Handling her with the delicacy but command that he handled Nellie, their mare. Grabbing and squeezing her with strength but a firm touch. Caressing her breasts with the sureness that he hoed weeds. She had wanted him so bad that she had forgotten where she was and had not noticed that she had placed her own hand on her breast.

She woke from this dream standing before the stove in horror. She had never lusted for a man before—she knew it was wrong. It was worse than wrong, it was a mortal sin. She had never been able to imagine how anyone could commit a mortal sin. How could one be so angry they could kill, or lazy they would miss Sunday Mass, or lustful they would indulge in sex outside of marriage? She had never even lusted for William after they were married.

But she had just lusted for Nick. She had not only wanted him, she had allowed herself to imagine him taking her, and she knew that her Church and her God condemned the wish as much as the action. She had for the very first time in her life committed a mortal sin. Fear and guilt took over. How could she be so evil as to wish to have sex with this man—just a hired hand—a man who did not even go to church on Sunday—maybe he wasn't even Catholic—how could she—such a horrible act—such a horrible thought. How could she betray Jesus whom she had vowed chastity. It was bad enough that she had married William and slept with him. But they had married in the church, it was a holy wedding and it was a sacrament and as William's wife it was her duty to have sex with him even if she had preferred to have kept herself pure for Jesus. How could she betray William? How betray Jesus? To want Nick in that way was to destroy her marriage. No crime against marriage was as great as adultery. All her life her church had taught her that the thought was as great as the action. She was an adulterer and she must confess to the priest and to God and maybe even to William.

She wanted to go to the church that very moment. She had a mortal sin on her soul—needed to go to confession. It was only Wednesday. She could not wait until Saturday night when the priest heard regular confession. What if she died with a mortal sin on her soul? She would burn in hell forever. There would be no mercy for the fact that she had managed to live thirty-two years without committing a mortal sin. It was the state of the soul at the moment of death that made the difference. She thought of walking the three miles to Badaxe, knocking on the rectory and asking Father Malonic to hear her confession. But she knew everyone in town would see her and figure that she had committed a mortal sin—they might think she had even had sex with Nick. Her sisters used to kid her about having such a he-man around when her husband was away. But they were only joking. If she went waltzing off to the priest to have her sin heard, they might think it was more than a joke. Better wait until Saturday. "But what if I die, I'll burn in hell forever. I'm not going to die. I'm not. I've lived this long. I'll make it to Saturday. Maybe I'll go to confession on Saturday and die in an accident on the way home. Then I'll go to heaven and be with Jesus. Yes Jesus, let me live to Saturday and confess my sin and then take my life. I deserve to die. I am so ashamed."

Agnes waited out what proved to be the three longest days in her life. That Saturday night, she got the children ready to go to confession so early they got to church one-half hour before Father Malonic arrived to hear confessions. Agnes never prayed so hard to God before. She asked Him to forgive her, and she talked to Him in all her shame as if he were standing beside her. When Father arrived, Agnes was waiting first in line for the confessional. No use to take a chance that she might be struck dead while waiting for others to confess their sins.

"Bless me Father for I have sinned. Father, I don't know how to tell you this, but this week I committed a mortal sin. I've never committed a mortal sin before. It was so horrible." Father could feel the tears run down Agnes' face. He had been hearing her confessions for many years, and he knew that there was not a more devout person in his parish. Sometimes her only sin might be that she wished Rita Monty wouldn't come up to talk to her after Church. Father paused and waited for Agnes to continue. Finally she said, "Father, I don't know what happened. There is this hired man who stays with us. Well I just started liking him more and more. I liked being around him more and more. At first, I thought this was good. A sign he was becoming one of the family. But then I noticed he was a man, that he smelled good that he looked good—that I liked him. The devil must have gotten hold of me, because I never thought it was bad. It just happened and I liked it and never thought it was bad. How could I be so evil?" She stopped for a moment. Father wondered if that was it. Agnes had decided that she liked Nick. Well, he could reassure her that this was not a mortal sin. God did not say you could not like someone of the opposite sex if you were married. Or did she sleep with him? No not possible. Agnes, his very holiest parishioner, committed adultery? It would be proof that the devil could take control of anyone. Agnes must have slept with Nick. She knew enough to know that just liking Nick was not a mortal sin. Maybe a venial sin but certainly not a mortal sin.

"Go on Agnes."

Agnes was surprised that Father knew it was her. Confession was supposed to be secret. But she was also glad. Father had to keep her sin a secret, so she had no fear of him telling others, and now that she knew that he knew it was her, it was easier to tell him of her evil thoughts.

"Oh Father, I was standing in the kitchen and I felt Nick come up behind me. He touched me with those strong hands, ran them over my body, touched me all over and I let him—I let myself enjoy it—I am so evil, so embarrassed—oh God, please forgive me—oh Father, please forgive me."

"Agnes, God forgives you, He forgives all sins. You have done an evil thing. You must not let it happen again. Maybe

Nick should leave. The temptation will be great once you have given into the devil. If he stays there, you may want him again."

"No, oh Father no, I can't stand to look at him now. The very sight of him repulses me and reminds me of the awful sin I have committed. It is punishment every time he sits at the table."

"Then, let that be your punishment. To feed the man you sinned with in your own home, before your husband and children. God has found for you the correct punishment. But Agnes, will Nick leave you alone. You may despise him, but will he want you again."

Agnes giggled a little. It was the first smile since she had those thoughts in her kitchen. "Oh, Father, Nick doesn't know. I did not tell him that I had those evil thoughts." Then Agnes realized that Father thought that Nick had actually touched her breast. She was humiliated that he would think such a thing of her. But she went on, "Father, while I had these thoughts of Nick, I began to touch myself. I did not know that I was touching myself until I gained control of my thoughts. I really didn't mean to do it. Forgive me God for this sin also."

Father reassured Agnes that there was no sin if she had not intentionally touched herself. If she was not even aware, then she could not have intended it. Father blessed Agnes, told her that God would forgive her sin if she was truly sorry and that her punishment was to feed the man who had caused her to fall and to be especially good to her family for the next week. "Agnes, next week I want to know if you were tempted again. It is good to face temptation. It can make you stronger. But we should not play into the devil's hand. If the temptations continue, Nick should go."

Agnes was never tempted again. The anguish she suffered over her fall from grace was too great and the very sight of Nick made her stomach feel heavy for the next few weeks. In time, the work of the summer began to take over Agnes' preoccupations and soon she could have Nick at the table with ease. Slowly things went back to normal, and time plus a busy summer healed Agnes' anxiety. Only when William approached her, and she felt like a used woman did the pain of having let herself be seduced by Nick return.

Nick stayed on to work on the Genotti farm four more years. The farm began to prosper along with the country as a whole. William announced that he was not going to continue to work on the road. He was making enough money from the cows and the tobacco that he could stay home and tend his farm. Nick seemed worried so William assured him that he wanted Nick to stay. Agnes was pregnant with her 10th child and Nick knew that the family needed the bedroom he was using. The next Sunday he left for the woods with his knapsack on his shoulder. They never heard from him again.

William tried to find Nick, so he could give him his share of the tobacco money. He never found Nick. After twelve years, William and Agnes gave the money, which had grown to one-year's income, to the Church to build a new two-room school. Nick's contribution turned out to be the single biggest gift raised for the new school.

II

Earth

II: Earth
(1934 -1943)

Gardening

"Agnes, is that all you do is work?" asked Frank, her youngest brother. "Have some fun once in a while. How many hours a day you out here fussing over this or that plant? Ten? You need your kids to do more of the work."

"What? This is not work. Scrubbing the bathroom is work—doing the dishes after the thrashers is work. Taking care of the chickens is work. Putting up with you is work. This is not work."

"Who you kidding? Not many things harder to do than raise a garden."

"Not many things more rewarding! When I harvest the fruit off a plant that I seeded and nurtured, that's joy—that's being close to God. Whoever said work was hard—work is doing something for money or something you don't wanna do but have to. Sometimes I think cooking is work, and you know what, it is. But making Easter dinner or cooking for the thrashers—that's not work because it's so much fun to create a dinner everyone, including me, is going to love. That's fun, Frank, and don't you ever forget it."

The joy of creation, the joy of making something useful and beautiful from tiny seeds gathered the year before or purchased at the store was her chance to be one with her God. If she could make tens of pumpkins from one tiny pumpkin seed, how could anyone doubt God's ability to make the universe from nothing? The proportions were the same. The universe was tiny for the Almighty God. The only difference was that she started from a seed, and God started from nothing. Not exactly nothing, for the seed of the universe had to have been in God's mind. Since God was so grand, he was able to pop the seed out of his mind into the creation of the universe. It was really nothing compared to the creation of all these pumpkins from one little seed. All this lettuce, corn, peas, beans from little seeds! The power of the creator—controlling the planting, the weeding, the location, the sunlight and the water—gave Agnes a power over the destiny of her garden that she did not have over any other part of her life.

Sometimes early in the morning with the rising sun coming over her left shoulder, stooped over her string beans or picking strawberries or corn, she looked like the Virgin of Gardens. A giver of life with no need for conception. She, God, and the universe made life, and they made beauty that gave meaning to all that looked. The power of creation was in her hands, and she molded one of the greatest creations possible. Agnes prepared her garden with the care of an architect, planted with the energy of the painter over his canvas and watched over the plants with the loving hands of a sculptor.

She learned to garden from a master. Her grandmother was born and raised on a truck farm just outside of Trento in Italy and her family had been feeding the finest families in the area for centuries. When she came to Badaxe, she provided vegetables for the local grocery store as well as her family. As a child, Agnes' favorite activity was to help her grandmother in the garden, so she absorbed her grandmother's knowledge and skill. Some even claimed Agnes' garden surpassed her grandma's.

The year William and Agnes moved to the Moundridge Farm, they decided that she should have the plot next to the road below the yard for her garden. William planted apple trees and grape vines on the west side of the plot, and he plowed the east half for Agnes' garden. She wanted the east side so her plants received the morning sun with no obstructions while being shaded part of the afternoon. Over the years, the garden crept to the orchard area and eventually across the road into the adjoining field as Agnes needed an ever bigger garden to feed her growing family.

She planted the regular stuff—potatoes, tomatoes, corn, watermelon, sweet peas, string beans, squash, pumpkins, beets, cauliflower, leaf lettuce, cucumbers, kohlrabi, cabbage, strawberries, leeks and onions. Most agreed she raised the juiciest sweet corn in Badaxe. Agnes picked her corn before the dew lifted, and she insisted strawberries tasted better if picked before eleven. She always had a large patch of strawberries, raspberries, asparagus and rhubarb, and she knew when a patch might die off, so she started a new one in time. On the ridge farm she maintained a fifteen-foot arbor of grapes to make jam if the children did not eat them all first.

Each year she planted one new vegetable. If it grew and her family liked it she added it to her repertoire of annual plantings. Early in the 1930s she planted a new variety that looked more like an undersized green tomato than a fruit. They called them "ground cherries", and Agnes got them to grow abundantly. She cooked them down into pie, and her family ate them before they cooled. She made ground cherry jam, and

William made a rare sound of approval when he ate it the first time. Agnes grew ground cherries thereafter.

One year she planted kale—no one liked it; another year sweet potatoes. She tried peanuts one year. They got a few and Gabriel and Lucy loved roasting them, and they got eaten. She planted several rows and got very few peanuts. She concluded that the harvest was not worth the land wasted, though by then they had plenty of land. To the children's disappointment she never tried to grow peanuts again. Her rule of thumb was if the plant didn't produce an abundant crop and get eaten, no sense giving it a second chance.

So it went, trying new food plants, keeping some on the following years, discarding others. Sometimes she weeded out plants that would have loved to take over the garden. Each year she cut back the rhubarb (she called it pie plant) asparagus and mint. Most years she cut back the raspberry stand and some years the strawberry patch. She never suffered when she weeded these plants that she had earlier nourished into life. For the sake of both the plants and the rest of her garden, she controlled their growth. If they grew too greedy and tried to take over, the plants got tough or might kill themselves out. Prune them, weed them, and they would flourish without suffocating the other plants. "Roosevelt should take heed and trim the filthy rich allowing the more deserving their share, and we could kick this depression in no time, I say."

She raised enough to feed her family for the entire year. She purchased one of the first freezers in Badaxe, and she put up corn and beans in the freezer but always saved room for the venison, beef and pork that would be added in late fall. She canned hundreds of quarts of corn, pickles, tomato sauce, beans, and peas. She put up forty gallons of apple sauce and ten quarts of blackberries for the long cold winters. She made one hundred and fifty pints of jams and jellies—strawberry, apple, currant, blackberry, green tomato, ripe tomato, ground cherry, raspberry, and black raspberry. Many of her children liked the green tomato jam the best, so she always made a few extra jars of it. When her family was the largest, she canned over a thousand quarts of vegetables and fruits to get the family through the fall, winter, and spring until she was able to feed them fresh food the next summer. Each fall the root cellar was filled with potatoes, beets and onions. William and the children picked and husked bushels of walnuts, hickory nuts, hazelnuts, buttercup nuts which all grew wild on their farm.

The biggest and favorite harvest of the family came from the bramble across Moundridge Hill. There blackberries grew wild in the woods and every year Agnes and her children picked gallons upon gallons of blackberries. She made fresh blackberry pie, blackberry jam, and froze gallons to be used to make pies in the winter. Everyone loved blackberries and they were always happy to push through the bramble and fight off the mosquitoes in order to pick the berries from the prickly bushes. During blackberry season they picked as many as ten gallons of berries in one day.

Agnes' pleasure came from watching the seeds pop up as green plants, distinguishing the weeds from the plants, hoeing out the weeds, and nurturing the plants. Plucking many buds and leaving so many to go to fruit made the vegetables bigger, riper and juicier. Agnes reasoned, "It must have been here, in the garden, that man discovered the very concept of creation. To make something from nothing. To nurture a seed into sprouting to a plant to a fruit—it is like having an idea, turning the idea into a plan and then putting the plan into action."

When she died there were a few hundred jars of peas, beans, corn, applesauce, beets, blackberry jam, stewed tomatoes, green tomato jam and ground cherry pie mix. Her children divided them among themselves and took them home to feed their families. For they knew—every one of them—that this was more than some jars of garden food. Each of her children hoped that somehow their mother's lust for life, for creation, for oneness with her garden and her Creator, would somehow pass to their children.

At her funeral, her youngest son said, "Mom was the da Vinci of gardeners; her garden the Mona Lisa of gardens. She was one with her garden, a believer in creation and redemption, the Dionysus of the 20th century, remaking life each year. It is the image of her planting, pulling out weeds, picking strawberries before the sun was up that I will always carry with me. Her care for and love of the land will always inspire me to plant, to create, and to care."

The Annual Butcher

Fall came and went, and the first days of winter approached. Winters were cold and damp along the Mississippi Valley. The wind rolled down the river and whipped up the coulees with a ferociousness that surprised strangers.

For Agnes the winters were a mixed blessing. The chickens laid more eggs and took less care. The garden lay idle. Clothes dried by hanging them in the basement which was easier than hauling them up the narrow back basement steps to the clothesline in the yard. It also meant William spent more time in the house. That meant more time for the two of them to argue. Worse, William went to sleep earlier and knocked more often on the wall at 4:00 a.m. for her to join him in his bed.

Winter was announced with deer season and butchering. William waited to see if he tagged a deer before he decided how many cows or pigs to butcher. Butchering day was an exhilarating time for Agnes. While William and the boys rounded up the animals chosen for the slaughter, Agnes got out the sausage grinder and meat saws to clean them. Every year she rolled the washing machine out of the way and pushed the old dining room table into the center of the basement and added the table leaves to form as big a work space as possible.

Agnes prepared the basement to process the meat, as William and the boys shot the animals, slit their throats to drain the blood, hung them by the rear hooves with the block and tackle, cut open the belly and gutted the animals. First they prepared the steer. Then two of the boys skinned off the hide with knives. Some years the hide was valuable enough to take the care to skin it without cutting holes in the hide. Other years the value was so low that they cut more carelessly because they'd throw the hide on the pile for the dump. The guts were separated out for fertilizer.

While the boys skinned the steer, William and the oldest son rounded up one of the best hogs. Some years William killed two hogs if he had not bagged a deer, or if he wanted extra sausage. The work all had to be coordinated between everyone. William pushed the process through in a day because he believed the meat would spoil if it hung too long.

This was the day that the meat for the family was put up for the year, and this was a meat-eating family. The potatoes, corn, beans, and peas that Agnes put up were part of the diet, but they all supported the real food of life—animal meat. All the instincts of hunter, provider and storer came out as they set about turning their livestock into food for the family. The ritual never changed other than which child did what. By the time Agnes and one or two of the girls got everything set up in the basement, William and the boys hauled in a slab of beef and a half of a pig. William took the hand saw and began cutting the carcass into sizes that Agnes and the children could work with. Some pieces were cut up for boiling beef, roasts, and hamburger. The fat was carefully removed to make soap. Agnes ground the beef into hamburger, started melting the fat to make soap over the stove she kept in the basement to can, and wrapped cuts to be frozen all at the same time.

The real joy came when the sausage was made and the slabs of prime rib were prepared for dry beef. William became an artist as he cut the pyramid shaped beef pieces to be dropped in the salt brine to cure. He mixed the brine the day before by adding salt until an egg floated in the mixture. He added salt and some secret ingredients to the chunks of pork he'd cut earlier with the right amount of fat and lean meat to make a sausage recipe that had been passed down unchanged by generations of Genottis. William said, every year, "I guess we been making this sausage since the time of the Council of Trent."

Earlier, Agnes laid out the salt, garlic, pepper, cinnamon, basil necessary to make the sausage. William picked pieces of meat from the two piles and tossed them into the sausage grinder. Agnes fussed with William that he was getting the wrong proportions. Too little fat and the sausage might mold, too much fat and it wouldn't taste right or age correctly. William ignored Agnes. In all the years he made sausage he never had a batch go wrong.

The pail filled with meat and Agnes poured the spices on with the same skill and experience that William mixed the meats. William told her to put in a little more garlic, but Agnes knew how to make the sausage so everyone would eat it. She always made one batch with twice the garlic so William would have some he liked. Agnes liked the extra garlic too, but she knew the children would never eat it.

Agnes stuck her arms into the pail of meat and mixed the seasonings in, dipping her arms into the meat up to her elbows. After she mixed the seasonings enough, she carried the pail of meat back to be run through the sausage grinder again. At the same moment William finished grinding the next pail full. He moved it over for Agnes to add the spices. Agnes slipped the sausage sleeve over the end of the grinder and picked up an intestine that one of the boys had cleaned and one of the girls had boiled to sterilize while she and William put up the meat.

William grabbed a handful of the mixed sausage and tossed it in the grinder like Jackson Pollock tossing a pail of paint at a canvas. He cranked the grinder and the sausage oozed into the intestine skin. Agnes held the skin in one hand and prepared the string to tie off sections of the sausage with the other. She wrapped the string around a section and tied it off without ever losing her steady grip on the entire link. After tying off six to eight lengths, she tied off the end twice. One of the kids cut the skin and took the link to hang in the attic. Agnes slipped the new end over the sleeve and the process was repeated. William hardly broke in his circular cranking of the grinder. Sometimes, he did not notice that Agnes had come to the end, and he kept cranking full speed. A bit of meat fell off the end of the sleeve. She grabbed it and tossed it back in the pail.

So the day went. The girls made dinner on butchering day, and after dinner the boys went out to milk the cows. When they came back about 8:30 p. m., Agnes was stirring the fat mixture to become lye soap and William was checking the room where the sausage hung to make sure there was enough air around each link to breathe, or he'd be doing a final check on the meat curing in the brine to be sure no pieces were sticking up in the air where they'd spoil.

Then everyone pitched in to clean up. The grinder was taken apart and taken upstairs along with all the butcher's tools to be cleaned. The scraps were gathered and hauled out to feed the dogs or bagged to be frozen to feed them later. The tables and work bench were scrubbed so no meat was left to attract mice and rats into the basement, and the floor was scrubbed. The table was taken apart and pushed back into the corner and the wash machine rolled back out for use the next day. The last action of the night was Agnes turning off the fire under the pot being used to make lye soap.

By then it was midnight and the boys had to get out of bed the next morning at 5:30 to milk the cows before going to school. Agnes would be up by 6:30 to make them breakfast. Muscles they didn't know they had were sore, but Agnes and her family were happy. They'd put up enough meat for the year. It was the last harvest of the season and God could pour any amount of cold and snow and wind on them, and they'd make it just fine into the spring.

Agnes lay on the bed staring into the darkness with the smell of garlic, cloves and red meat permeating the room. Yes, life was good. Food was plentiful, the house was warm, the children were healthy, and she had warm feelings for William—

at least tonight she did. As she closed her eyes and drifted off, she had a yearning for William to knock on the wall at 4:00 a.m.

Fourth of July

On the Fourth of July, St. Francis Church threw a big party and everyone came. It was New Year's, Christmas and Independence Day all wrapped up in one.

Agnes and all the parish wives baked chickens and pies and cooked tons of risott. Everyone cooked up their best for the most important feast of the year.

In the churchyard a huge bingo table seating a hundred players was set up and every year the Zaboglio family would call out the numbers. In the Father's garage, William set up his ice cream stand and sold two-scoop ice cream cones for ten cents. The Veneris ran the beer and pop stand. Fred Jamboys, William's best friend, ran the roulette wheel.

For the children there was a fishpond, ring toss, softball, bingo as well as the ice cream. Every year Agnes tried to give the kids at least one dollar plus spending one dollar for the dinner. The boys also would collect bottles and mole's feet to get more money for the Fourth. Most of the children liked it because it was a chance to play with their school friends in the middle of summer vacation.

Agnes could see her family come together for the Fourth. William got more pleasant to live with. All the girls pitched in to help bake pies. The boys chopped off the chicken's heads and helped pluck the feathers after Agnes scalded the chickens.

The days before the fourth were filled with hard work in the hayfields and picking strawberries in the garden. Sometimes

Agnes picked strawberries until 11 a.m., and then filled the crock she used to make bread and poured two cups of sugar on the berries, let that sit for a while and then mashed them into pulp with the wood potato masher. She then skimmed the cream off the four bottles of milk in the refrigerator and poured the cream on the berries.

When the boys came out of the hayfields sweating, dirty and hungry, Agnes had the huge bowl of smashed berries and cream and three loaves of bread on the table. The kids placed a slice or two of bread on their plate and then poured a cup of berry cream over the bread. They would eat one, two—sometimes five cups of cream berries. Agnes knew there was no reason to put anything else on the table for only the berries, cream, sugar and bread would satisfy these workers on a hot muggy Mississippi River day.

Everyone worked hard. No one wanted to make hay on the Fourth of July—they had to get the crop in before then, and get the corn hoed for the last time. "Knee high by the Fourth of July." It was a safe saying for the corn was almost always waist high by Independence Day.

The morning of the Fourth, everyone was up early. Gabriel got the cows in fifteen minutes and the milking was done by 7:15. Breakfast was gobbled and the risott cooked for the renowned Badaxe dinner.

The pies, chickens, risotto were piled into the car and Agnes and William drove off to the church. One of the girls rode along if there was still room; otherwise they all walked to the picnic.

Agnes carried the food into St. Francis' kitchen. She laid her pies next to the growing pile. She smiled for her apple pies and her ground cherry pies were the best, and she knew it. They were always eaten first. Even Agnes' children would try to get first in line to get one slice of her ground cherry pies. After Agnes' pies would go, everyone would then eat the strawberry pies. They were the hit of the Fourth dinner after Agnes' pies. Now in truth Agnes' risott was better than her pies. She sautéed onions and fried the rice in butter, added fresh chicken broth and let it simmer. Two minutes before it was cooked, she added a stew of saffron that had been raised in her garden. She knew how much cheese to make the rice melt in your mouth. The risott dishes looked alike—and were often poured together in a large pot. Otherwise, everyone would have insisted on Agnes' risott too. It was better this way—for it may have been hurtful for the other church women to have Agnes' risott prized too. The party slowed about 5:00 p.m. when many farmers had to go home to milk their cows.

By the time they returned to pick up their wives, the place had about emptied out. In the meantime, Agnes along with many of the kitchen staff filled in the spots left by their husbands at the bingo table. Agnes took her egg money and played bingo until it was all gone. Every year she'd win a prize or two but it wasn't the winning. It was playing and paying for Christ. Sometimes she'd play five cards at a time—but more often she played three. It was just enough to keep her mind fully occupied. It was the one time a year she was having so much fun, she forgot about the farm, the children, the chickens, the garden and her husband.

Falling to sleep she wondered if this might not have been her life—not playing bingo—but praying and playing for Jesus—had she only followed her dream.

Hot Potato

Agnes' garden, children and God began to take all of her time. William's indifference to the three most important things seemed to matter less because Agnes had less time for William or to even think about William. After Giuseppina was born, Hannah, Alex, Matthew, and Marie had come along about every sixteen months. William had talked about using birth control and had purchased some new fangled latex condoms when he was in LaCrosse. But they sat in his drawer under his clothes because Agnes was not going to sin by using artificial birth control. William had suggested they use rhythm if Agnes would not let him use the condoms. She wanted more children, and she thought that her God preferred that they not interfere with his plan for populating the earth. The church said it was not a sin to practice rhythm—if William wanted to abstain, Agnes would go along with it. She had five healthy children and it would have been enough. Since she never enjoyed sex much, it would be a relief to abstain for ten days or so every month; but it did not matter much for William could not go without his regular dose. In fact, it seemed William wanted it more when he tried to abstain so the result was they actually had more sex when she was ovulating.

Other than having to make love with William several times a week, Agnes did not see much of him. He was in the house for meals, but he never said much and never helped feed the children. He did help keep them under control, because William could not stand a bunch of kids fooling around, talking at the same time or jostling. So meals were quiet in Agnes' house, and she enjoyed that for the children were plenty noisy when William was out in the barn or fields.

Life had fallen into a comfortable routine. Agnes got the children up, fed the baby, made breakfast for her growing family, cleaned up after breakfast, worked in the garden in the summer, sewed in the winter, made dinner, cleaned up the kitchen, got the children down for a nap, cleaned a part of the house, made supper, fed the chickens and collected the day's eggs, cleaned up, told stories and rocked the children to sleep, did some final cleaning, undressed and more nights than not let William make love to her. On Sundays, she went to church in the morning and took a few hours off in the afternoon. It was a life her mother had lived, her sisters and friends were living and it kept Agnes too busy to wonder if there might be something else. On occasion, when she was in her garden alone, she'd think about being a nun, and she'd long for a life where every thought and action would be just for Jesus. It made her sad, because she could not help to think it was her calling but as more children came there was less time for such idle thoughts.

Most of the time, Agnes was glad that William was a stern disciplinarian. She subscribed to the "spare the rod spoil the child" method to raise her children, but she just could not use the rod herself. William, on the other hand, could not stand to see his children be rowdy. If they talked too loud or at the same time or tousled with each other in William's presence, he yelled at them in a powerful and frightening voice. If that did not stop them, William used the razor strap. He did not have to do that very often, because for weeks after he beat one of the kids, the house was deathly silent when William came in. Of course the children made up for their pent-up energy when he was gone.

Agnes hated it when William whipped the children hard like that, and she often asked him to be gentler. At the same time she believed it was good for the children, so she wanted William to whip them. Why couldn't he be a little gentler?

In October 1933 Pina and Hannah's teacher had taught her students about Halloween. She told them about the souls of people in purgatory coming out of the grave and asking for prayers from relatives to help them get into heaven on All Saints Day. Their teacher told them how the Halloween costumes had originally been designed to keep the ghosts away from the living. Pina and Hannah had enjoyed telling the smaller children about the ghosts of Halloween. Especially when Matthew got scared because he was always acting as nothing scared him. Pina and Hannah could see that the stories of the dead souls from purgatory coming out on October 31 were frightening Matthew. So they made the stories grow. That summer, Alvin Francoli who scared every kid in Badaxe, had died. Marie looked Matthew right in the eye and said, "Alvin Francoli will be looking for youuuu. He'll be wantin' you to say some prayers to save his eviiill soul." Agnes saw the fear in Matthew's eyes and smiled as she remembered her childhood when stories like this could be so real. The children had asked Agnes if they could use old pieces of cloth to make Halloween costumes. Sure that the ghosts of purgatory were going to come and get them, they worked harder than they had on anything to make costumes so scary they would chase the ghost of Alvin Francoli away.

October 31 came and the children had put their costumes on as soon as Hannah and Pina got home from school. They ran around the house and in the yard scaring each other and practicing so they could scare the ghosts of Halloween. Agnes heard Matthew screaming "Alviinnn Frannnnncoli get away! I'm scarier than you, get away."

Agnes made supper and enjoyed the intensity with which the children expressed their fear. When she called them for supper she said: "Kids, take off your costumes. You don't want to get food on them." Matthew began to whine, "Mom, I don't want to take my costume off. What if the ghosts come during dinner? I got to be ready." Agnes had to think fast because William would get angry if the children wore their costumes to supper. "You know, if you spill food on your costume, the ghosts won't be scared. They'll know you're human because you need food, and they might come right up and lick it off your costume. The costume won't scare them away." Off came the costumes in a flash and the children sat down to eat as fast as possible, so they could get up from the table and get the costumes back on to protect themselves from the ghosts and especially Alvin Francoli.

William came in for supper. Agnes had made a pot roast, cooked carrots and boiled potatoes. She cut up the meat and passed it around. The children were jabbering in their excitement about Halloween and the ghosts. William put up with it for a while, but Agnes knew he'd be yelling at the children soon. She hoped he wouldn't yell too much because she didn't want him to spoil the fun the children were having being scared. The children were so anxious they just kept talking about ghosts and Alvin Francoli and giggling. They were trying to be quiet because they all knew their dad didn't like them to talk at the table. Still, they were so excited, they kept talking and poking each other and laughing. All the time they kept one eye on William in anticipation when he would begin to yell. Agnes was surprised he did not say anything, but she was also anxious because she could see his anger growing. What was he waiting for? Did he want to see if Agnes disciplined the children? "Quiet," she said, "you know Dad likes it to be quiet when he eats." "Quiet." Things quieted down for a minute, but the children could not hold either their fear or their anticipation of Halloween. "Quiet" Agnes said again as the noise rose.

Before she could say "Quiet" the third time, William grabbed a handful of steaming hot boiled potatoes and reached back behind his head and threw the hot potatoes at her children with all the force he had. "Shut up!" he yelled. The potatoes hit the kid's faces with a force that shocked them into silence. Absolute silence. Agnes sat still. She could not eat. She watched the children sit in frozen silence. Then one by one raise their hands to wipe the potatoes off their face. Matthew ate the potatoes from his hands. Agnes and Hannah scraped the potatoes onto their plates. They licked their fingers and picked at their other food. William continued to eat as if nothing had happened.

William finished his meal, stood up and said, "I got to milk the cows," and left for the barn. The children finished their meal in silence. Agnes said, "Better wash your faces." One by one they got up and washed the remaining potato off their faces in the basin. Hannah went to her room, Giuseppina started to sew a button on her blouse, Matthew and Alex went outside to play but Agnes never heard a word from them all night. Agnes put Hannah to bed early and began to clean the potatoes off the walls of the kitchen and then did the dishes by herself.

Agnes did not have to tell the children to go to bed that night. In fact, they were all undressed and in bed ten minutes before bedtime. William came in after chores, but Agnes had nothing to say to him. They went to bed, William touched her the way he did when he wanted sex, but she turned her back— he rolled over and went to sleep.

Saturday Night Baths

Saturday night was the time for baths; for Agnes to get her family clean for Sunday church. First the smallest children took their baths while the older children cleaned the dishes or milked the cows. Agnes scrubbed them, cleaned inside their ears, and around their little butts. If they were boys she scrubbed their little dicks, and they would always laugh. She wondered why little boys laughed and men became beasts when a woman touched their privates.

The girls took their baths next. One at a time, but she made three of them use the same water. They always complained about that but Agnes knew they would overflow the septic tank if everyone used new water. Plus it would be wasteful of God's gift of water to change it after every bath. So the girls rotated from week to week who went first. By the time the older boys came up from the barn, the girls would be finished. The boys didn't mind using each other's bathwater. They sure didn't want to take a bath. Every week, Agnes had to fight with them to get them into the tub. She understood why the girls fought to get the first bath. The boys fought to be last. They were so dirty from working the fields and in the barn all week. Why wouldn't they want to get clean? She did not understand. But get clean they did, for Agnes was not about to let them go to see Jesus on Sunday morning anything but as clean as possible.

One Saturday night was like the next. At the end of it, with the children all in bed and William sound asleep, Agnes took a breath, cleaned the tub and drew herself a tub of water a little hotter than she had for her family and then crawled in for a long quiet soak.

She sometimes wondered if she wasn't being too selfish because she drew the biggest tub and hottest tub using the most water, the most electricity and the most space in the septic tank for her bath. Still, each week she did it and most weeks the guilt feelings quickly faded into dreams and thoughts as she lay back in the tub and began to spend the most pleasurable moments of the week.

Hannah Acts Up

Agnes did not understand what happened to Hannah. She had been the best of her children. She was always quiet and she helped around the house. Ask her to do something and she did it. Alex was always working with William in the fields so Agnes rarely asked her to do things about the house. Pina was always talking and jabbering to a point of distraction. She took three times as long as Hannah to do a task. Agnes figured Pina couldn't talk and work at the same time.

Hannah came home from school, changed and came right into the kitchen to help. She set the table and fed the baby. After dinner, Hannah started the dishes immediately, scrubbed the kitchen floor and picked up the dining room floor. Then she went off to her room to study until either Agnes or William told her that it was bedtime. She shut off the lights and went to bed. No arguments from her. If she had not finished her homework, she got up earlier in the morning. Sometimes Hannah was studying by 4:30 a.m. in order to complete her homework. She studied more than Alex or Giuseppina, but she never got better grades. Agnes wondered about that and figured Hannah wasn't given as many marbles by Jesus.

For the past month she was doing strange things. Sometimes she stared at a wall. Agnes said, "Time for the dishes" and Hannah did not move, did not say anything and did not help out. Agnes hit her one night, but Hannah did not move. Just stared like Agnes wasn't there. She began to answer the phone when the phone was ringing for other families. Sometimes she'd tell the caller to quit bothering her; other times she told them funny stories. Once she said she was from Mars and Vito better not call on her, or she'd destroy his corn.

Agnes was reluctant to tell William that Hannah stopped helping around the house and was acting strange, because she knew that William would yell at Hannah and maybe whip her with a razor strap. That would only make things worse.

One rainy day, William came into the house, and he and Agnes made love before the older children got home from school. The preschoolers were all napping. William and Agnes got out of bed a few minutes before the children came down the hill from Moundridge School. William picked up the Tribune and began to catch up with the news. "God, I been so busy I haven't read the paper in a month of Sundays," he said to himself as much as to Agnes.

Pina, Hannah, Alex, Matthew, Marie and Mark came in from school. Though the school was only a few hundred yards up the hill, they were all soaking wet from the rain. Everyone went to change into dry clothes except Hannah who sat right down on the couch like she wasn't wet. She started to talk to her dad about squirrel hunting and carp fishing. She'd never shown any interest in William's hunting and fishing before, so he was taken back and pleased that she showed interest. He didn't even scream at her for sitting on the chair in wet clothes.

Agnes listened to the conversation. It was so bizarre, because Agnes knew that Hannah resented the time William hunted and fished and also thought it horrible that nice little innocent animals were killed. Hannah started to talk about these things like she was an expert. In fact both Agnes and William were surprised at how much she did know about hunting and fishing.

The phone rang two shorts and a long. It was for Fred Beratti. There were thirteen families on the line and each had a separate ring, and everyone knew everyone's ring. Two shorts and a long was Fred Beratti's. Hannah got up and went to the phone, picked up the receiver and began to listen. William hated it when the local gossips listened in on a phone call, and he made it clear to Agnes and to each of the children that they were never to listen to other people's calls.

William sat with his mouth open when Hannah picked up the handset and began to listen. He was not used to his family openly defying his commands. Here Hannah was boldly and without fear breaking one of the most sacred rules in the family. Before William or Agnes was able to react to such behavior, Hannah began to shout into the phone. "Leave him alone, you whore. Why are you calling him again? Stop it. You are a whore. You sell your body. I hate you." William jumped to the phone, grabbed the phone away from Hannah and said as calmly as he could into the phone, "I'm sorry, I don't know what got into her."

William held Hannah tight. She was writhing and hitting William to free herself. No child of William's was going to hit him. He pulled back his hand and whelped Hannah beside the head with a blow that stunned her. When she spun out of the daze, she was a changed person. Her body went into contraction, and she limped off to her room, changed her clothes and returned to work in the kitchen where she moved in slow motion and looked like she might be swimming in a thick milieu.

William looked at Agnes and asked, "How long this been going on?"

"Maybe three, maybe four weeks. I thought she was gettin' better until today. What we gonna to do with her, William?"

William said; '"It seems pretty obvious she's possessed. Let's take her to Father Duffy in the morning. I think she's possessed by the devil. Hopefully Duffy can exorcise her." The thought of the devil possessing her daughter frightened Agnes. How could the devil have entered her home? They were good Catholics. They went to church every Sunday, and Agnes said at least one rosary every day. How could the devil take over Hannah? The devil was powerful—he could come into anyone's body. She heard that the devil possessed the holiest girl in a faithful family in France. Was Hannah so holy that the devil found her to be the ultimate challenge? Agnes found that hard to believe. Nor did she want to believe that Hannah was so evil that the devil found a natural home. She was an ordinary little kid; a little quieter and nicer than most.

Agnes was pleased that William wanted to turn to Father Duffy for help. He never had much to say good about any of the priests, and he disliked Duffy. Sometimes on Sunday morning if

William nodded off, Fr. Duffy found a way to mention his name in the sermon. This was Father's way of keeping everyone alert and everyone in the parish knew it. So if you had your name mentioned in the sermon, every one figured you were nodding off. Now William asked for Father Duffy. Was William's faith increasing?

William went into town to ask Duffy to come right out to exorcise Hannah. Father was as surprised as anyone that Hannah was possessed by the devil. He told William to wait for him in the rectory while he prepared the necessary holy things and spent a moment with God to seek his help in the battle. In truth, Duffy was so taken back that he needed a few moments by himself to comprehend such a thing. Then he needed to prepare himself to take on the devil since the devil often left the bereaved and jumped right into the exorciser. He'd been a parish priest for fifteen years, and he was thankful that he had never been called on to take on the devil. William looked troubled and Agnes must be beside herself. "I'd better pull myself together," he thought, "and get to the Moundridge farm to help them. It is why I am a priest." These thoughts did nothing to make the trip up Highway 56 any more pleasant. Duffy asked William a lot of questions. He wanted as much information as possible—it might help to conquer the devil. Both William and Father were aware that there was right at that time a case in France where the devil stayed in the little girl possessed and jumped between the girl and the exorcists whenever someone tried to exorcise her. The parish priest, the bishop and the specialists from the seminary had all been possessed by the devil every time they tried to remove him from the little girl. There was talk of taking the girl to the Pope in Rome.

The more information Duffy absorbed, the more likely he was to succeed before the devil's grip became too deep on Hannah. William was of little use. He was only able to say what Hannah had done that day and that the devil was working on Agnes for she had not told him about Hannah's behavior before. "Hannah's been possessed for some weeks and Agnes said nothin'. She always tells me everything and in fact it was this secretiveness of Agnes that made me realize that Hannah wasn't being just a bad girl but was indeed possessed by the devil and the devil had influenced Agnes. No doubt about it. Agnes wouldn't behave this way."

They drove into the farmyard. Father could see Hannah on the swing tied to the old oak tree in the yard. She was just sitting on the swing. Father did not remember ever seeing a young person just sit on a swing and not swinging. Was the devil resting to take him on? Certainly the devil was aware that William came for help, and that he had answered the call.

Father got out of the car cautiously. William sat behind the driver's seat with his arm on the rolled down window and stared at Hannah. For the first time in his life he felt absolutely helpless. He could fix the machinery if it broke down, he knew what to do when a bull got too feisty, he dug wells, made it through the worst of the depression and up to now kept his children and wife in line. He never thought he'd face a task he could not handle. After stopping to talk to Agnes, Father moved toward Hannah and for the first time William realized that Duffy was scared. Priests were not supposed to know fear. They were chosen by God, and they did not have the emotions the rest of us had. William saw Father Duffy was scared and immediately he liked him more than he had.

Agnes heard the car drive up, and she came out to greet Father and to assist in any way. She had kept an eye on Hannah ever since William had said in front of her he was going to get the priest to chase the devil out. Agnes thought William was foolish to announce to the devil that he was going to get the priest. That gave the devil time to dig deeper into Hannah's soul and gave him more power. As she anxiously awaited Father's arrival, she began to realize that secrets could not be kept from the devil. Even if William said nothing, the devil could read one's thoughts like God could.

Maybe Father could chase out the devil and Hannah would go back to normal. William never had much faith—not that he wasn't a good Catholic—he went to church every Sunday, went to communion most of the time and to confession once in a while. To William, church-going seemed a waste of money and time, but Agnes was so firm in her beliefs he managed to do the minimum to prevent any fights. The more she clung to her church the more William pulled away emotionally even if he continued in the external manifestations. Agnes thought, "If Duffy can chase the devil out and return our girl to us, William'll believe for sure."

After William left, Hannah started to beat her head against the wall. At first, she hit her head softly like she had done so many times before in the past few weeks, but now the pounding continued to grow until she was flailing her head against the plaster. It was the devil, and Agnes guessed the devil was angry because William had gone to get Father. She was afraid to confront Hannah, but finally she grabbed Hannah around the waist and lifted her away from the wall. Agnes half expected the devil to enter her body. She felt nothing except the kicking of her little girl. She carried Hannah out on to the porch and sat on the steps. Hannah fell into Agnes' lap and Agnes rocked her gently. After a few minutes, Hannah quit kicking, and then she quit rocking and finally she became perfectly still. She did not move. Agnes held her for a long time, and she felt Hannah's body stiffen almost rigid. Agnes wanted to shout, but she did not, she wanted to cry but couldn't, to squeeze Hannah back to normal but was helpless. Finally, she remembered that there were dishes to do, and there would be no help from Hannah tonight. "Hannah, mother has to go do the dishes now. Why don't you go sit on the swing and I'll do the dishes. I know you are tired tonight, so I'll do the dishes. It's getting late. Get up now so I can do the dishes. Hannah, get up please. Hannah." Agnes realized that she raised her voice on that last "Hannah" and that might lead to Hannah flailing around again. She lifted Hannah up, carried her to the swing, sat her on the old wood seat, put her hands on the ropes and gave her a little push. Hannah hung on to the ropes, but there was no other sign of life. Her feet dragged on the ground as the swing brought her through the middle. Hannah hung on and stared ahead like she wasn't there. Then the swing came to a stop. Agnes reached down to give another push, but realizing the futility of it and being thankful that Hannah was quiet, she turned and headed for the kitchen. When Hannah was like this, Agnes preferred to have her on the swing because she could see her from the kitchen sink. Agnes went through the motions of washing the dishes while thinking about Hannah and what happened. The difference was that the dishes got washed though Agnes was paying little or no attention to the dishes. Her thoughts about Hannah only zigged and zagged. Nothing made sense and the thoughts led to nowhere. In what seemed both the next moment and an eternity later, Father and William drove into the yard. She put down the dishcloth and walked to the porch door, opened it and walked toward Father to greet him.

"Hello Father, thank you for coming so quickly. Hannah is on the swing. Can you help her?" Father realized how distressed Agnes was and while he kept his eye on Hannah, he paused to comfort Agnes. "I'll try Agnes, but I can promise nothing. The devil is powerful, and he can hang on to little girls with deep penetrating fangs. You of all people, Agnes, know that God is more powerful than the devil and if our prayers please him the devil will be gone." Agnes wanted the devil gone. She wanted her girl back. Father wanted the devil gone. He did not want to be possessed himself, and he did not want a personal fight with the devil.

He left Agnes and headed toward Hannah. Hannah did not move. Father moved closer and closer. He finally reached her. There was no movement from Hannah. She stared into the same space though Father was now in her line of vision. He reached out and touched her forehead, no reaction. He blessed her with a sign of the cross—nothing. He took out a crucifix and laid it on her forehead—nothing. Father then laid his hands on Hannah and said some words that Agnes could not hear. No reaction from Hannah. Father shook her—still no reaction. Father put his fingers on her eyelids and opened them wide and peered into her eyes. He got up and came over to William and Agnes.

"I don't think she is possessed by the devil. He would have responded to the blessing, cross and rosary. We can be thankful for that. From how she feels to the touch and the look in her eyes, I think she is mentally ill. I don't understand mental sickness very well, but I've seen it before and I think Hannah is mentally ill. The doctors are better at treating mental illness than they used to be. They have some medicines that can help. I'll call the doctor, and we can take her to LaCrosse to be examined. We'll have to wait to see how he finds her."

"What is this mental illness?" Agnes didn't know about mental illness. She had never seen someone mentally sick before. Was it caused by something like falling down, or did it come like a cold? Her thoughts were moving in circles and coming back. Her Hannah had this mental sickness, and so she better find out what it was so she could care for Hannah. It was clear that it was a serious illness and every serious illness demanded care from a mother.

The next day Father called and said that they had an appointment for the following week with the doctor. Agnes was relieved. If the doctor was willing to wait a week, it couldn't be so bad. If Hannah had a broken arm they'd take her right away; so it must not be as bad as a broken arm. Even if she had a bad cold, the doctor wouldn't make her wait a whole week. The doctor would see her and help her feel better.

On the appointed day, Agnes got up earlier than usual. She put on her Sunday best and then dressed Hannah in her Sunday outfit. Going to the Doctor was a rare event for Agnes, so she dressed in their finest. The doctor's appointment wasn't until 9:30 a.m. and LaCrosse was barely twenty miles away. William wanted to leave by 7:30. It was only 7:00, and she and Hannah were ready to go. This wasn't like Agnes. William always wanted to leave so early that she was never ready when he was. Today, she was ready and she had Hannah ready, and they were waiting for William.

Hannah was restless. She had not said a word about going to the doctor or to LaCrosse. Hannah had never been to LaCrosse, so she could be expected to be excited about the trip.

Going to the big city was a big day in the life of any Badaxe child. Hannah understood they were going somewhere, but she did not know where. It might be just as well Agnes thought. If she realized she was going to the doctor for her "mental" sickness it might only make her worse.

Suddenly Hannah reeled out the door and ran to the dirt pile in front of the house. She threw herself on the pile and began to turn and roll on the dirt pile intentionally dirtying her new dress.

Jack

The depression hung on like rust on a mower left outside all winter. As hard as Roosevelt was working to kick the country into financial health, the years without money seemed to be endless. Things had gotten a little better but not much. At least William had been able to quit his job on the country roads. William had now owned his farm for fifteen years and he'd not missed a single payment. In fact, he had made the last farm payment to Peter just three months ago. He was proud of that fact, and he never missed an opportunity to let anyone who would listen know it. The milk check brought in enough they were able to put a little in the bank every month.

William purchased a jackass to help around the farm after Sally, their hardworking mule, died in 1936. William called the new ass Jack. For a jackass, Jack was not very stubborn. He was a strong animal and hauled things for William all day without ever balking at a job. Sometimes when William had Jack pulling logs out of the woods all day, Jack would stop late in the afternoon. William said, "Hell, Jack did a hell of a job today. Can't blame him for letting me know he's had enough for the day." William let Jack rest and then led him off to the barn to rest for the next day. Word got around that Jack was strong for a jackass, and the neighbors began to ask William to bring Jack around to stud their mares.

At first William took Jack to his or Agnes' brothers farms. He didn't mind that as they lived close and it only took half a day out of his time. If he was busy, they were willing to wait until next time their mares came into heat. Soon more people—some William did not even know—wanted him to bring Jack over. One day William said to a stranger who lived over on Veneri Hill, "Sure, but it'll cost you five bucks." The stranger took out five one dollar bills and gave them to William. From then on William charged everyone including his brothers five dollars for a stud fee. The money came in handy to buy little things for around the house and the farm and to let them give an extra ten dollars a year to the church. Agnes was very happy they were able to donate to the church. They had put a quarter in the collection plate every week when they first got married. With the depression, there were times she only donated one dollar in a whole year. With two stud fees she donated ten dollars extra during Lent, and William did not begrudge her that.

Jack's fame began to grow and sometimes William took Jack so far he did not get back the same night. Matthew and Alex were old enough to milk the cows and do the chores, so William was able to stay overnight with the farmer who had hired Jack and head back the next day. The first night William was gone Agnes missed his warm body next to her. She remembered how much she had missed him when he went away week after week to work on the road and how hard it had been without William there every day. This time William was back the next day and Agnes was happy.

A month later, William headed back to Veneri Hill and told Agnes he'd have to be gone overnight again. As the day went on, Agnes decided to make a chocolate cake for the children and cook hamburgers. William did not like chocolate cake or fried hamburger. Agnes loved chocolate cake but had not baked one since William quit working for the road. Her children would be pleased; she began to look forward to supper.

The children smelled the chocolate cake when they came from school, and Matthew said "Yum, Mom, I smell chocolate cake. Are we having it for supper? Please Mom, let's have it for supper."

Agnes said "yes" and the children said in one voice, "yeah." Agnes was pleased.

That night after all the children were put to bed, Agnes noticed the silence. She was alone and at first she was not sure how she felt about that. She took out the tatting she was working on and sat in William's rocker and gently rocked while she tatted. Her mind wandered to sitting on her granddad's lap on his rocking chair and her granddad telling her stories of the old country. He'd tell about hills so tall that the bluffs of the Mississippi River would be just the first step in a many stepped ladder. He called the hills the Alps and said that he and his dad used to climb half-way up the Alp Mountains to take their sheep grazing in the summer. Sometimes there was only the two of them in the mountains for weeks at a time. He told other stories about his mother and how they all packed up one day and headed toward Le Havre, France to grab the first ship they found to America.

She remembered Father asking her to teach the first grades at school and how much she enjoyed teaching. Agnes taught Alvina Kenlsey and Jerome Jamboys as first graders and she recalled how they learned to read and add and subtract. Now they were full-grown, married and had children.

Agnes remembered dreaming about becoming a nun. She laughed a little when she remembered dreaming about taking that long river road all the way to LaCrosse. With their car, they could travel to LaCrosse in less than an hour. In her childhood dreams, she and her dad had to awake before dawn and drive all day to get there as the sun was setting. She smiled, but she also longed to be able to have that dream again. To go to the convent, to spend her life in prayer and quiet. To offer herself to Jesus as a virgin. It was a pleasant dream that was a far distance from her life to keep her children fed and clothed. Every day was one of cleaning, cooking, changing diapers, settling disputes, feeding the chickens, mending clothes, raising and canning food and letting William make love to her. The days were long and noisy without much chance to think of Jesus let alone say a prayer or two. She went to church every Friday for the Stations of the Cross and Sunday for mass. She wished she had more time for Jesus. She put down her tatting, walked over to the dresser and took out her rosary. With William gone, she said a full rosary and went to bed when she wanted to. "In the name of the Father, the Son and the Holy Ghost." Fifty three Hail Marys and six Our Fathers later, Agnes had forgotten where she was and had joined in union with Jesus and Mary. The hustle of the day seemed less and the quiet of the night seemed more.

She enjoyed not having William in the house. She took in the moment—no one asking her for something. Time to say the rosary without being rushed. She could go to bed if she wanted to, or tat more or say another rosary. She liked the feeling. Though she was not tired, she decided better to go to bed because she had a long day tomorrow. She rocked for a few more minutes and listened to the silence and stared into the darkness beyond the window. She leaned over and switched off the light and continued to rock.

She got up, walked through the house without turning on the light and headed into her bedroom. She lifted her dress over her head and undressed completely. She picked up her nightgown to put it on but stopped. Without William here, she could sleep naked with no worry that he'd become aroused. She tossed the gown down and crawled into bed. The quarter moon was hanging in the sky directly out Agnes' window. For a moment she felt like a school girl imagining she was sitting on the moon ledge with feet dangling. Agnes became aware that she had not looked at the moon for a long time. She began to think back when she last looked out the window or up in the sky and enjoyed the moon. She tried to remember, but she couldn't—at least not since her wedding day. Had she not once looked at the moon in all those years? Not possible she thought, but she could not remember when. She looked back at the moon and began to feel the light shine on her naked body. For a moment she closed her eyes to let the light flood over her. It caressed and warmed her. She let the light penetrate in a moment more before she opened her eyes to soak in the color and the light. When she opened her eyes she thought for a moment that she saw Jesus in the moon looking at her and the light of the moon was the brilliance of his eyes looking at the earth. It wasn't possible; it was the moon and the moon was a part of God and that part of God was shining at her. She wanted

God to like her. She wanted to be perfect for her Jesus so he would love her, and he would take her into heaven with him forever.

"Jesus, I love you. I wanted to serve you, to be a nun. You know I wanted to. But you called me to be a wife and mother and so I am. I want to be a good mother. I want to raise my children so they will love you. Maybe, just maybe, I will be lucky and you will call one of my boys to be a priest and one of my girls to be a nun. Let Mark be a priest. Marie said she wanted to be a nun. My heart fluttered. Please, Jesus, call one of them to you.

"It is hard to be a mother, Jesus; harder than it is to be a nun. Every day the children try me. Especially Matthew. He can be so mean. The other day Alex said he had squirted blood milk into her mouth. I did not want to believe a son of mine could do that. But I think he did. I tried to dismiss it—I told William because I did not want to take care of it. He said, 'If he did it, she probably had it coming.' Later he switched Matthew, so I think Alex must have told him too.

"Jesus, I love you. I want you to love me. I need your help every day to be a good mother. I know you are here and that you help. But do not forget me for I cannot raise these children without you. Sometimes I wonder why life can be so hard. The kids fighting with each other, William wanting sex and his meals and nothing else from me. When we got ahead, the price of milk fell, and we are behind again. Roosevelt promises the end of the depression, but it ain't ended here, I'll tell you that. Then I remember how hard you had it. Preaching all day, telling people to love only to be hung on the cross—betrayed by your disciples in the hour of need. My life is pretty easy I guess."

Agnes spoke aloud, "Jesus, I thank you most for helping Hannah get over her illness. I know she still struggles some, but she found a job, met a most wonderful man. I think they may get married soon. Thank you, Jesus, thank you one thousand times. Jesus, thanks for being here—for looking out for me and my family. I love you, we love you—even William—I think he loves you."

The thoughts whirled in Agnes' head as she stared at the moon. "Hail Mary, full of grace, the lord is with thee"...

The moon slipped past the window and the room was dark. Agnes rolled on her side and closed her eyes. Sleep came and the next thing she heard was the alarm telling her another day had arrived.

Nine Lives

Agnes knew how mean Matthew was, but she did not believe this. Matthew had begun to milk the cows when he was seven years old and had at that age gotten Alex and Mark to help work. Now Mark was only five but Matthew often made Mark work alongside him. By the time Matthew was twelve, William had made him responsible to milk the twenty-eight Holsteins that supported the family. Matthew also worked the fields alongside any man. At age nine he could toss a shock of grain like the strongest men in Badaxe. Matthew had dunked Mark in the milk trough until he felt like he was drowning. He had squirted fresh bloody milk from the cows that had recently birthed into Alex's and Luke's mouth when they did not do what he wanted.

Still, Agnes was horrified when Matthew yelled at Luke that he would kill Ginger, his cat, if Luke didn't feed the cows. Now Luke was only five years old. Agnes watched as Matthew lifted the shovel over his head and told Luke to feed the cows or get ready to bury his cat. Luke had already learned to hold his own in the game of "chicken" and maybe to protect his boyhood.

Agnes and Luke's hearts stopped together when Matthew swung with his strength and the back of the shovel crushed the cat's head. Matthew gave the cat and shovel to Luke and told him calmly to bury the cat behind the corn shed. Luke took the cat and the shovel and headed toward the shed. She went back to hoeing the tomatoes, tilling the ground but in slow motion. How had she given birth to this? Had God punished her for not hearing his call to her? Was life based on raising tomatoes, corn, cows only to harvest them at their ripest, a message too cruel for young people? Had her husband abandoned life and his family after those years of the Depression? Had they all learned only to punish?

Agnes noticed, too late, that the tomato plant was in the path of her hoe. She tried to stop the forward motion but the hoe cut the tomato stem before she was able to stop it. She leaned on the hoe and let the weight of her body and her life rest. Then Luke walked from behind the corn crib to over the knoll to the sand hill where he had so often played with his cat. She thought it best to let him be alone.

As Agnes was walking toward Luke to comfort him, she saw something move out the left side of her eye. She turned and saw Ginger running toward Luke—"Do cats really have nine lives?"

Thrashers

It was hard to believe that it was already August in the summer of 1942. Luke was already 7 years old. Agnes was closing in on 40. There was little time to reflect on that. Today the thrashers were at her home. William was up by 6:00 getting everything set up for the day. He'd driven the over-sized thrashing machine down from Vito's place the night before. Sometimes he'd set the machine up the night before, but Vito had so much grain this year that he didn't finish his place until 9:00. It was 10:00 p.m. by the time William drove the machine into the field below the house. He shut the Hart Parr off, came to the house and plopped into bed.

By the time the teams came at 8:30 everything had to be ready. They had one day to do the whole job because tomorrow they were scheduled to be at John's place, and William's grain was also heavy this year. It was going be a long day, even if they got started on time.

Vito, Angelo, Howie, John and their oldest boys showed up promptly at 8:30, and the work began in earnest. The men went to work in sets of three: one drove the tractor and wagon through the field, and the other two speared a shock of grain together with their forks and heaved it over their head on to the wagon. Earlier William had used the grain binder to tie off sheaves of grain that were then stacked into shocks of 6-9 sheaves so the grain dried enough to be threshed. They proceeded up and down the fields this way all day. A few of the bigger boys actually tossed a shock of grain by themselves. No one could do that all day long, but a couple of the boys were able to toss a full shock half the time.

Jean Veneri, Agnes' sister-in-law, came over to help prepare the dinner. Now, a thrasher's dinner in Badaxe was a sight to behold. Agnes butchered a dozen chickens the day before. Luke and Mark caught the chickens and chopped off their heads. They were still too young to go to the other farms to thrash. But they were old enough to run the place while all the other men were gone. In fact, they often milked the cows by themselves on the evenings when the others were out late.

Agnes saw the excitement of thrashers day on Luke and Mark. They would go in the fields and toss shocks of grain tomorrow, and they would sit at the table and try to eat as much chicken, risott and pie as their full-grown cousins.

She had some concern that their excitement was heightened by too much pleasure from chopping the chickens' heads off. They sometimes fought over who had cut the most heads, and they laughed in a child-like way imitating the chickens flapping about the yard after their heads were chopped off. They sometimes laughed so hard they had to grab for their breath.

Agnes appreciated the fact that her nine and twelve-year-old sons were strong enough to chop the chickens' heads off without grimacing. Some city kids (the name given to children who lived in the town proper of Badaxe) had never chopped a chicken's head off or shot a squirrel. Agnes did not want her children to grow up sissies. Nor did she want them to take glee in killing an animal. It had to be done, it was right to be done, but it should be done with neither glee nor squeamishness.

After the chickens were killed, Agnes, Lucy, and Zita dipped them in a vat of boiling water to loosen the feathers. The trick was to raise the temperature of the chicken's skin, thereby stretching the pores so the feathers could be plucked more easily without partially cooking the chicken, thereby reducing its flavor the next day. Immediately after plucking the chickens clean, they gutted them. The necks and gizzards were boiled to make broth and then cut up and prepared to be used for stuffing.

Several pies had been prepared and baked the day before. This year Agnes made apple, ground cherry, and strawberry pies with crusts made with as little water as possible.

On the day the thrashers came Agnes mixed the stuffing, stuffed the chickens and began baking. At the same time, she cut several onions to be sautéed for the risott. Her biggest pans were arranged on the stove, and she boiled potatoes, cooked five quarts of beans, and sautéed four onions and ten cups of rice. She poured three gallons of chicken broth over the rice. As it cooked she grated four pounds of cheddar cheese and boiled a cup of saffron. She poured the saffron water over the cooked rice, mixed in the cheese, poured the water off the potatoes and beans, took the chickens out of the oven, and served them all up to fourteen very hungry thrashers.

Ronald Andretti was the champion eater. He'd take a whole chicken—stuffing and all—three cups of risott, four large potatoes, a half-dozen serving spoonful's of beans. After he finished this, he'd take a quarter of a ten-inch apple pie and a quarter of a ground cherry pie. He washed it all down with a quart of milk.

Agnes saw Luke trying to eat as much, except he didn't take any potatoes and beans and only a leg and thigh of the chicken. But he ate two pieces of pie as big as Ronald's.

After the men went back to the fields Lucy and Zita cleared the table that was set up outside. Then Agnes, Jean and the two girls filled their plates and went out to the yard table to eat what was left. While they ate, the thrashers were picking the shocks up on the field just past Agnes' garden. She watched them toss the shocks as if they weighed fifteen pounds instead of more than fifty pounds. Then Agnes' eye caught Luke and Mark. They were thrusting their forks in to the shocks and tossing them on the wagons with the men, shock for shock.

Then Mark said something to Luke who put his fork on the ground and leaned on it, back bent over like a man of fifty. Mark walked toward the shock and thrust his fork in the top, dropped the fork handle on his knee, leaned back and lifted. To Agnes' amazement the shock of grain lifted off the ground, floated over Mark's head and landed in the wagon with the grace of a woman waltzing. Mark bowed toward the next shock, again thrust his fork into it and lifted. This time one bundle fell off as the rest of the shock glided into the wagon. Luke pushed his fork into the fallen bundle and lifted it on top of the rest.

Mark laughed a little, and then he walked to the next shock, and he and Luke went back to partnering the grain into the wagon. Agnes was amazed at their strength, and yet she also felt the humiliation Mark experienced when he had failed to toss the second shock in. His step into manhood was short-lived.

Then began the drudgery work. Everything had to be cleaned up—wash all those dishes and cut the leftovers up and refrigerate them, so they could be used for future meals.

The team of thrashers didn't finish by 5:00, but some of the men had to leave to milk their cows. Matthew, Alex, Frank Veneri, and Ronald Andretti and William's brother Geno stayed on to finish the job. Luke and Mark came in for supper. They ate warmed-up risott and another piece of pie. After a small unsuccessful fight to get Joshua to help them, they headed to the barn to milk the cows. By then both boys were exhausted. They hardly had the energy to lift the pie to their mouths. They headed toward the barn to milk the thirty-two cows they now had.

Agnes wasn't one to dwell on how hard her life and her family's life were. In fact, she felt blessed that they had no debts, plenty to eat, and enough work to keep everyone out of mischief. Tonight as Luke and Mark shuffle across the yard looking more like miniature fifty year olds than lively boys, she asked herself if she and William demanded too much too early of their children.

Twins

Father Duffy came to see Agnes in the hospital; something was wrong or Father would not be there. She hoped it wasn't the twins. They were so tiny, but they were so beautiful. And twins. Agnes had already birthed 12 children, but she experienced a new sense of life when she gave birth to the twins. While every birth was special, Agnes had not felt so special since she gave birth to Pina some twenty years earlier.

Father Duffy confirmed her worst fears. After a little chit-chat, he came right to the point. "Dr. Gallagher says the twins are fragile. They are underweight and he's worried about them. I knew you want them baptized. I know you want to take every precaution, so I suggest we baptize them now. We can do it right here. I know it's not the same as at church, but it's most important to baptize them, and we should do it now. William asked Geno and Stella to meet us here to be their godparents.

They're outside." Stella was Agnes' sister and the wife of William's brother Geno.

Agnes heard the death toll. The twins receiving baptism at the hospital did not mean certain death. How many times had she told the children at Sunday school that receiving the last sacraments did not mean death? It meant preparation for heaven in case death came. She knew a lot of people still living who had received the last rites. Her mother had received them thrice.

She didn't want to have the children baptized like this. Why couldn't it wait until they got home to do it with all her family there? What was the hurry? The twins couldn't die. She was 41 years old, and they would be her last children. Dr. Gallagher had told her that she could not have any more. She was glad for that. Fourteen was enough for one woman. The twins had to live. She didn't want her career as birth-giver to end in double deaths. She looked at Father and said, "Yes, of course. Please baptize them. We want them to go to heaven if they die. How horrible if they had to burn in hell because we did not baptize them." Father left the room. Agnes suddenly felt as if someone had crushed her chest and collapsed her lungs. She sucked in; using all her concentration to breathe, and then she exhaled and sucked in again. Her body was numb; she looked to see if her legs were still there.

Father came back with William, Geno, Stella and a nurse carrying John in her right arm and James in her left. Agnes studied the nurse carrying both so she could learn how. She was so envious of the nurse, to be able to carry those tiny and beautiful babies down the hall. "Jesus, let me out of bed. Let me carry my two sons out that door, down the hall, into the car and home. I want to nurse my babies in my own home."

She tried to lift her head off the pillow. The nurse leaned in and handed the babies to Agnes. The blood of life rushed through her veins. The boys were so tiny and yet their touch filled her with vitality. They were life, and life was to give life. For the very first time Agnes felt the fullness of her own giving—with two children, near death, and she weak from a difficult childbirth. Life had a way of being absorbed in cooking, cleaning, gardening and taking care of the chickens.

With these two cherubim in her arms, Agnes felt the milk that made life. It was in the giving of birth, of touch, of milk, of care, as much as the giving of food and shelter and cleanliness that made life possible. With her two children in her arms, Agnes thought: "If I had the strength, I could will them to life. Father Duffy is being an alarmist. These boys will live because I have given them life as I have given them twelve brothers and sisters, I will give them life. They will live from my milk and it will sustain them. I will hold them. I will rock them, and they will grow strong as their brothers have grown strong. My love will give them life. I will love them. I do love them." The thought sounded foreign to Agnes. "Love." It was not a word she used. "Yes, my love will give these babies life," she whispered to herself.

Father looked at Agnes and James and John, and while he had always had the godparents hold the baby at baptism, he dare not take those two delicate babies away from Agnes' arms. He said, "Geno and Stella, stand on the other side of the bed. Agnes, hold James and John as they are, and I will baptize them from here." Father kissed then lifted a purple stole over his head and took a moment to straighten it across his chest. He folded his hands and bowed his head.

"Jesus, these two lives were brought to this earth by Agnes. She and William have twelve other holy children, and they thank you for these two new souls. We ask you to let them stay a full life on this earth. You have given life, and we ask you not to take it away before its time. Yet, we know of thine mysterious ways. If you will, we will understand if you call these two souls to heaven early. If you choose to bring these souls to you early to honor you in heaven, we will find thanks for your blessing. We will suffer, and it will be painful, but we will never doubt your wisdom, your choice or your ways."

Father took a small bottle out of his pocket, unscrewed the top and poured a little of the holy water into his hands. As he said "I baptize thee in the name of God the Father, Son and Holy Ghost", he poured a little of the water over James' forehead. He poured more water in his hand and repeated "I baptize thee in the name of God the Father, Son and Holy Ghost," as he poured the water over John's forehead.

He asked Geno and Stella to promise to always be ready to do what was necessary to be sure that John and James stayed in the fold of the Church. "Agnes, may God be with you and give you strength in this difficult time. Pray and God's will will be done. Let us say a rosary together to ask God to let these children live and to bring happiness to you." Father led the rosary with Agnes, Stella, Geno and William responding. Then they left, and Agnes lay exhausted with her two offspring. John in her right arm and James in her left. Her eyes did not stay open. She dreamed that she rolled over first to the left and then to the right suffocating both.

When she woke they were gone. Did they die in her arms and the nurse stole them away in her sleep? In a panic she reached for the emergency pullstring to call the nurse, and then pulled on it again and again and again.

When the nurse came into the room, Agnes was white—she gagged and struggled out the words, "The twins?"

The nurse smiled. "Oh, they're okay. You fell asleep, and I took them back to the nursery. They're fine, Agnes." The nurse sat on the bed and took Agnes' hand to comfort her. Agnes smiled and fell back to sleep.

One Week Later

A week passed and Agnes regained her strength. James and John were more active and their red skin had toned down, so they looked more like regular babies—just a lot smaller. Each day Dr. Gallagher came to see Agnes and said the twins are doing better than can be expected. Finally, yesterday he said, "I think they will make it. They really look good and their vital signs are improving." Today, Agnes asked the doctor if they could go home.

"Not just yet" he said. Agnes stared ahead, and she felt James sucking on her—but she wasn't sure that she herself was still there. Her mind processed thoughts slowly—the doctor is here—he said John had pneumonia—he would not live—James was in danger—but he looked good—he was sucking strong—certainly he would make it.

The doctor realized Agnes could not speak. He reached for her shoulders—touched her—said, "Hold on." He wanted to assure Agnes that James would make it—but he could not.

He told the nurse, "When James is finished, return him to the nursery. You may have to take him from her. I don't think she'll know." Agnes saw the nurse take James. She picked him up, turned and walked from the room hovering a little above the floor. Agnes' eyes were focused on a speck on the wall but indeed she saw nothing. Her mind stopped, her feelings dried up. She wondered if she had been frozen into a statue, she tried to move to reassure herself that she was alive. Nothing moved. Was this a state of consciousness after death—frozen in time? She wondered if the shock of John's death killed her and death was a gradual slowing down of the mind until it froze like a bolt not used eventually rusting into nothingness.

The day passed this way. Something that looked like a nurse with a baby came in. She attached the baby to Agnes' breast and the baby moved its mouth in exaggerated sucking motion. Agnes felt nothing. It wasn't there, it could not be there; there was no feeling, no motion except his lips chopping away at her stone breasts. Finally, he stopped, the nurse floated over, took the baby, floated out the door. Agnes felt a sense of relief; it was the first thing she felt since dying. Maybe there is feeling after life.

She saw a man in a white jacket enter. He moved toward her, reached out his arm toward her. She wanted to block it, she did not want him to grab her, but her arm did not move. His arm kept coming toward her, getting bigger and bigger until he grabbed her shoulder. He shook her and Agnes could see her body move. He must be strong to move a solid stone statue like me. The doctor shook her harder and Agnes began to feel the pressure of his push. Slowly she began to realize where she was—in the hospital—her sons dying—a doctor shaking her awake and she wasn't dead. If only she could be.

The doctor's eyes told Agnes that John was dead. She'd seen those eyes many times. The tears rolled down her eyes before the doctor said "I'm sorry Agnes. He was so tiny—we couldn't do anything. I'm truly sorry. Once he got pneumonia, we couldn't do anything."

"How's James?"

"It's too early to tell, so far he is not showing signs of pneumonia. But he is so tiny, he is weak. He's had diarrhea today and it is taking his strength. We can only pray."

"I want to see him, I want to hold him. Now!" The doctor nodded to the nurse who left to get James. When she returned Agnes took James and held him against her heart. She felt his warmth and he seemed to feel her love. His body reached for his mother. His legs kicked and his arms reached in all directions. The doctor was reminded his medicine was not as powerful as the mother's.

Agnes' tears turned into sobs and for the first time in her life she began to cry hysterically. James reached for her and his hand settled on her breast as if he were comforting her. The nurse handed Agnes a wet cloth and she wiped her tears, but the tears and the sobs continued.

"Oh Jackass in the Sky, why, why—why now? Why take my child? What have I done to deserve this? Why finish my life as a mother by taking my baby?" Her thoughts began to replay her life. She saw her drunkard father preventing her from going to the convent—her wedding to a stranger—sweat rolling down her chest while canning, the hours and hours of childbirth, and those hundreds maybe thousands of times a bald fat man entered her to get his own pleasure. There were endless years with no money to buy even soap at the store. William was working on the highway and running the farm and getting nowhere. "Jesus, what happened to this life? It was good with you in it—having you in communion—praying to you. It made this awful life not so awful. Why are you abandoning me now? I want the joy of having my last baby live? Please let James live. Please."

Jesus did not hear her. James died the next day. The funeral was quiet. Father Duffy and William, Agnes and the two corpses. Father arranged to get two small cans from the funeral home to hold the bodies. After the services William carried the cans to the car, opened the trunk and put them in. Father helped Agnes out of the church and into the car. The three of them drove up to the cemetery. Matthew was already there. He was leaning on a posthole digger. As Agnes approached Matthew, she could see he had dug two holes the size of a hole for a post. William handed the two cans to Father who said some silent prayers and then dropped the cans into the holes. Agnes took the shovel and with no apparent emotion filled both holes—alternating the shovelfuls.

William, Agnes and Father walked back to the car. Agnes wanted William to take her hand, to hold her. He got in behind the wheel and started the car. Father held the door for Agnes and said "I'll walk back to the church." As they drove off Agnes saw Matthew packing dirt into the graves and Father walking not toward the church but toward Matthew. She thought she saw a tear on Matthew's face.

William drove up 56 in silence. They came over Moundridge where the school was that James and John might have learned to read. William drove into the yard, got out of the car, went into the house, changed into work clothes, went to the machine shed, started the tractor and drove out to the field. Agnes sat in the car for a few minutes and then walked slowly to the house. She went into the baby room, sat on the rocking chair and began to weep. Gabriel came in, saw her weeping, climbed on her lap and gave her a sugary two-year-old hug

III

Fire

III: Fire
(1944 -1953)

A Matter of Time

Agnes could not tell if William was in shock or relieved after the twins joined their Maker too soon. Dr. Gallagher warned her, "Your body cannot withstand another pregnancy. Next time, not only will the baby die, his mother will as well." Agnes felt she provoked such a harsh sentence when she asked when it would it be safe to have another child. She had found Dr. Gallagher to be kind and gentle. After a few days of fury at his crude remarks, she came to believe he was just taking her welfare as his responsibility. Never for a second did Agnes consider not having at least one more child. Her mother's last pregnancy ended with a stillborn. Agnes was seventeen and thought at the time that she was more distraught than her mother. Her mother seemed to take it in stride—part of being a woman on the frontier. If anything she should be thankful her other pregnancies all ended in healthy children and all were alive and well. The stillborn was not and could not be baptized, so he could not be buried in the Catholic Cemetery nor have a funeral mass, so there was no funeral or graveside ceremony. Agnes was angry at the time and, for the first time, felt doubt of her church's teachings. Her mother was stoic and resolved—Agnes never witnessed a tear.

Many years later, on what would have been the birthday of her brother Charles, her mother said, from nowhere, "The greatest regret in my life is that I did not have a child after Charles. No mother's last child should be born dead." Agnes' mother never said another word about it. After John and James died, Agnes visited her mother. Before she could bring up trying to have another child, Mary Margaret said, "Agnes, it is different. You have twelve children, I only had seven, I was younger than you are and I had no health issues. I could have had another child, but the pain of losing Charles was too great. I should never had said something."

Agnes was not to be deterred. She would have another child. Dr. Gallagher would care for her. William, even if he did not want any more children—and Agnes was sure he did not—would not be able to stay away from her. She would have another child—it was just a matter of time.

Birth of Maria

Giuseppina gave birth to Maria on October 15, 1946. Agnes had given birth to her last child three months before so the joy of birth was fresh in her memory as she and William drove across the state to be with Pina on the birth of her first child—their first grandchild.

The first part of the trip Agnes found herself settling herself and Leonardo into the car and getting over the anxiousness of starting out on a long journey. Pina lived about five hours away, and Agnes could count on one hand how many times she'd taken a trip that long. She was concerned about traveling with a three-month old, but Leonardo was soon asleep, and once William got out of the Mississippi Valley bluffs, Agnes relaxed into the trip and began to enjoy the rolling fields of Central Wisconsin. It was much flatter than her home area, and she began to wonder why her ancestors crossed this land that looked so much easier to farm, in order to settle in the hills and valley of Badaxe. It seemed strange for she knew they come to Wisconsin when there was still plenty of land to be claimed.

Leonardo was asleep; William was occupied driving; there were no children to feed; no garden to hoe and harvest. Agnes heard silence she had forgotten existed as their old black Ford headed east. She felt calm grow from inside to the outer layers of her skin. Her feet, ankles, and legs went limp. Serenity edged up her back, across her shoulders, into her neck, and up the back of her head. She closed her eyes for a moment to feel this lack of tension. It was a strange feeling. So quiet. So at ease—she did not recognize it.

About the time she was trying to remember if she had ever felt this tranquil before, a swelling grew in her stomach. For a fleeting fanciful moment she wondered if she were pregnant—she hadn't slept with William since Leonardo was born, and besides, the doctor told her she could have no more children. The fullness grew warmer, and, from deep inside her, it grew to an image of Giuseppina full with her firstborn. William never liked to talk when he drove on strange highways, and today Agnes was glad, for she was enjoying this inexplicable maternal sensation.

Sooner than she could believe, they drove into Pina's yard. Oliver, Pina's husband, told them it was a little house, but Agnes had not thought this little. It was more a toy house than a little people house. She smiled at that image.

Leonardo woke up suddenly when William shut off the engine. Agnes opened the back door and took him into her arms. William knocked on the door. No answer. He knocked harder. Agnes thought they'd have to hear that no matter where they were in the oversized dog house. There was no answer. Pina said they'd be home for sure. Maybe they went to the grocery for some last-minute things. The neighbor lady came out and stared at them suspiciously. About the time Agnes was ready to explain that she was Giuseppina's mother, the neighbor lady said, "You must be Pina's family. She's a spitting image of you. But you missed 'em. They already gone off to the hospital." Pina was yelling something fierce. Could hear her all over the neighborhood."

William got directions from the neighbor, and they headed to the hospital. Agnes noticed William was more worried than when he drove her to the hospital to have their babies. He always cared a lot for Pina, and Agnes was pleased to see him worry, but another side of her was hurt. "Couldn't he care more for me?" That thought dissolved as her own anxiety and anticipation for Giuseppina took her attention.

They drove to the hospital yard, got out of the car, crossed the parking lot, and went up to the receptionist. "Um, um, we're Giuseppina Modell's parents. She's here? We came to see her. She's going to have a baby. I think she's here. We're her parents. We drove down from near LaCrosse to see her. Be here when she has the baby. Is she here?"

The girl behind the desk said, "Yes. She just arrived a little while ago. The doctor's with her. She might have the baby any moment. She's in Room 226. You can go to the second floor. Tell the nurse you're here. There's a waiting room on the second floor. You can wait there."

Agnes and William walked up the steps and found the nurse and asked for Giuseppina. "She could give birth any minute." The nurse said they could not see her, but she'd tell Giuseppina her parents had made it.

Agnes wanted so to see Pina before she went into labor. She'd be frightened and Agnes could calm her down. She wasn't a very strong woman, and she hated pain. They were too late, so Giuseppina had to make do by herself. Maybe it was for the best. She'd have to be strong to raise a family, care for Oliver and become a mother and a real wife. Agnes knew you learned a lot about being a wife after your baby was born. Before that you were lovers, girlfriend more than wife. With the first baby, you overnight became both mother and wife. It might take more strength than weak Giuseppina had to become mother and real wife at the same time. So being alone to give birth might help her to be stronger. "But she's not alone. She has Oliver and it will help them come together. Help him realize he is a husband."

She saw so much of William in Oliver. Pina had been such a favorite of William's it was natural she would marry a man like him. That is not to say Oliver looked or lived like William; he'd been in the navy and had traveled about the country and had been to Europe, while William had never left Badaxe. Oliver wasn't a farmer. His parents owned a golf course, and Oliver now worked as an engineer on a railroad.

The real things—a meanness that kept him alive, a distance that prevented any real intimacy, a sternness that was frightening—Agnes recognized those traits too well. Giuseppina would have a difficult life with this man, but she had her religion, her family, her upbringing. She'd survive it, and if she got stronger, she'd survive it with dignity if without happiness. God would reward her for her suffering. It was for the best.

Mixed Marriage

Alex called from Madison. "I'm getting married." Michael had asked her last night, and she said she surprised herself by saying yes. She wasn't ready to be married, but Michael was her dream man, and he loved her so much, and he said he wanted to get married before he went back to Korea. "Mom, I wasn't thinking about getting married. But Michael is dead serious. He says he is afraid I won't wait for him while he is fighting in Korea and that he could not bear to wait for a letter from me saying I found another man. He says he'd rather break it off if I won't marry him. He loves me and treats me better than anyone ever has. I was not thinking about getting married, but when he proposed, and said he wanted to get married before he went back, I said 'yes.' Somehow I knew it was the right answer. We haven't set the date but it has to be this month."

Agnes let Alex talk. She liked Michael, and she had noticed how he paid attention to her when Alex had brought him to the farm to visit. She had never remembered William looking at her like that or paying so much attention to her. Michael opened the door, let Alex walk in front of him, and helped her if she spilled something. He always seemed to be aware of Alex. He played with the children and particularly enjoyed the baby, Gabriel. He'd be a worthy father because he liked children. He had been friendly to Agnes and tried to talk to William. She liked him.

"Will he join the church?"

"He said he'd be married in our church, Mom. He's even talked to his family, and they said they planned to come to the wedding if it was in our church. You know they are staunch Lutherans. Lutherans really don't like Catholics. It will be as hard for them to see Michael be married in a Catholic Church as it would be for you to see me get married in a Lutheran Church. Mom, I told him we had to get married in St. Francis in Badaxe and he understood."

"Will he convert, will he become Catholic?"

"He can't, Mom. Even if he wanted to, he can't tell his parents he was gonna to join the Catholic Church. His parents would disown him."

Agnes did not say anything. She'd had to suffer through Giuseppina getting engaged to a non-Catholic who said he wouldn't join the church. When Agnes told Pina, "You can't marry a non-Catholic. God will not approve," Pina told Oliver he had to become a Catholic or she would not marry him. He started to study Catholicism and in no time he began to believe, and he was baptized before they were married. Agnes would have preferred Giuseppina had married someone who was raised Catholic, but love being what it was she was glad Oliver had converted.

Alex was saying Michael would not consider becoming Catholic. Agnes' stomach sank, she felt like someone had deposited a lead cake at the bottom of her stomach. The unimaginable was happening. One of her children was marrying a non-Catholic who would not convert to the Church. Would God forgive her? What would her sisters think and say? Could Agnes attend the wedding, even if it was at St. Francis?

"Mom, you there? Hello. Are we disconnected? Mom, you there?"

Agnes did not speak and she heard Alex say: "God damn phones, we got disconnected again." Agnes heard the phone click, so she hung up.

How would she tell William? How would she tell the rest of her children? How could Alex do this? Sure love has its own way of doing things, but one had to say no to love if it meant marrying a non-Catholic. The Church did not approve. Alex thought she'd get married at St. Francis, but Agnes had never known Father Duffy to marry a couple when one of them wasn't Catholic. Father Duffy liked Agnes and William, and he especially liked Alex, but he'd never married a Catholic and non-Catholic before. Agnes could not understand what made Alex think he'd marry her to a non-Catholic.

"Where did I fail? Hannah married a nice Catholic boy, but Pina had gotten engaged to a non-Catholic who only joined the Church when she refused to marry him unless he did." Agnes did not mind that too much, because she knew a lot of devout Catholics who had joined the Church so they could marry a Catholic. She had hoped Oliver would be one like that. So far he wasn't. She suspected he might not always go to Church when he wasn't visiting them in Badaxe.

Now Alex was saying she was going to marry Michael, and she wouldn't ask him to become Catholic. Agnes was supposed to be thankful his parents would come to a Catholic wedding. "No way, why shouldn't they come to a Catholic wedding. It is the only true wedding. People married in the Lutheran Church are not married. It isn't the same thing."

Agnes began to think of ways she might convince Alex to either ask Michael to become Catholic or to not marry him. Alex was strong willed. "Nothing I do will persuade her to ditch Michael. William could—but he won't. He was much more upset Giuseppina was marrying an eighteen-year old than that he was not Catholic. I don't believe he cares if the girls marry a Catholic. Sometimes I wonder if he'd go to Church himself if he didn't know I'd make him go. Alex never listened to me and anything I say to her will only make it worse. She might become mad enough to go and get married in a Lutheran Church." That thought turned the lead brick-cake into a nauseous bubble that jumped into her throat.

It took her awhile to calm down. Her only hope was to find a way to convince Michael to become a Catholic. She played out in her mind how she could get him to convert. Father Duffy might convert him. But he might not meet Father Duffy. He would refuse to marry them and there would be no reason for him to meet Michael let alone have the opportunity to convert him.

They would have to be married in a church in LaCrosse or Madison. "Guess they wouldn't have no reason to get married in LaCrosse so they will get married in Madison." Agnes knew that some priests would marry a Catholic to a non-Catholic even though the Pope had condemned it. Father Duffy said the Pope had asked priests not to marry non-Catholics. They were not baptized so they should not receive the sacrament of Matrimony. Apparently the Pope had not "officially" forbid priests from marrying a Catholic to a non-Catholic, so some bad priests did it any way. There must be at least one priest in Madison that would marry them. He could find a way to let Michael know about the Catholic Church. Agnes was so sure her religion was not only the best, but she believed anyone who knew about the Church would be converted. Only people who were ignorant of the Catholic Church stayed non-Catholic. It was why Lutherans and Baptists and other Protestants said all those horrible things about Catholics. It was how they kept their parishioners ignorant about the Catholic religion. They did not want all their people joining the Catholic Church. All Agnes had to do was to find a way to make sure Michael learned more about the Catholic religion.

The phone rang. "Hello"

"Hello, Mom." It was Alex. "We must have been disconnected. Mom, I'm going to marry Michael. We'd like to get married in Badaxe at St. Francis. But you have to agree to it. Otherwise, we can get married here. I think we will either get married the third or fourth Sunday of October. Mom, I know you are disappointed, but I love Michael and he loves me, and I know I will never find another person as good for me."

"Father Duffy wouldn't marry you, if Michael doesn't convert. You know that."

Silence. "I guess you're right. I'd forgotten how pigheaded he is."

"Alex! How dare you talk about Father Duffy that way?"

"I'm sorry, that was not fair. But he sure is stubborn about not marrying a couple when one isn't Catholic. Well, we can get married at St. Thomas. One of my friends married a non-Catholic there just a couple of months ago, so I know Father Malic is willing to do it."

"Alex, can you get Michael to study the Church with the priest at St. Thomas? Even if he won't convert, it is important for him to know about your religion. He'll let you raise your kids Catholic won't he?"

"Yes, Mom, he agreed to that. I won't marry him if he won't let me raise our kids Catholic. He understood."

"Well, all the more reason for him to study and understand the beliefs and practices of the Catholic Church. If he doesn't do it before you get married, he might never do it. Then it will just be harder to get him to understand why the children have to go to church and why communion is so important and about confession. You know Protestants always make things up about confession. He should understand what it really is."

"Okay, Mom, I'll ask him. I think he'll go to the classes they have at St. Thomas. I'll ask him to. I'm sure he will, Mom.

"Mom, we want to come up for Saturday and Sunday. We need to make plans quick. Figure out who to invite. I thought we would talk to Father Duffy, but you're right, he probably wouldn't talk to us let alone agree to marry us. I'll talk to Father Malic before we come up, and we'll set a date. We'll get there in the late afternoon. We can stay until after supper on Sunday. I guess you will all have to come here for the wedding. We have a lot of things to plan, who to invite, how you are going to get here, if you stay overnight where you will stay."

"Good, I'll see you Saturday. We better hang up because this is costing you too much money."

Agnes hung up. "Damn" she thought. Why did Alex have to fall in love with Michael? Sure he was nice, and he treated Alex like a queen, and he liked kids. But he was not Catholic, and he would not convert and it would lead to nothing but trouble for them. Their love would fade and when they needed God and the Church to help them through their marriage and raising a child, they would not have that together. It would be trouble. Agnes wished Michael might be called to Korea before the wedding. Maybe they would call it off. She had not ever thought of Alex getting married. She was pretty and she always liked boys. She had a different boyfriend every week and was so independent. She could care for herself and did take care of herself. Why did she want to get married now?

Agnes went for a walk out the back door and up to the sand pile where Pina, Hannah, Alex and all of her children since played. She sat at the side of the sand pile and picked up a handful and let it run through her fingers. Then another handful and another. She wanted to understand. She could not imagine herself allowing herself to date a non-Catholic let alone falling in love with one and marrying one. It was not possible. How could two of her children have been so foolish? Hadn't she raised them as good Catholics? They had learned at school the evils of mixed marriages, and they had seen plenty of examples. Everyone knew Olga and Herb Beffa fought all the time over religion. Herb was not a protestant. He did not believe at all. Olga was always trying to get him to take her to church, and he would not do it, or, if he did, he went to Veneri's bar and got drunk while she was in church. Marrying a non-Catholic was bad. It just did not work. Why did Giuseppina and now Alex get involved with non-Catholics? Father Duffy would preach two-three times every year on the evils of mixed marriages. Didn't they hear him? Why? Why? Why?

Agnes resolved herself to teach her other children better and to find a way to make Michael convert to Catholicism. It was the only thing she could do.

She picked up another handful of sand and poured it over her half covered foot.

Grandma Veneri

Agnes had little time to accept the fact her father had died when her mother, Mary Veneri, became ill. Agnes was the oldest child of the Veneri family, and she had that special relationship to her parents that only oldest children have. She visited them every Sunday after church. She did not remember missing a Sunday since she had left home to marry William. Oh, she had not visited them when she was too pregnant to go to church or too ill after birthing to attend. After her father had died a little over a year ago, she also visited her mother during the week.

None of Agnes' brothers or sisters had been so faithful about visiting Grandma (everyone called her Grandma and even when Agnes and Mary were alone, Agnes called her Grandma). She enjoyed visiting her mother and never thought of it as a chore or duty. She accepted that the oldest child would show more care and visit more often. She sometimes wished Roberto would visit more often. Ever since he came back from the war he seldom visited anyone and only came to see his father and mother once a year though he lived only a few hundred feet away. Mary and Bart seem to understand something had happened to Roberto in the war, and they accepted his aloofness. Agnes felt she should also accept it even if she thought he should visit his parents more often. The fact she stopped every Sunday, while her brothers and sisters drove right on by to spend the afternoons with their own family, never seemed unfair or peculiar to Agnes.

The doctor said Mary Veneri was going to die. The priest had come to give the last sacraments and Agnes' brothers and sisters had come to say goodbye. Death was in the air and Mary,

Agnes, the rest of the family, the priest and the doctor had all come to accept it. Well, the doctor had not accepted it, and he wanted the family to admit Mary Veneri to the hospital. Mary wanted to die at home, and she had told the family many times since Bart died that he was so happy to have been able to die at home. No one wanted to admit her to the hospital even if it meant that her life might be prolonged for a few days. There was something right about dying on the time schedule God had created rather than one a doctor realigned. All agreed one ought to be able to die at home. Dying in a hospital was a cruel way to end one's life—in a strange place with strangers in control running around like they owned not only the place but you. They had all heard tales of the nurses kicking the next of kin out of the room just before death became final. No one could understand the cruelness of such an act. Everyone wanted their wife or husband, child or parent at their side when the last moment came. Why did they send them out of the room? Did they think we did not know death? That we did not deal with death face to face? There wasn't a person here who hadn't had a score of dogs, calves, horses, cows die in their arms. Death among the parishioners came on a regular basis. They all attended over a half dozen funerals every year, and they had all held the hand of a dying person as they took their last breath. Death was bad enough, but to die in a hospital away from one's family and home was a punishment they did not deserve. No one in Mary Veneri's family was going to let that happen to her.

Agnes agreed to stay with Mary overnight. Her breathing was turning hoarse and the end was nearing. Everyone had chores to do and family to care for, so they must take turns to spend the last days and nights with Grandma. As the end neared, it seemed natural to all that Agnes would spend the night and the next day and night if necessary with her mother.

Mary laid on the bed, her back propped up a little to ease her breathing, her eyes one-fourth open so it was hard to tell if she were sleeping, awake or unconscious. She breathed loudly, but there was no other motion. Agnes took her mother's hand and talked to her for a few minutes but as she got no response she fell silent. She remembered Grandma when she was Mother, beaming at Agnes' First Communion, the two of them washing dishes together and laughing when Dad was out milking the cows, Mother pouring sand over her hair in a sand pile she'd forgot they even had, walking to church together in the snow when Dad was too hungover to drive them, the look on her face when she first saw Giuseppina, the pride of a new grandmother. I wonder if she knew how many more times she would become a grandmother and a great-grandmother. Agnes started to count the grandchildren and great-grandchildren her mother had. She got up to thirty-three but wasn't so sure she had counted all the great-grandchildren. She started to count again, and then laughed a little at the idea that somehow counting Grandma's offspring might keep Grandma alive.

She was going to die; she was ready to die; she had said many times over the last year that she wanted to die; she wanted to join Bart in heaven, life without him made no sense. She'd joked if she left Bart alone too long in heaven, one of those single women would be snatching up such a handsome man. Agnes wondered about Grandma's new-found expression of love for Grandpa. She'd bitched plenty to his face when he was alive, especially when he went on one of his binges. Agnes' father liked his alcohol and while he controlled his need for it most of the time, every few Saturday nights he'd hit one of the three taverns (sometimes he'd hit all three) and come home soused to the gills. Grandma would become so angry if he was so hungover the next day he couldn't make it to Sunday Mass. Some times she'd go a week without talking to him. Other times she'd call him names a Christian woman wasn't supposed to know—let alone use. Agnes had thought Grandma might actually be glad to have the old geezer gone. Sure she'd expected tears and a few months mourning, but she thought Grandma might be relieved to have him out of her life. She'd thought about it herself. If William died, she'd be devastated. The pain of his death and the fear of living without his support would bring her to her knees. When she'd think about a life without his bickering; without his yelling; without his insistence she get his approval to spend a nickel; and without his anger and cruelty to the children, she knew life could be tougher, but she concluded she and the children would be happier without William. She envisioned whole days with no one yelling and going to the grocery store and buying two dozen wieners, and everyone enjoying them without some cheap SOB complaining how expensive they were. Besides, he didn't do anything on the farm anymore anyway. They'd get along great without him. She thought her mother must have had the same thoughts. Somehow things changed after Bart died. Now Grandma only remembered the good times they had together and how much she loved him and did not really want to go on without him. Agnes wondered if she would feel that way if William died. "Grandma's just old and afraid she won't be able to manage on her own. But she has me. She knows I will always be here to take care of her. Why did she need that old drunkard around?"

Suddenly loneliness overcame Agnes. Grandpa and Grandma were always there. She visited them every Sunday.

She called Grandma anytime to talk or ask how to do this or that. When Grandpa died, Agnes felt a loss, but she was never so close to him anyway, and she still had Grandma. Now Grandma was going to die. If things got bad, where would she go? During the depression, she always knew she could turn to Grandma if they ran out of food or clothes or money. Sometimes they would get down to the last dollar and not know where the next pound of flour was coming from. It was horrible, but Agnes had survived it because she knew Grandma would give her five dollars if she really needed it. She was proud that she had never had to ask, but knowing that it was there was the assurance that had allowed her to survive. Grandma always knew when one of the children did not have clothes to wear for school. She'd show up with a pair of pants, a shirt—even shoes.

When William got too mean, Agnes had slipped away to visit Grandma and it made things better. When the children were small, she'd carry the baby and walk the two miles to Grandma's just to get away from William. He never liked it, and often called her a mommies' baby, but he was mellower when she returned. Even now, Agnes would escape to her mother's. William spent less and less time at home as he often spent the entire day at Levi's store or Jamboys' garage. When he was home all day, Agnes was likely to go visit Grandma. Where would she go when Grandma was gone? Agnes began to feel, for the first time in her life, a loss of belonging. With what was she connected? She had always had her parents, her husband, her children, her Jesus. They had assured and reassured her of her connection to life. With her mother going, that connection was shifting under her, and she did not recognize the sensation. Was it through her mother that she connected to her past? Was her mother her connection to God or was God her connection to the world? She had always thought it was her belief and love in Jesus that gave her life meaning. She did not understand how some people struggled so within themselves to find truth. Roberto was in a constant struggle. Why didn't he accept the teachings of the Church? Now, Agnes saw her relation to life, the world, even to the Church and Jesus as something that passed through her mother. Would it all be severed when her mother died? Would she be as stranded spiritually as she would be financially without the assurance her mother was there; could be turned to in need?

She was not able to answer that question and it frightened her.

The night crawled along. Mary never moved except to exhale. Her eyes stayed half open and her body perfectly still except for slight movements in her chest and the vibration in her throat that created the death rattle Agnes knew too well. Agnes' mind stayed alert, both watching Grandma for the slightest movement that might indicate this was the last moment and replaying vividly her own life with Grandma. She remembered helping Grandma hide some money behind the picture of the Virgin Mary. It had been many years ago and Grandma had saved enough of her egg money and other money she'd received from Grandpa that she had wanted to hide it. Agnes never knew how much it was but her mother had asked her to help re-paper the back of the picture so it looked like it had never been tampered with. She had said she wanted to save some money for a rainy day and for the time Republicans would get elected again. Agnes had suspected she was really saving some money Grandpa did not know about. Agnes had forgotten about it until now. She wondered if Grandma had stashed more money in other places. Did she have some under the mattress? Behind other pictures? Maybe the money wasn't behind the Virgin Mary anymore. Maybe Grandma had taken it out and spent it or come to her senses and put it in the bank. Roosevelt had fixed things so the Wall Street crooks, robber barons and bank moguls could not create another depression with a run on the banks.

Agnes had no reason to believe anyone else knew about Grandma's hiding money. After Grandma died, she'd look behind the picture to see if the money was still there. If it was, she'd look behind other pictures and in the bureau and even under the mattress. If there was money she'd use it for a memorial at the church. Agnes knew Grandma wanted to give something to the Church, but she didn't think she had a will. Agnes knew her brothers well enough to know they would not want to give anything to the Church. So she decided right then and there if there was money hidden no one knew about, she would keep it to give it to Father Duffy for the Church. "Maybe, just maybe, there is enough money to buy the rose window Father Duffy has been preaching the Church needed. No, a rose window probably costs more than a thousand dollars; Grandma couldn't have hidden that much money." If Agnes had saved her egg money for her entire life she would not have had a thousand dollars.

At three o'clock in the morning, Mary Veneri stirred, Agnes reached for her hand, Mary's eyes opened a little, she looked at Agnes, and her hand squeezed Agnes' as she tried to pull Agnes toward her. She was so weak the tug was barely perceptible. Did she want Agnes to come closer? Agnes leaned down to be closer to her mother at her last moment. Mary pulled a little harder. What did she want? For a moment Agnes thought Mary might be asking for a hug but Agnes had not hugged her mother since she was a little girl. As close as they were to each other, hugging was not an acceptable form of expression. Mary squeezed harder and continued to pull on Agnes hand. Agnes hesitated, she wanted to reach over and hold her mother, to let her know she loved her and that her love would go with her to heaven. Grandma pulled a little harder. Was it what she meant? Grandma's breath rattled deeper, her body contracted and went limp. Agnes reached her arms around her and held her tightly. It was a moment too late. Agnes put her head on Grandma's chest and the tears came spontaneously. Her mother, her best friend, her connection to the past was gone.

Agnes stayed in her mother's arms for a long time. She could not stop the convulsions. Death was not new to her. She had lost two sons, she had been with Grandpa when he died, and she, like others in her village, had known death from before memory. But this was her mother who had been so central to her life—her sense of being—even her happiness felt permanently shattered.

The morning light was coming in the windows when she finally lifted herself from Grandma's chest. It had been the middle of the night when Grandma died. Agnes wondered if she had fallen asleep. She got up, walked to the picture of the Virgin Mary that had hung in Mary's bedroom from the time of her marriage to Bart. Agnes took the picture off the wall, noticed that the paper back was glued to the frame; the same as when she and her mother had glued it there. She took the picture into the kitchen, took out a kitchen knife, cut around the paper, took out the fasteners with the tip of the knife, inserted the knife under the cardboard backing and lifted. "My God, the money is still here." She noticed a hundred dollar bill folded over some other money. She lifted it and unfolded it. There was another one hundred dollar bill. She counted one, two three four five six seven eight nine ten bills. They were all one hundred dollar bills. Agnes had never seen so much money in one place in her life. She wondered if she had ever seen that much money period. It was the first time she had seen that many hundred dollar bills. In fact, she only remembered ever seeing one hundred dollar bill before. When some fat guy from New Jersey came and bought their best milk cow, he had given William a one hundred-dollar bill for the cow. William had showed it off for several days before he took it to the bank. Wow, one thousand dollars. The bills became sun shining through the rose window in Agnes' mind. "It will make the perfect memorial for Mom."

Agnes went back into the bedroom and took down the picture of Christ. She noticed the back had also been glued shut, she opened it and there was two hundred more dollars. She went to her mother's bureau, opened the drawers to search for more hidden money. She went through all the drawers and found nothing. "Maybe she hid some in the mattress." She lifted the sides of the mattress. She recognized a place that most would not have seen where the mattress seam had been repaired. "No, Mom didn't really hide some money in her mattress?" She took scissors and a needle out of the sewing kit and opened the seam. It was a little spooky doing this with Grandma on the bed, but Agnes felt sure her mother would approve. Grandma had mentioned she might buy the window, except she was afraid if she lived too long she'd wind up in the poor house. Grandma wanted Agnes to do this and must be directing her where to look. Agnes opened the seam and yes there was money stuffed in the mattress. Agnes could not help laughing. She looked at Mary and said, "I'm sorry." She reached in and pulled the money out. There were tens and twenties and another hundred dollar bill. Agnes counted the money. She couldn't believe it. There was $1200. Agnes had no idea Grandma had this much money in the whole world, let alone buried in her house. Agnes took the needle and the thread and began to sew the mattress seam. She heard the door open. She looked at the clock. It was only 5:00 a.m. Who would be here so early? She got up and walked quickly to the front room. She did not want to be caught with the money and Grandma's mattress open. Someone might think she was stealing the money. It was Sara, Agnes' sister.

"How is she?" Agnes stared at Sara a little too long before she remembered that only she knew Grandma was gone. "She's in heaven with Jesus." Sara was shaken. Somehow she wanted to believe Grandma was better. Sara had always been the one that thought things would work out.

Sara walked into the bedroom to see Grandma. She was stiff. She looked at Agnes who offered her the arms she had not been able to give to her mother even at the last moment. They cried in each other's arms for a long time. Finally, Agnes said, "Sara, Grandma has a lot of money hidden in the house. I think she would want us to take it and give it to Father to buy the rose window for the church. It could be a memorial to her and to Dad. Would you help me search for the money before we call anyone and tell them mother is gone? You know Raymond and Roberto will never agree to use the money for the Church, but I know Grandma wanted to donate the money for the rose window."

"The rose window will cost more than a thousand dollars. Possibly two or three thousand dollars."

"Grandma's got that much here. I've already found $2400."

"No!"

"Yes."

"I can't believe it. $2400! You got to be kidding. $2400. If there is that much do you think it's right we give it all to the Church?"

"You know Mother would want us to. You know she was thinking about buying the rose window as a memorial to Dad. I think we have to do it. I've thought it out. We can take the money and hide it until after we get our inheritance. Later we can give it to Father and tell him that it is from our share of the inheritance. No one will be the wiser. It's the right thing to do. Will you help me? Let's look to see if there is more money. We'll split it in two and take it home and hide it until it's time to give it to Father."

Sara looked at Agnes, "Is this my sister who is talking like this? My sister who wouldn't take a nickel from a millionaire is now talking about taking Grandma's money and hiding it from her brothers and sisters?" Agnes' logic made sense. Grandma had not made a will. If she had made a will she would have given money to the Church and divided what was left among her children. It was right to honor what her will would have been.

Agnes and Sara searched the house for more hidden money. Sara looked through Grandma's bureaus. She even lifted the browned white paper at the bottom of each drawer and yes she found a few more ten and twenty dollar bills. Agnes continued to take apart each of the pictures in the house, but she did not find any more money. Finally, they gave up looking, sat down to count the money and found they had $2800. They divided the money and each put $1400 in her purse. Agnes went to the telephone and dialed the operator to connect her to Frank and Jean's line. They were on a separate trunk line from Agnes and Grandma, and they had to be called through the operator. Frank answered the phone. "Frank, Mom died during the night. Would you call Philip, Johnny and Rosa? I'll call everyone else." It was all they said to each other.

Agnes hung up then picked up the phone and rang two shorts and one long which was Roberto's number. "Mother died during the night. You better come over."

Agnes cranked a short-long-short. It was Father Duffy's phone in the rectory. He would be up and praying silently by now. She hated to interrupt him from his prayers, but he would want to know Grandma had died, and he would come immediately to the house to console the family. He had given Grandma the last rites, so he would not do it again. Some times when he had not given the last rites, Father would give them even if the body was cold. Everyone knew the last rites were only good if the soul was still in the body; the Church's teaching was that the body died when the soul left the body. All the same, Father thought it was best to give the last rites even if the body appeared to be dead. One never knew and it was better to err on the side of the person dying than on the side of caution for the sacrament. Not every priest in Badaxe had believed that, but Agnes was glad Father Duffy did. He had also heard Mary's last confession before she became too ill to talk. "Mom is ready to face Jesus and she must be in heaven. There should be no need for such a holy woman to spend time in purgatory. Mom was never a candidate for hell." The idea that Mary Margaret would go to hell was too ludicrous to have even thought it.

Father Duffy knew it was Agnes calling for he said "Agnes, are you all right?"

"Mother died in the night. She was ready for heaven. Thank you, Father."

"I'm sorry Agnes, but she lived a holy life, and she was ready to die. Did she go peacefully?"

"Yes. She woke before she passed away. She looked at me to say goodbye and that was it."

"It's good. I'll be right over."

Agnes called the rest of her brothers and sisters who lived on her party line, and then she called William's brothers and sisters, her aunts and uncles and Mary's friends.

Since they were all on party lines with five to nine homes on a line—and the people of Badaxe tended to listen in especially if there was a call so early in the morning—by the time Agnes finished calling, everyone in the parish knew Mary Margaret Veneri had passed away in the night.

By 6:00 a.m. Father Duffy, Stella, Roberto, Frank and Jean Veneri and a dozen people from the town had come to see Grandma and to offer there condolences to Agnes and the rest of the Veneri family.

Most stayed only for a short time, as they had to return to the farm and milk the cows or to prepare breakfast for the family and get the children off to school.

Frank called the undertaker in LaCrosse. There was no need to discuss who would handle the funeral for every Catholic in Badaxe had used Francini's Funeral home from the time anyone in that room could remember. The man at the end of the line said they would be right down to pick up the body. He asked Frank if he would like to return to LaCrosse with them to pick out the casket. He said he thought his sisters would come up later in the day.

People came and went through the early morning hours. The undertaker came, covered Mary's body and removed it through the side door, loaded her in the hearse and drove off to LaCrosse where her body was prepared for a viewing the next day. Everything came as one might expect. Except, there was one small peculiarity that no one noticed. Agnes and Sara, who normally put their purses down upon arrival in someone's home, kept their purses around their shoulders with their left arm planted firmly over the purse.

A few weeks later, Bart and Mary's earthly possessions were counted and the wealth was divided equally among the nine children. To everyone's surprise this relatively modest farm couple had managed to accumulate enough money for each of the nine children to receive ten thousand dollars in cash. They would auction off the farm in July after Raymond's lease ran out and divide the proceeds from the sale of the farm, the equipment and the cattle on the farm.

Sunday Movies

Agnes loved Sunday afternoons in the winter because Father Duffy showed movies in the church basement. Each Sunday after dinner the entire family would pile in the car and make the drive to St. Francis. The children loved the cowboy movies, especially Gene Autry and Roy Rogers. The older girls loved the romance stories, and Agnes liked the religious movies the most.

Since Leonardo was born, sometimes Agnes had to stay home. Sometimes Zita or Emma stayed with Leonardo. A couple of times Agnes took Leonardo to the movie, but he was too restless. Before the movie everyone would coo over him because he was so cute. When the movie began Leonardo became a nonentity. Most of the audience never saw a movie except the St. Francis movies and Leonardo was no competition to the magic of the film. Leonardo didn't like this, so Leonardo would raise Cain. First he pulled on a shirt, then tried babbling and when they got no results he'd let her rip. Leonardo made sure Agnes spent most of the time in the churchyard. It was better to stay home with him. Agnes decided the fairest thing was for Emma, Zita, and Lucy to take turns with her to watch Leonardo.

Emma hated to take her turn to watch Leonardo. Being three miles from town and going to a small one-room school with only her closest neighbors, she loved going into town to play with kids her age and to flirt with the few boys in town who were not her cousins. Emma loved boys and liked teasing them more. She was the tomboy of the family and she loved to play with the boys. Sometimes she'd wrestle with them, and she liked that because she could be tough on one hand and touch the boys who she invariably had a crush on. Sometimes she'd "accidentally" grab their crotches as she tussled on the ground. She liked that the most. Paradoxically she'd grow up, get spurned by the man of her love and never marry.

Emma hated to give all this up to stay with Leonardo, and she made Agnes feel uncomfortable when it was her turn. Agnes also hated to give up the movies. Orsola, Mary, Jean always came early, and they would get up quite a gossip by the time the movie started. Plus Agnes loved the religious movies.

She never missed one, and she especially liked the movies with nuns.

Zita preferred to stay home with Leonardo. She was so shy that being in a crowd made her uncomfortable. While she enjoyed the movies enough, she hated the time before the movie. Sometimes she'd sneak behind the schoolhouse, but then she was always afraid someone would see her and tease her for hiding there.

Taking care of Leonardo was fun. It was the most fun when no one else was home because Leonardo would give all his attention to pleasing her. Zita never had anyone else ever try to please her. She was a plain Jane who was most content when cleaning a room in the house by herself. No one ever recognized that she too needed attention and needed to be pleased. Agnes thought Zita was happiest when left alone cleaning or canning.

On February 15, 1948, Agnes was excited about going to the movies. Stella and Sara would both be there and the movie was based on the life of St. Francis of Assisi. Agnes had seen the movie before for Father had shown it two of the past three years. Assisi was her favorite saint, and she loved how the movie portrayed him as a holy man with a singular vision. She could have watched the movie every Sunday. However, it was her turn to stay home with Leonardo. She decided she would take him and hope for the best, but then Zita volunteered to babysit for Leonardo.

Agnes, William, Mark, Emma, Luke, Lucy, Joshua and Gabriel headed over Moundridge and down route 56 to St. Francis. It was a cold, windy winter day, but you might have thought it was a spring holiday to see the faces of this family going off to the Sunday movies. It was like Father Duffy had brought the Fourth of July to every second Sunday of the month during the Badaxe winter months.

Of course only William and Agnes talked in the car. The children knew to be quiet. On this Sunday Agnes kept quiet too. She didn't want to have a fight with William, and she knew that would happen if they started to talk. So it was a silent car that drove through the snow banks, but it was one that appeared to be filled with music.

William pulled the car into Badaxe and drove through to old Zaboglio's house and turned left to make it up the hill to the churchyard. The back of the car spun out a little on the corner. William gave the car as much gas as he could without spinning. He'd driven these roads since his dad had first owned a car, and he knew he had to have the maximum forward movement without spinning the wheels to drive up a snow-packed driveway. At the top, the back of the car spun out from under the car and William's heart sunk a little. He hated backing down the church road. He was so fat that it was difficult to turn around, and with the car full of children sitting two-deep in the back seat, it was even more difficult to see. The car found a few pebbles of gravel sticking through the snow and the tires grabbed them enough to pick up some speed. William pulled the car out of the slide and over the tip of the hill into the flatter churchyard. Agnes sighed in relief. William was always harder to live with if he had to back down the church hill. He often blamed Agnes and it was a week or two before things got back to normal.

She wanted to see Sara and Stella. They had recently moved to farms north of LaCrosse but came down for the movies once or twice a year—and Agnes loved to visit with them. If they had to back down the hill it would be another ten minutes before she'd get to visit them and the movie would start in fifteen minutes. She said a silent prayer to Jesus for letting the car stick to a few gravel pebbles.

Sara and Stella weren't there, but Jean and Orsola and Mary Andretti were and the movie was about to start before Agnes realized she had not seen Sara and Stella. Maybe the excess snow had kept them away.

Albert Pasquali played Saint Francis so well everyone there had no doubt that he was indeed St. Francis. This audience had seen few films—and the realism of this movie was so real all were mesmerized. Agnes felt herself drawn inside the film. Walking at a distance—wishing to talk to the holy man—recognizing before others that he was more than a good man and a good priest. She was too shy to approach him. He was too holy for her plain soul, and she could not address him. So she watched Francis—through much of the movie—from the corner to the left of the camera view. She never thought of herself on a Hollywood movie set, but in Italy in the thirteenth century helping quietly and unbeknownst to St. Francis as an obedient sister in the Order of Poor Ladies. She made sure there was a little less suffering in the world. Somewhere near the end of the movie—Agnes drifted into the present—she saw herself as the twentieth century Assisi dressed in black—only her face showing in her Franciscan robe—giving food to the poor—comfort to the sick-struggling with sinners to wrestle their souls from the devil. Agnes—the nun of our time—unobtrusively relieving pain, reducing suffering, bringing food for the soul and the body to the world's less fortunate.

Today she dared to see herself—totally unacknowledged during her life of derision, die alone from a disease contracted in her services to the poor in far off Africa. Only Mother Superior and her sisters Sara and Stella came to the funeral.

Knowledge of her sacrifices spread—first in Africa and then in Badaxe and Wisconsin. Soon the Pope heard of her exploits and came to Badaxe to visit her grave. While there, the Pope prays to her to help alleviate a drought in central Africa. At that very moment, thunder clouds roar over the drought area and it rains for two days and two nights. The Pope realizes the power and holiness of Agnes and begins canonization procedures.

Agnes is startled out of her thoughts with the clapping sounds of her fellow parishioners who have all been deeply moved by this story of their favorite saint. Agnes realizes she has missed the end of the film. She knows the story by heart and catches up by whizzing the scenes through her mind as the basement lights are turned on.

Agnes is quiet as the Genotti family drives the three miles up 56 to their Moundridge home. As they approach the ridge, Mark sees smoke on the other side. He yells, "There's a fire!" William picks up the speed a little as the worst thoughts enter his head. Agnes' mind races, has the barn caught on fire? Some hay hadn't cooled correctly? Maybe Beffa's place was on fire? No. It had to be in the woods behind our barn—but how could that be in the deep snow? Some oil or gas lit up in the garage? Damn! Why a fire now? Things are going well. Last year with Truman's Farm Support, we made more money in one year than ever in our life. We built a little nest egg for the first time since the depression. The farm is paid for. The doctor said we could have no more children. Five of our children have left home and it wouldn't be so long before they'll all be gone. Things are good. This fire has to be at Beffa's—it can't be ours—

but it must be. Things are too good and it isn't the way life is supposed to be.

William cries a little too loudly, "Those damn movies you have to go to! If we'd of stayed home, I could have stopped the fire before it got so bad. Why do you and the kids like these damn movies so much? They are silly. Just a Hollywood trick making a show about Francis Assisi to sucker people into paying a lot of money to see it. If everyone who saw this movie paid ten cents, the movie people would be rich—a lot of people saw this movie. A lot of ten cents and a lot of bullshit, and now my farm is burning to the ground." He felt helpless because the roads were so snowy he dare not drive faster. William sped over the ridge and the back of the car slid out so far—every Genotti thought they'd go over the bank into the forest. William was determined to get to his farm to save it. He drove the car out of the spin as much by willing it as by skill. They drove down the hill to see not the barn, not the forest, not the garage, but their house on fire. William saw his life's hard work go up in flames. Gabriel, who had received a train for Christmas, his first real toy, feared it went up in smoke. Joshua knew they'd never save the sausage that filled his small bedroom that he'd given up, so they would have more sausage and dried beef. Agnes saw Leonardo trapped inside. Zita would not be smart enough to take him out of the house.

Agnes knew God was punishing her for indulging in going to the movie—for letting Zita take her place because she had wanted to see St. Francis so much. For sure, Jesus was punishing her for dreaming of becoming a saint. She was too unworthy to be a saint. God was now telling her so by burning her baby. Where was Zita? Was she also burning?

William drove into the yard. Six farmers/parishioners who lived further up the road were there—standing and watching the fire. Some had run into the house and started to hand out the furniture. It was obvious the house was too gone to save—the thing to save was what could be carried out.

The Genotti family was frozen. Agnes cried "Leonardo" and everyone realized he must be in the fire. Mark flew out of the car and dashed through the flames coming out of the doorway. Finding nothing and seeing he was not able to get out through the fire that now engulfed the front, Mark jumped out a back window, ran for the ladder in the garage and threw it up to the second story. He ran up the ladder, tried to raise the window of Zita and Leonardo's bedroom but it wouldn't budge—he flung his arm through the pane and yelled for Leonardo. A cloud of smoke rushed out almost toppling Mark off the ladder. He fought for his balance as he reached in and unlatched the window. He opened it and climbed in. He pushed his way through the smoke yelling Leonardo—Zita—Leonardo—Zita—Leonardo.

At this moment old man Beffa drove up. Everyone was scurrying about frantically. He heard Mark yelling Leonardo—Zita—Leonardo. He grabbed William—shook him out of his frozen stupor and said, "Zita and Leonardo are at my house."

William yelled to Mark, "Leonardo's safe—Zita's safe—get out of the house." Mark's feet appeared through the smoke, found a rung and in no time he was on the ground. Everyone had stopped hauling furniture out while they thought Leonardo and Zita were in the house. Once Herb announced they were at his place, the entire gang went eagerly to get things out. They hauled out the refrigerator, radio, freezer, kitchen table, chair, and some bedroom furniture from the first floor. The house was going up fast. "Get away! Get away! She's gone."

William watched stunned as he saw his home of twenty-five years go into flames. Agnes ran into the flaming house and grabbed her silverware that her mother had given her for her wedding. She ran to the car to put the silver in it for safety—she ran back and took her dishes out of the cupboard and her pots and pans. The men were all busy carrying heavy things and the women helping outside. Agnes wanted the everyday things she needed to care for her children. She never thought to save her brooches or a single necklace or Sunday dress. The things from the kitchen were the most important.

The doorway to the kitchen flared up and someone yelled—"Stop! Don't go in again!"

Agnes stood frozen. Eyes staring at the flames and smoke. She envisioned the flames consuming her dresser, her garnets, her new Christmas dress, the pancake turner, the wood stove she cooked on for twenty-six years. She imagined the jam jars blowing up with the applesauce and rhubarb jars. A life's work and a year's labor gone. How would they eat until the new garden came in? They could butcher another cow and pig to replace the meat, but there was no way to replace the fruit of her garden that was burning in the basement.

Agnes imagined her china popping, the kids' bedroom furniture upstairs in flames—in her mind it all burned one piece at a time as the fire cracked in the cold wind of the freezing winter night.

The Genotti children had just had their first real Christmas. Gabriel had gotten a train, Joshua a tricycle, Luke and Lucy new bikes which they had kept in the basement. Dad wanted them to put them in the shed, but they insisted on keeping them in the basement. Their hearts sank as they saw Christmas go up in smoke. The older children realized that this fire would set the family back and it might be years before they saw another Christmas with gifts.

By now the entire ridge population had gathered. Most saw the smoke as they were returning from the movies. The rest came when they got the fire warning over the telephone. Everyone on the ridge was on two lines so the operator only had to ring for help twice. They couldn't do much except watch the place burn. There was no fire engine within twenty-five miles and the fire had gotten too far anyway.

As the fire subsided, talk got on to where everyone could stay. William, Agnes, Mark, and Emma would stay the night with Matthew who had rented a farm over the ridge less than a mile away. Lucy was invited to stay with her best friend Barbara Beratti. Luke would stay with Trussonis. Herb Beffa said Gabriel and Joshua could stay with them. Gabriel liked that—for Jenny Beffa was his best friend. Then everyone remembered that Leonardo and Zita were still at Beffa's. Herb said they could stay too. Agnes said no. She insisted they come to Matthew's with the rest of the family. She could see Leonardo was frightened and Zita was upset. "They'll need their mother tonight."

Moving to Dad's Farm

Agnes' mother had died a year before the house burned. All the Veneri children were surprised at how much wealth Bart and Mary Margaret had accumulated in a life of hard work.

Agnes and Sara found $2,800 hidden inside the house, and they had secretly given it to the Church to buy a memorial rose window to replace the plain window above the altar.

The rest of the estate was divided among the children. The farm which had rundown considerably under the care of Raymond, Agnes' youngest brother, was put up for auction. Agnes had no idea what it would sell for as the world of business was handled by her husband. She knew she had inherited $10,000 as her share of the estate, and she would get one-ninth of the sale of the farm.

The bidding started at $9,000. Agnes thought, "I should buy this farm. My parents lived their entire lives here—I am the oldest. I can have this farm for their memory. The boys are pretty grown up. We should have more than one farm to sell them." She bid $9,500. William was stunned and angry. Agnes was bidding without consulting him, but he couldn't do anything in the crowd. Someone bid $10,000, Agnes said $10,500—the other bid $10,900. Agnes hoped the biding would stop if she bid $12,000. It was her money. She got it from her parents. She did not want a stranger to have her farm, and she wanted something for Mark or Luke or Joshua or Gabriel or Leonardo to have when they grew up. So she made her final bid $12,000. It was too big a jump and all the opposition fell quiet. The auctioneer made a final call—12—anyone 13, 13, 12 and 1/2, 12 and 1/4—12 and 1/4—12 and 1/4—going—goooinnng—sold to Agnes Genotti for $12,000.

Agnes' heart stopped. She'd never spent $100 in her life without asking William first. In fact, she'd never spent $100 in her life on anything. She stood up and bid for this farm. Spent her entire inheritance on the place. She felt good—but she was sweating in the thirty degree cold. She had made a leap in one impulsive moment. She had saved the farm from the hands of a stranger. She'd invested in her children's future, and she had done it without getting William's permission first.

They settled up the paperwork quickly. William signed all the papers with Agnes, but he didn't say a word. Agnes thought, "Did I pay too much? Could I have had it for $11,250? Should I have bought it at all? Can we farm both places? Wasn't one place already too much for William?" Matthew and the three oldest had left because there wasn't enough to keep them. Maybe with the new farm Mark would stay and farm it, and she would pay him to farm it. Or she would rent the farm to him 60/40 like Matthew was renting from Uncle Geno. She did the right thing and she knew it. William's silence made her doubt and fear.

When they got in the car, William still said nothing. They drove out of the yard and up toward the ridge farm. About a mile into the ride—William's anger could be contained no longer, and he let go in a ferocious voice. "What the hell was that? How could you be that dumb? It's all run down. It's three miles from our place. How can we farm it?" He yelled and yelled. Agnes said nothing.

Now a year later, it was obvious there was only one thing to do—fix the old Veneri place and move in. After the fire, they all lived with Matthew at Geno's place. Geno had a bigger house, and it was just over the ridge to milk the cows and care for the farm. The children were as close to school being about equal distance on the other side of the road where the ridge school sat at the top.

The Veneri place had a pump outside the front door and an outhouse in the backyard. The Genotti's had had indoor plumbing for nearly ten years, and they weren't about to go back to this. So the first task was to dig a septic tank, put an electric pump in the well and put plumbing in the kitchen and add a bathroom. William had learned plumbing when he worked the summer after he graduated for a company that dug wells, and he had installed all the plumbing in the ridge place. He built a small bathroom out of part of the kitchen and began to run the pipe to the well and toward the septic tank. He went to LaCrosse and bought a toilet, bathtub, and an electric motor to power the pump.

He had to wait for the ground to thaw to dig the septic tank, but he gathered all the stones and was ready. Before the final thaw he put Luke and Mark to digging the eight-foot deep hole needed. William did not want the working on the house to interfere with the first planting. So Mark and Luke broke through the frost with the pick and dug the round hole eight and one-half feet below. Agnes was so thankful once the plumbing was working. She remembered pumping water and heating it every day of her youth. She wondered why her mother had never added a pump. Clearly they had the money to modernize their home. Maybe she got so used to pumping water and heating it—going outside to the bathroom in the twenty degree below zero weather, she never knew how much more comfortable it would be to have indoor plumbing. Was she afraid to look too wealthy?—but others had put in plumbing before Mary Margaret and Bart had rented the place to Bart Jr.

"Well, I guess I'll never know," Agnes realized she hadn't thought about it when Mary Margaret lived there. When she visited, she trudged on out to the outdoor toilet and helped her mother with the dishes after dinner. I guess you get used to it and do not notice what you don't have if you never had it.

Agnes was used to indoor plumbing, and she hated going out to the backyard to use the outhouse. She used a portable pot under her bed, so she didn't have to go out in the middle of the night. It was a concession to comfort that surprised Agnes. She'd thought she was hardier and going out in the night in winter wasn't so hard.

The three months before William got the plumbing in were miserable. Not as miserable as it could have been. They might have had to build a new house on the ridge farm if Agnes hadn't purchased the old homestead. Agnes knew they could not afford a place as big as the one they had or her father's home. She would have hated living in Geno's place even if Matthew was renting it and technically could have the whole family there. They would be living off of William's brother Geno and his wife Stella. Stella would be generous—but she'd now and then remind Agnes of how generous she was. Agnes loved her little sister Stella, but she hated it when she played more generous than Agnes could because Geno was a bit more successful than William.

The Veneri house was smaller than the ridge home but Agnes had little trouble adjusting. The kitchen was large and the dining area was big enough to hold everyone. Best of all; Agnes got her own bedroom. The two bedrooms on the first floor were tiny and William did not want one of the children sleeping in a room next to Agnes and him. So he agreed to let Agnes have her own room. She enjoyed going to bed alone and not having William pulling at her panties.

William didn't touch her for the first week and Agnes sighed with relief. She was sleeping so well the inconvenience of the outhouse and no running water seemed less and less a burden.

William settled in and one morning about 4:30 he woke and wanted some. He wasn't about to go to Agnes' room which only had a single bed. He jerked a few times but it wasn't what he wanted.

He reached up behind the bed and knocked on the wall three times. Agnes heard the first knock while still asleep. It was a far away sound reaching into her consciousness. The second knock woke Agnes; by the third knock she knew what William wanted, so she crawled out of bed and walked through the door that joined their bedrooms. Her reprise was over.

Spring Time

It had been a long winter. The Mississippi River had frozen over by Thanksgiving and Agnes only remembered one other winter, before she had started school, when the river had frozen over so early. One December day, she had looked out her kitchen window to where the garage had been and only saw snow. At first, she thought the garage must have burned down in the night. Then she realized it had snowed so hard the garage was covered for she saw the snow slant down where the east roof had been. A month later, she came home from the Sunday movie and thought Leonardo was burning up with their house.

Today the sun was shining, the last patch of snow against the south hill had melted away yesterday, and Jake, the local handyman plumber, was coming to help William turn the old hand pump into indoor running water. They had decided to use some of the large kitchen space to make a bathroom with an indoor toilet and a bathtub. Agnes had been raised in this house and the outdoor pump had served them well. However, since she had running water on the Ridge place for many years, she had found the need to pump water and heat it for a bath once a week a very challenging chore. She didn't mind pumping water needed to drink and cook. Zita and Emma pumped and heated the water needed to do the dishes. It was pumping and heating water for herself and all the children to take baths every Saturday night that was too much. To top it all off, she rarely had enough water to enjoy sitting in the tub.

Jake started to convert the hand pump into one of the newfangled electric pumps. Somehow the electric pump could create enough pressure on water in a very small tank they would not need a cistern to hold the water. No more stinky water and fishing around for a dead rat several times a year. Every year three or four rats had drowned in the cistern and turned the fresh water into a putrid smell that stayed in the house for hours and in the water for days after they found the rat and pulled it out of the cistern. Agnes would be glad never to have to do that again in her life.

William promised he'd get up early and plow, disk and rake the garden before Jake got there. Agnes was looking forward to working in Grandma's garden. "Funny, how I've come to think of my own mother as Grandma," she thought as she looked at the weeds that had overtaken the ground that had been Grandma's and soon would become her garden. In a couple of hours, William would have plowed, disked and raked the garden smooth. When Agnes was a kid, it had taken her dad a full day and sometimes two days to prepare the garden for Mother. With his little Model A tractor, William had the plot ready for planting by 10:00 a.m. Agnes was ready. She was eager to plant the first seeds into the ground. Planting some seeds would be proof that the long cold winter was over, and she would be planting seeds in her garden. She'd planted in this garden every year of her youth and had helped Grandma just a few years ago before she moved into town. Though Grandma had not lived here for four years and Agnes had been in the house since February, she still thought of the house and the place as Grandma's. Agnes knew it might still snow before summer really came and that it probably would. She also knew she still felt a little funny every time William made love to her in Dad and Mother's bedroom. Now as she looked out her living room window at the newly plowed garden she began to feel that it was her place. It wasn't Dad's place, it was her place. "This will be, no it is, the home for me and William and our family. It is ours, it is mine. I bought and paid for it—sure it was what I got when Mom died that let me buy it, but I took that money and I bought the place. Now that our house burned down, this is going to be our home. No, it is already our home." She looked out the window and held on to the moment for a few minutes. Then she was off to the kitchen to cook breakfast.

Fifty, 1952

Agnes turned fifty, it was Easter and Lucy had promised to make dinner to celebrate her mom's birthday. It had been a good year. Some months the milk check had topped $400. There were some years in the 30s when the year's milk checks did not equal $800. William had sold five cows for over $200 a piece and had gotten $350 for one. Mark had raised an acre and a half of tobacco and sold it for nearly $1200. For the first time William had given Agnes a few hundred dollars to buy some things for the house. Yes, her fiftieth year on earth had been a fruitful one and there was no reason not to think that her fifty-first year might be better. Giuseppina, Hannah, Alex and Matthew had eleven children between them. "Two more grand kids and there will be as many as I raised," she thought.

On the radio they had said it would be another good year for farmers. Prices should be up and the weather was expected to be good for the entire year. Truman was President and things were good despite him. He had less than one year left as President, and many people were talking about Eisenhower running.

"If the country could prosper under such a dolt as Truman, it will get much better under Ike. He is such a brilliant man." FDR had always been such an obvious choice. It had been clear who to vote for and it would be clear again this year. Except now, it would be a change. She had never voted Republican in a presidential election. In fact, she had never voted for a Republican except for Joseph McCarthy for Senate and for William's cousin Mark Genotti who had run for county seat. In recent times people were talking about McCarthy running for President. That would be a tough call—between McCarthy and Eisenhower. Agnes wasn't sure which way she would vote. She'd never had to make a choice before. It had always been obvious. "Well, no need to think about it today—maybe only one will run. Besides, it's Easter and my birthday. No need to idle away thoughts on politicians."

Agnes had on a new Easter bonnet and a new dress. Except for 1948 she had never bought both in one year. She felt good in her new clothes and a little too proud she thought. She remembered that her house burned down the winter after 1948. Please, Jesus, don't send another disaster. I'll stay humble, and we'll share our fortune with you and the Church.

Everyone in the Church seemed to have a new dress and hat. Some men had new suits. "William should buy a new suit," she thought. He's been wearing the one he has for over twenty years. Agnes had let it out twice and it was still tight. It couldn't be let out anymore. Sometimes he didn't wear his suit to Church. He'd just wear a pair of pants and a shirt. Agnes didn't like that much, but she never said anything. If she got him a new suit that fit, he'd wear it more often. She resolved to get him a suit for next Easter. Agnes blessed herself as she came into the church. She held her genuflection a little longer than usual and thanked Jesus for all the fortune in her life. She entered the pew and bowed her head in a silent prayer. She wanted to see everyone's Easter bonnet before mass began, so she looked around to see what everyone was wearing. Everyone else was looking too and Agnes nodded silently to them. Agnes' eye caught Mary Lou, Joe Malin's daughter, who was nothing short of stunning in her new outfit. She was beautiful, intelligent, and she knew how to buy clothes. Lucky girl. Mary Lou's grandmother was a sight. She was at least sixty, and she was wearing an oversized feather hat. Why couldn't she dress her age?

Father entered in his Easter robe and the mass began. Agnes soon forgot everyone's new Easter clothes and even forgot her own as she became one with the newly risen Christ. Jesus had come down to earth to save her soul, and he had been crucified in redemption for her sins, and he had risen from the dead to join his Father in heaven. Agnes' faith in this story was unwavering. If her faith was in doubt, it was because she was so sure the story was true it took no faith to believe. Her love of Jesus was without fault and her hope for a life in heaven was marred only with her self doubts of her own worthiness. She knew she would go to heaven if she died without a mortal sin on her soul. The Church was clear about what constitutes a mortal sin and Agnes had come within a mile of one only once in her entire life. If she kept her faith and kept her ways she would be saved. She knew the ways of the devil, and she knew that he loved to tempt the holy most of all. She had seen people more devout than she lose their faith. The devil got to them somehow and stole their faith, and she knew that the loss of faith was the one unforgivable sin. She prayed to Jesus to always let her believe.

Agnes had committed her share of venial sins. Sometimes she'd get too angry at her children. She had been known to say "God damn it." She'd gossip about her neighbors and sometimes coveted what they had. She'd enjoyed a little too much some men in the parish, but she had never lusted for one. Today she looked back over her entire life and could not remember ever stealing anything except that one time she stole two root beer barrels from Zaboglio's store. When Father consecrated the host and lifted it above his head, Agnes joined Jesus in a complete union. She always felt close to Christ. Today she felt closer than ever. Jesus had taken over her soul. She knew at that moment that she was absolutely prepared to die. When she accepted the communion host on her tongue, she thought for a moment that she had gone to heaven. Her entire body was weightless, and she was unaware of her own and the entire parish's presence in the Badaxe church. There was only Jesus and Agnes—that must be what heaven is.

Agnes remembered Lucy was cooking Easter Dinner and her birthday dinner. It wasn't too vain to think Easter dinner was also her birthday dinner? She wondered on the short drive to the farm how it was going. Lucy was making a pot-roast, mashed potatoes, gravy, a string bean and cheese dish, risott and a birthday cake. She'd cooked all these things before, so she should do fine.

Agnes was surprised when she came into the house because Lucy had set the table and had picked flowers from the garden. Under the bouquet were two packages. Agnes had never had flowers for her birthday and it had been a long time since she had received a present for her birthday—she remembered it—William gave her a cast iron pot the year before the Depression hit.

Lucy was in control of the dinner. Agnes did not see the cake but she smelled it. Had it fallen and Lucy was so embarrassed she fed it to the pigs? Best not to say anything. Everyone sat at the table—Mark, Zita, Emma, Luke, Joshua, Gabriel and Leonardo. William went to the bathroom before joining in. Lucy said "Now everyone just wait; I'm going to serve Mom like she was in a restaurant. I want you to imagine that we are all in a restaurant and I'm your waitress. So you have to be on your best behavior and wait until I serve you." Agnes liked the idea of going to a restaurant—she'd never been to one. Go out to a restaurant for her birthday? It might be fun, but William would never take her, so she knew she would never go. Today she would make like she was in a restaurant. Lucy was a little uppity and always wanted things too fancy, but Agnes decided to enjoy it today. William said "a little fancy for your britches aren't you Miss Muffet?" If William had said that to anyone except Lucy, Agnes knew the party would have been over. William liked to tease Lucy, who was without any hidden pretense his favorite child. So she could be "a little too fancy for her britches."

Lucy put the potatoes in Agnes' finest serving bowl. They were steaming hot. Next, she served up the pot roast which she had earlier cut up for the family. She had made a bean dish, but also served corn. Everything was laid out on the table. Lucy served her mother first. She sat down and said "Now, the rest of you can dig in."

After everyone had filled themselves on the dinner, William started to get up from the table. Lucy jumped up and said, "Wait a minute." She went out to the back porch and was gone a little too long. The door opened and in her hand she had a birthday cake with candles on it, and she began to sing, "Happy Birthday".

The rest of the family joined in. Agnes was having a regular birthday party. She'd never had a birthday party in her life. Her mother didn't believe in them, William was too awkward and life had been too busy with all the children. Agnes thought, "Lucy is a bit of a party girl and a show off, but she made me a party and I like it. Things are good, and we should celebrate, and Easter and my birthday on Easter—that's worth celebrating."

Lucy gave Agnes the knife and said, "You cut the first piece." Agnes cut all the cake because that's what she did. She took the first piece and gave it to William. That's what she always did. Lucy said, "Ma, it's your birthday. You have to take the first piece." Agnes didn't know about that because the first piece always went to William. She looked at him and he nodded. Agnes took the first piece and everyone cheered. She scooped a piece into everyone's plate. "Wait! Wait till everyone's served before you eat any," Lucy said. Before anyone took a bite, Lucy handed one of the packages to her dad and the other to her mother. William awkwardly handed the package to Agnes.

Agnes was stunned; William had not given her a present in over twenty years. She opened it and there was the watch she had seen last time she was in LaCrosse with Lucy. She had so wanted the watch, but she did not feel she should spend so much money on herself. Somehow Lucy had gotten Dad to purchase it. Agnes could not remember being so touched. She reached over and squeezed William's hand. Everyone burst out singing "Happy Birthday to you..." Agnes took the other package and opened it. There was a little note from Lucy. "Happy Birthday, Mom—I love you." She opened the package and took out a red brooch that went perfectly with her new red dress.

The next Sunday, the family packed into the car and went off to church. Everything seemed like another Sunday. Agnes remembered the Sunday before and regretted only for a moment that this Sunday was not as special as the last Sunday. Easter only came once a year and birthdays only came once a year and what made them special is that they were special. If every Sunday was special, it would be too much, and we all might forget to thank Jesus for the special times and the hard times we have. Jesus made life worth living and a special day might make it a little nicer, but without Jesus it would be meaningless. Agnes enjoyed last Sunday, but she didn't need it, and she would not miss it much. On the other hand, without Jesus and without mass every Sunday, life would have no meaning, and it could not be endured.

First Communion

There was only one day more glorious to Agnes than First Communion—and that day was not Christmas or New Year's or Easter or even the Fourth of July. Nor was it marriage or confirmation or baptism. The latter were also sacraments in her Church, but First Communion was the event that she built her faith around for First Communion meant her child had reached the age where he could receive the body and blood of Jesus. The only thing that could have made Agnes prouder, happier and more fulfilled would have been the calling of one of her sons to the priesthood. For then Jesus would not only enter the body of her child, but he would have entered their very soul.

Agnes prayed every Sunday to Jesus to send the calling to one of her children. "Jesus, I never went to the convent. I know you wanted me to. I'm sorry. Now I can send one of my sons to be a priest. It's better. You need priests, but you have to call one. Please, God. My life will be full only when one of my sons gets ordained."

Her greatest moment of happiness had not yet arrived, but today was the thirteenth time she celebrated one of her children receiving First Communion, and none were sweeter than the thirteenth one—Leonardo would be her last child to receive First Communion. She also knew it was the first of many more First Communions for she was a grandmother a dozen times, and she had every intention of attending every one of their First Communions.

The week before Agnes had taken the white "First Communion" suit out of storage, cleaned and pressed it with care. She had bought the suit for Matthew. They were in the throes of the Great Depression and the cost of the suit had been an immense strain on the budget and the family, but Agnes wanted her son dressed in white to symbolize the purity of the soul in preparation to receive the body and blood of Jesus. It could be no other way. Now the suit was to be worn for the seventh and final time.

The day before Leonardo's communion with Jesus, Agnes butchered three chickens to prepare a special dinner. She plucked the chickens, boiled the necks to make broth for risott as she peeled two dozen apples and turned them into three sumptuous pies. She made William go into town to buy film for their Brownie and the girls cleaned the house better than it had ever been cleaned.

The night before Leonardo's big day, Agnes prepared his bath and instructed Leonardo in friendly but no uncertain terms that he was to clean himself better than he ever had, and he was to wash his hair. No one in the Genotti family ever took a bath except on Saturday night and if you missed a Saturday night, you waited a week. The boys liked to miss a week and sometimes even two weeks, but washing one's hair was a rarer activity. None of the boys washed his hair every week—maybe once a month and sometimes less. Leonardo knew that tonight he had to take a bath, and he had to wash his hair. He wasn't quite sure what all the fuss was about. His mother didn't often put her foot down so when she did, Leonardo, like his older brothers, minded without question.

First Communion. It happened to every boy and girl in Badaxe at age six or seven. It happened to every Catholic all over the world at about the same age. Birth was magical, but it was a routine activity for the life of a mother in Badaxe, and baptism followed birth as naturally as exhalation follows inhalation. It is part of the necessary force for life to go on.

Holy Communion could only be received by someone old enough to know the difference. It was, at least in theory, the first self-aware choice that the new person was choosing of his own free will—to be one with Jesus. The child had no say about birth or baptism. Having obtained the age of reason, each of her children had chosen to take Communion. Since Agnes remembered her own Communion so well, and remembered embracing the body and blood of Jesus with such desire and fervor, it was only natural for her to assume all her own sons and daughters had chosen to take Jesus' body and blood with the same enthusiasm. It never entered her head that a seven-year-old in Badaxe would no more consider not taking First Communion than they would have considered jumping off a one-thousand-foot cliff. Not one seven year old from Badaxe had ever said "no, I don't think I want to take communion, I think it is a barbaric ritual." To Agnes, it only meant that the choice to take Jesus in communion was as obvious as the choice to eat. While one was free not to, why would one be so foolish as not to make the right choice?

On Sunday Agnes dressed in her Sunday dress, put on her brooch she had received from her mother on her First Communion and brushed her hair a few more times than she would have on any other Sunday morning. Leonardo had gotten dressed in his white suit with shirt and tie. He did not have the tie tied for he had never worn a tie. In fact, he had never worn a suit. Agnes stood behind Leonardo and tied his tie. She straightened out the collar of the little white shirt and repositioned the suit on Leonardo's shoulders. Leonardo looked in the mirror and admired his white look. He was most uncomfortable in these clothes. He liked his look but hated his feel. Later he would wonder if that moment made him hate wearing suits and ties. Years later, he would give up one of the jobs he liked the most and for which he was paid the most, because they insisted he wear a suit to work every day.

Leonardo and his fellow communionites walked down the aisle all dressed in white and took the first pew. Agnes heard, "Here comes the Bride" repeat itself in her earworm as she thought, "Yes, it is a little like a marriage—the young boys and girls giving themselves to Jesus until death and beyond." As the Mass began, Agnes' mind took her to the future, "Leonardo might be my best hope. He is quiet and I have never seen him get angry. He prepared more for First Communion than any of my older children."

When Agnes accepted William's proposal, she had made a deal with herself and her God. If one of her boys received the calling, she and William would give their full support. Even then she bargained with her God, "If not a priest, then give me a nun." During the sermon which she had heard many times before, Agnes found herself reliving each disappointment, "Giuseppina was too much in love with herself, Alex was too much a tomboy and too crazy about boys. I thought Hannah might be my nun, and she had convinced William to agree to send her to school. The convent did not want her after she went crazy. I don't know why; she never had a relapse after she came back from the hospital.

"Matthew is too mean and too hungry for money to be a priest. Mark has a certain fervent dedication that might make him a stellar priest. But Mark was too happy to get out of eighth grade to consider more school, and a priest would have to go to school for twelve more years." Besides, William wanted Mark to take over the farm. William wanted to pass his farm on to his oldest son and since Matthew was already gone, the next in line for the farm was Mark. Even though William was only fifty-three, he was ready to retire. He told Mark he wanted to rent the place to him when he turned sixteen.

Agnes had given up hope that any of her eldest children would go off to the seminary or convent. She was taken by quite a surprise when Marie asked politely if she could attend the convent to take a look at becoming a nun. It was a strange way to think, Agnes thought. She had not wanted to go to the convent "to take a look." She had wanted to attend to become a nun. Was Marie serious? How could she want to "take a look" at a calling from Jesus? You had the calling, or you didn't have it. What is this "I'll take a look."?

Agnes told Marie she'd think about it and talk to William. As much as she wanted a nun, she did not understand what this "take a look" meant. Plus it would be expensive. The church would expect them to pay for Marie's studies in the convent. William would not like that. Agnes knew she'd have to fight William to get him to pay for the convent or seminary, but she knew exactly how she'd win the fight when one of her children was ready. She had played it through her head many times; she'd never played a scene when one of her children wanted to "take a look."

On Saturday, when she went to confession, she asked Father about it. Should she send her daughter "to take a look?"

"I want my daughter to be a nun, but she has to be called. How can she take a 'look'?"

Father smiled at Agnes' strong but naive belief in "the calling." He explained to her when he went to the seminary, he did not know he would be a priest. He thought it might be the correct thing to do. The calling from God came only after years in the seminary. Others came who thought they had been called, and many never completed their studies.

"The calling can come later, in fact, often does."

So Agnes faced William. "Marie wants to go to the convent in LaCrosse. She will start on September 7. We'll need to buy her some extra clothes and pay the church for her tuition."

"How much?"

"It's $125 a year."

William gulped. He could still remember when he had worked a whole summer on the road for less money than that.

Agnes expected William to go into a rampage; to tell her how this was impossible. Marie wasn't serious; she wasn't holy enough, not smart enough, and it just plain cost too much. William didn't say anything. He recognized Agnes was determined to have a nun. Marie was as likely to be called as any. It wasn't a fate he liked, but he felt helpless. He didn't mind losing Marie. She worked half the time in the house, and although she was a steady worker she wasn't strong like Alex was, and she was slow. She always seemed distracted. She'd be no great loss for William. Besides, Mark was doing more and more of the farming.

One hundred and twenty-five dollars to send her to the convent? And every year, for four years? Five hundred dollars! William had never spent five hundred dollars on anything in his life except for his farm and his best tractor.

He grunted something like a "yes" and left the house to go work on his machinery. Agnes could see his pain, but she was happy he recognized that it was the right thing to do.

Marie went off to the convent. She stayed for two years. She was happy there, maybe too happy. Her grades were average, and she often got in trouble with the nuns. When Agnes and William visited the convent, Mother Superior would ask if they were sure Marie had the calling. "Sometimes we think she doesn't."

When Marie came home for the summer after her second year, too quiet and self-reflective, Agnes came to accept that she wouldn't be going back to the convent. Agnes never thought Emma or Zita were convent material. "Luke is too interested in girls and Lucy in boys. Joshua doesn't seem so interested in anything since he got rheumatism when he was about ten. Gabriel is too interested in everything and is a trouble maker at school—and he always has his mouth in trouble. Leonardo is my best hope. I can prepare him for it I know..."

Agnes' thoughts were interrupted when Father Duffy asked, "Leonardo, What are the seven sacraments?" Leonardo answered without hesitation, "Baptism, Holy Communion, confession, confirmation, matrimony, ordination and Extreme Unction."

"Yup, he is gonna be my priest," Agnes thought with confidence and pride.

Pa Genotti Comes to Die

Agnes had to put her foot down this time. She liked William's dad and knew that her children were crazy about him. Gabriel and Joshua in particular loved Grandpa. They often went out together to pick hickory nuts in the fall and be gone all afternoon and come home with about an hour's worth of gathering. Grandpa liked to tell stories and the boys loved to listen to him. Sometimes Gabriel would tell Agnes one of the stories Grandpa told, and he'd be all excited like it was the first time the story had ever been told. Of course Agnes had heard it many times before for Grandpa loved to tell the same stories.

Agnes saw that her children received attention and love from Grandpa that they never gained from their dad. She was thankful for that. Grandpa was 96 years old and had only been sick a couple of times in the past decade. Agnes had been honored to care for him those times. When he got sick for what looked like his last time, William had brought him home and took it for granted Agnes would care for Grandpa until he died. It was not easy, but she had to tell William this was not right. She had taken care of Peter when he was too sick to care for himself. He could linger on for years. Agnes still had ten children at home. More importantly, Peter had nine children besides William, and they should all share equally in taking care of Peter during his last days.

It took courage, but after a month she said to William in a tone he recognized to be final, "William, each of your brothers and sisters should take turns caring for Peter. He is healthy enough to move from house to house. It is not right that one of us should be his sole caretaker. He has been here a month. I suggest you take him to Vito's." William did not want to do that, but he heard the finality in Agnes' voice and decided to drive over to Vito's and suggest to him that they take Grandpa for a month and then move him to someone else's home.

That afternoon, Agnes packed up Peter's belongings, and William carried him to the car and drove him to Vito's. Agnes could see that her children were upset because they enjoyed going in to see Grandpa at his bedside. He was too sick to get out of bed, but he was not too sick to talk to his grandchildren or play checkers. Gabriel looked her in the eye and said, "How could you kick Grandpa out of our house when he's so sick?" and ran out of the house before she could answer. No answer would have been satisfactory, so she was happy he did not wait for one.

Ten months later, Peter moved back in. He could no longer feed himself and Agnes had to take the time to spoon-feed him like a baby. After a couple of days, Lucy came in and asked if she could feed Grandpa. "You sure you don't mind? I can feed him."

Lucy said, "Mom, I'd like to feed Grandpa. He was always so nice to me." Agnes was relieved. The next day, when Gabriel and Joshua found out Lucy was allowed to feed Grandpa, they came and asked their mother if they could feed him. "Lucy's feeding him. Why don't we just let her?"

"I want to feed Grandpa, I can do it," Gabriel said.

"Me too," Joshua chimed in.

"Okay, okay, why don't you take turns? Let Lucy feed him today, Joshua you can feed him tomorrow and Gabriel you feed him the next day."

"Whoopee," Gabriel and Joshua ran outside to play. Agnes was pleased her children wanted to help.

Grandpa got worse. In a week, he could barely eat anything, and Agnes had to take over feeding him so he would get some sustenance. When the children came into see Grandpa, he no longer answered their questions and Agnes wondered if he recognized them. The children were worried and confused, so Agnes tried to explain about old age and dying. In Badaxe, death came regularly and you got used to it. Still, it was hard to see Grandpa dying since he had been such a good friend to her three youngest.

The month dragged on and Grandpa got worse. When it was time for Grandpa to be moved to Vito's, Agnes thought maybe they should not move him. She began to think he had come to her to die. She had always been his favorite daughter-in-law and sometimes she thought Peter liked her more than his own daughters.

Vito and Arlene showed up on Sunday after mass to take Peter to their house. William and Vito lifted one side of Peter and moved him into the back seat of Vito's car. Agnes stared in silence. Lucy, Gabriel and Joshua were playing behind the lilac bush, pretending not to pay attention. Agnes saw them glancing at Peter as he was hauled away. She wondered if they knew this would be the last time they would see him. Agnes and William would go to visit, but they would not take the children. No sense letting them see Grandpa get worse, plus it would be too much for Grandpa and for Vito and Arlene to have all the grandchildren running around.

A week later, the phone rang and Arlene said, "He's gone, passed away in his sleep last night."

Agnes woke William and told him. His dad was dead after 97 years. He'd been born in Badaxe, one of its first sons, and he'd spent every day of his life here except for a little over a year when he'd gone to California to work for one of his uncles. He had ten children and they had begotten 73 grandchildren. It was a good life, and he was a good man who was loved by his children and grandchildren. He had always been generous and Agnes knew he had given away his entire life's earnings before he died. There would be no estate to divide of what had been the richest man in Badaxe. He was in heaven. No need to stop off in purgatory for this man who had loved and was beloved.

She did not know how to tell her youngest children Grandpa was dead. Her mother had died a couple of years ago and her father the year before. The children had not seemed too upset at their deaths. Grandpa Peter had been their friend. He had picked hickory nuts with them and told them stories of his youth and stories of the old country he said his dad had told him.

The Hay Hole

Agnes heard a terrible noise at the front door. It sounded like Gabriel and Joshua were fighting over who would get in first. William was home and the children knew it, and they would not fight near the house when William was home. Plus there was a terrible moaning. Whoever was at the front door was in some kind of trouble. Agnes ran to the door and saw Gabriel struggling with the door. He looked drunk—real drunk more than she had ever seen her brothers or father drunk. He could not get the door open, he was moaning and trying to open the door but it kept slamming shut under his own weight. Then Agnes saw there was fresh blood in Gabriel's hair and it was running down the far side of his face. "My God, what happened?" Agnes reached for the door and tried to open it, but Gabriel was pulling and pushing so hard she could not get it open. Gabriel looked at her like he saw her but didn't see her. His eyes were wide open, but darting here and there. He either could not focus on her or worse did not recognize her. "What happened? Gabriel, what happened?" Gabriel moaned in different pitches. Was he trying to talk? My God what happened? Was he crazy? Did he knock his head so hard he was crazy? Did a cow kick him? Did he fall off the horse? He'd fallen off the horse last year and landed on his head. He had just gotten a cut then. Did the cow kick him crazy? It had happened to one of her nephews a few years ago. Cow kicked him in the head, and he'd never been right since. "Oh, God, don't let that happen to Gabriel!" Agnes called for William. "Dad, come quick," she yelled. She saw Gabriel mix fear with the horror in his eyes. He had heard her call for William. My God even in this state he could fear the old man? "Maybe this is a good sign," He must have heard her.

"Gabriel, back up a little. Let me open the door. I'll open the door for you, you just back up a little. No, no just move to the right a little—hang on to the wall." Gabriel was trying to move to the side. He weaved a little to the right and then to the left and back. His hands were scratching at the door like a wildcat. "Oh my god, what happened? Please, God, please."

"Just push yourself to one side or the other, Gabriel, take it easy, take your time, just push your hands against the screen and push yourself to the side." William appeared behind Agnes. "What's up?" He asked in the tone he used when someone interrupted his reading the newspaper. Then he saw Gabriel struggling at the door. "What the hell you doing? Get away..." his voice stopped as he saw the terror in Gabriel's eyes and the blood in his hair and on his face. Gabriel pushed hard and slid to the right and then fell to the ground. William pushed the door open pushing Gabriel's legs out of the way because they had fallen in front of the door.

Gabriel did not move. "Please don't be dead." Agnes picked up his head. It was lifeless. "Wake up. Wake up." She shook his body, slapped his face gently. "Gabriel, don't go to sleep. Wake up." Agnes remembered that she had been told not to let a person in an accident fall asleep. It was important to keep them awake, or they might fall asleep and never wake up. No, Gabriel must wake up. He can't die. "God, even if he is crazy the rest of his life, don't let him die." She shook him harder and William leaned over and slapped him in the face.

William yelled, "Gabriel, can you hear me. Wake up. Don't go to sleep. Stay awake." Gabriel stirred. He must have heard William. "Come on, open your eyes. Damn it, open your eyes," William's voice was louder. Agnes kept shaking Gabriel and pleading, "Stay awake, come on wake up, don't go to sleep, open your eyes."

Gabriel's eyes opened, he looked wildly in all directions. He grunted. He moved his right arm. He grunted some more and moved his arm. "Ooooooooooooooo,jooooooooooooo, uuuuaaaaa" It sounded like "off" or "use" or "Joe." His right arm kept moving in different directions. "What is he trying to say?" He couldn't mean Joe; He did not know a Joe. "Gabriel, are you trying to tell us something?" He nodded. "What is it? What do you want?" Gabriel grunted harder and quicker. He tried to point somewhere. His arm kept pointing all over the place."Jssssssh, ooosssssssh, jjjjjjjj, jjjjjjj, ooooooh, jjjjjh." No complete words came out. Only an incessant pointing and a grunt that sounded like jjjjjjj."

"JJooooss." he blurted.

"Joshua? Is he hurt too?" Gabriel nodded yes. "Where is he? Where is he?"

Agnes' mind raced. Where was Joshua? Where could he be? If he was with Gabriel, why didn't he help him to the house? He could see that he was hurt. Was he so afraid of William that he'd let Gabriel alone hurt like this. He couldn't. Was he hurt worse? Maybe he was dead someplace. Or unconscious? "Where, where is he?" she was screaming in panic.

Gabriel kept trying to point, and then he went silent. "Gabriel, Gabriel wake up, come on, don't close your eyes, open your eyes, come on, where's Joshua? Where is he, wake up, don't die, wake up, come on, where is Joshua?"

William shook Gabriel hard, "Where is Joshua?" Gabriel pointed and struggled,"bbbbbbbbbb aaaaaa."

Agnes looked at William, "I think he's saying barn, please look in the barn, maybe he's there." William ran off to the barn. "Gabriel, come on Gabriel, is he in the barn?" Gabriel said nothing, he quit trying to point. "Dddddd eeeeee dddddd"

"It's okay. We know he's in the barn. Dad went to find him. He'll be okay?"

"Nnnnnnooooo, dddddddeeeeeeaaddddd."

"Take it easy, keep your eyes open." Agnes could tell that Gabriel was responding to her voice, so she kept speaking. He was working to keep his eyelids open as his eyes were darting in every which direction.

William came out of the barn carrying Joshua. "He's out, but he's still breathing. Let's take them to the hospital in LaCrosse." The rest of the children had gathered around. "We're going to take them to St. Ann's. Mark, call the hospital and tell them we're bringing in two kids who fell down the hay hole and apparently landed on their heads on the cement. Tell them both of them are bleeding and knocked out."

"Agnes, I think they'll be all right. They must have fallen down the hay hole from the second floor. I don't know how it happened. Thank God they are both breathing. Let's get them in the car and take them to St. Ann's."

Mark picked up Gabriel and carried him to the car. He kept saying to Gabriel, "Stay awake you dumb asshole; stay awake; how'd the hell you fall down the hay hole, come on keep them eyes open." William put Joshua on one side of the back seat, and Mark put Gabriel on the other side. William and Agnes got in the car and William drove off to LaCrosse as fast as his old Ford would go.

Agnes kept the boys awake on the trip to LaCrosse. William pushed on the horn and turned his lights on when they came up behind a car. Everyone knew it meant an emergency, so they got out of the way. In fifteen minutes they were at the hospital. The nurses rushed the boys into the emergency room. Dr. Gallagher, who had assisted Agnes in the birth of both the boys, was there. He assured Agnes and William that he would do his best with the boys and hurried into the emergency room to check them out.

"Jesus, spare my boys. They were probably fighting—they are always fighting. I should have stopped them long time ago. It should have been obvious that one of these times they would really get hurt. Forgive me, Jesus, save them and I will be a better mother; a firmer mother making them obey me. Dad was right, they tussle way too much. Jesus, forgive me." She took out her rosary and began to mumble Hail Marys and Our Fathers; not stopping until Dr. Gallagher reappeared.

An hour later, although it seemed more like 24 hours later, Dr. Gallagher came out and told Agnes and William that the boys were fine. They'd taken a hit on the head, but they were young and could take it. He wanted them to rest in the hospital for another couple of hours. "Why don't you go have something to eat or go shopping and come back in two or three hours? The boys will be ready to go home by then."

Agnes said she wanted to go to Sears and Roebuck. "Shopping, what you want to go shopping for?" William was only teasing this time. They left and headed to Sears.

IV

Air

IV: Air
(1954 -1963)

Sunday Outings

Agnes was happiest on Sundays. She, William and the children went to the first mass at 8:30 a.m. By then Agnes had fed the chickens, prepared Sunday dinner and made sure all the children were clean and dressed right for Sunday Mass. Not that there was much choice on how to dress. Everyone had only one Sunday outfit to wear, and they wore it to church every Sunday—and to funerals and weddings. There were no other occasions special enough to wear their Sunday outfits. At mass, she said prayers aloud with the members of St. Francis.

While the church was always full for the 8:30 a.m. mass, the 10:30 mass only half filled the church. Some town folks who did not have to get up at 6:00 to milk the cows couldn't make it up for 8:30 mass either. A few visitors from Stoddard or LaCrosse came to 10:30 along with a half-dozen farmers. No one ever said anything, but there was no doubt only lazy people went to the 10:30 mass.

As Father consecrated the host, a tingle crawled up her spine. She felt a contraction in her womb. Agnes' mind was becoming one with Jesus. No moment was more magnificent than when she knelt at the altar to receive the Body of Christ from the priest—she became one with Jesus. Sometimes she felt like time stood still—if only for a second as she swallowed the unleavened bread. She had to pull herself out of the afterglow— for others had to receive Communion—Agnes blessed herself and stood—a little weak—then moved slowly, reverently back to her pew. She knelt in total peace with Jesus. No thoughts, no prayers; just acceptance. She liked it when she could be among the first to receive communion because she could stay closest to Jesus in the silence of the priest repeating "Corpus Domini Nostri Iesu Christi custodiat animam tuam in vitam aeternam, Amen," as he gave every parishioner communion.

When Father went back to the altar, Agnes was bumped back into the present, Often she had difficulty following the priest as he read the Last Gospel, but always she responded to "Benedicamus Domino" with a firm "Deo gratias".

As the priest left, the parishioners began to file out of the church. Agnes lingered for a last moment in the arms of Jesus and then walked to the rear of the church. Before exiting she dipped her hand in the holy water—turned one last time for this week to the Tabernacle which held the unused hosts containing Jesus' body and made the sign of the cross as she unhurriedly genuflected.

As she descended the church steps, every shaded part of the church yard was alive with chatter. Most of the parishioners saw each other only on Sunday and for the most part only for the fifteen minutes they lingered after church.

Agnes greeted everyone. There could be no enemies in a body of parishioners who had shared the Body of Christ. Then Agnes settled in with one of her sisters, and they would talk about the weather, the garden, the children, and the church. In fact, it made no difference what they talked about. It was the talking itself that counted. After spending the week only with William and the children, just talking to a friend was enough. So this week's talk might well repeat last weeks. There was no need to reach deeper—to talk was joy and relief enough.

Sometimes on the way home—with nine kids stacked in the back of the car, Agnes looked over at William and said, "Let's go to Jake and Liz's. Liz said 'come on over.'" There would be a tense moment of silence. If William said nothing, the hearts of everyone sank for it meant he wasn't going to go. If he agreed, a scream of joy took place inside everyone in the car. No one of course dare express the joy or sorrow in William's presence, so a stranger watching the car on that corner coming around Malin hill, might see no difference in this family's reaction from anticipation to ecstasy or disappointment.

Going to Jake and Liz's was the greatest. For Agnes, it was a time to catch up on all the gossip from Liz. For William, he could smoke a cigar with Jake and talk about how the crops were doing and what the weather would be like this week. He felt more at ease with Jake than with anyone except Fred Jamboys. With Fred, he didn't need to talk. In fact Fred and Jake may have been the only people besides his brothers whom William could talk to with total ease.

For the children, going to Liz's was the best. She made the richest cookies in town and put them out to eat—as many as everyone wanted. Once, Gabriel ate a whole Baker's dozen of double chocolate chip cookies. At home they could never eat as many cookies as they wanted; they got one maybe two.

Frequently Liz would have store bought wieners. Once or twice a year Agnes would buy wieners for a Sunday treat. Everyone only got two and the old man would complain from the time Agnes bought the wieners until after they were eaten about what a waste spending money on store bought wieners. Liz's wieners always tasted better. You could have a third and if the old man didn't notice even a fourth.

Liz laughed, and when she didn't laugh she smiled. Agnes and William did not fight. Liz and Jake's two boys shared their toys. Sometimes Agnes looked out over the yard and saw how happy her children were. She knew if she had a man like Jake, she could make a life where her children could play like this. Sometimes, but not very often, she'd recall how Jake had wanted to marry her. She had said no because she was going to be a nun.

Most of the time, after lunch, Agnes and Liz sat on the porch and talked and talked and then talked some more. Often they would both talk at the same time. Agnes might be talking about Sara and Liz about tomatoes, but more often they rehashed Father Duffy's sermon.

Cheaper by the Dozen

Agnes was clearly excited as she came across the churchyard to get into the car to drive home. She could hardly wait to tell her family what she had heard. She often had some gossip to share with William or the family, so everyone got a little excited because this must be really juicy gossip for Agnes to be so excited.

"You wouldn't believe it. It's too perfect to be true. You won't believe what they've done now. It is perfect for us."

By now all seven children in the back seat were leaning into the front seat and even William was listening with anticipation.

"Unbelievable, just plain unbelievable. Dad, I want to see it, I want us to take the kids so we can all see it. It sounds so fabulous. Let's go next Sunday after mass."

"Ma, what you talking about?"

Agnes could barely get it out. "They've made a movie called "Cheaper by the Dozen." about a family with a dozen children. Stella said she saw it last week in LaCrosse and that we'd love it. She said it was about a family that had twelve children—like us—well, we have 13—but a big family like ours. The parents are into efficiency. I think they make a living helping others be efficient. Stella said the parents try to make their family live by their idea of efficient. She said we are ever bit as efficient by necessity as they are and that we will recognize many of the situations the family gets into. She said any farmer with a large family had to be more efficient than the parents preached, or they would lose their farm. She seemed positive we would absolutely love it. It's playing in the Strand Theater right on State Street. You know which one—we drive by it to get into LaCrosse. Let's go next Sunday."

"How do you know you can even get in? What if we drive all that way, and they have sold all the tickets?"

"Stella says they always have tickets."

"Why don't we wait until it comes to the Church? Father will get the movie here in a couple of years."

"I want to see it now. It's a movie about us. A couple with a large family and how they get along. Stella says it's about us. I want to see it. I want to take the kids. Let's spend a little money and go. We been doing good lately. Let's go see the movie."

The next Sunday, after church and dinner, the entire family—except for William piled into their 1948 Chevy and drove to see the first movie any of them had ever seen in a real movie house. Not one of them was disappointed as each had someone on screen to identify with and all were enthralled by the life-like figures on the big screen.

Infested with Communists

Agnes did not know much about Joseph McCarthy, but what she knew was encouraging. Most importantly he was a Catholic. Almost as important he was from Wisconsin. She had heard he was trying to protect America from traitors who would sell out America to communists who were the people we were fighting in the cold war. She was aware he was getting a lot of attention and people at church liked to praise him or condemn him. Some of her friends loved him and thought he should run for President against Truman. Others thought he was a kook and was more dangerous to America than the feared "pinks" McCarthy loved to rail against.

Agnes had little time for politics as she was too busy raising thirteen children, a garden, four dozen chickens, and participating in church activities. She voted, and up to now the choices on the national, state and local level where obvious. She had first voted in 1928. Al Smith was Catholic so it was a no-brainer even if he was a Democrat. With Republicans like Kohler and La Follette heading up the party in Wisconsin, Agnes found it easy to stay with the party her dad had supported his whole life. On the local level, more often than not, one of the candidates was a relative and that person got Agnes' vote.

After Hoover failed to handle the depression, most of Badaxe, including Agnes, voted for Roosevelt and then became strong followers of Roosevelt and then Truman as they demonstrated their support for farmers. McCarthy's rise reminded Agnes she once voted only for Republicans, and she definitely favored the talk about McCarthy running for president. But then the Republican Party chose Ike. Agnes was disappointed, but she had already left the party of Truman and was not about to vote for the other guy who had a funny first name. Still, she wished they had picked McCarthy. No matter, she decided to vote for Ike at the same time she cast her vote for Walter Kohler for Senate.

On March 9, 1954, "See It Now" aired another episode on the issue of McCarthyism, this one attacking Joseph McCarthy. Titled "A Report on Senator Joseph R. McCarthy", it used footage of McCarthy speeches to portray him as dishonest, reckless, and abusive toward witnesses and prominent Americans. In his concluding comment, Edward Murrow said:

"We must not confuse dissent with disloyalty. We must remember always that accusation is not proof and conviction depends upon evidence and due process of law. We will not walk in fear, one of another. We will not be driven by fear into an age of unreason, if we dig deep in our history and our doctrine, and remember that we are not descended from fearful men."

In April 1954, McCarthy was also under attack in the Army-McCarthy hearings. These hearings were televised live on the new American Broadcasting Company network, allowing the public to view first-hand McCarthy's interrogation of individuals and his controversial tactics. On December 2, 1954, the Senate voted to censure Senator McCarthy by a vote of 67-22, making him one of the few senators ever to be disciplined in this fashion.

No television station had a signal strong enough to reach Badaxe, so Agnes had not watched any of these proceedings, and she had neither the time nor the inclination to follow these stories in the paper or on radio. Nevertheless, the stories made their way to Agnes as they did to anyone living in the United States. While some of her sisters kept their faith in McCarthy, Agnes gathered enough information to decide she could no longer support McCarthy or any of the things he stood for. Fed up with the Republican Party she opted to vote for Ike's opponent in 1956 and was an enthusiastic supporter of the Democratic candidate in 1960.

Early Retirement

"SUGAR! SUUUGAAAR!" If Agnes and William heard it once they heard it a thousand times while they fixed up the old Monti house for their retirement years. It was enough to make Agnes think they had made a big mistake to buy this house for their retirement. Old man Gelphi who lived down and across the street was bent on calling "SUUGAAR," his pet name for his wife, a few dozen times a day. It was a laugh the first few days, but it was enough to drive Agnes crazy after the novelty wore off.

Agnes was looking forward to retirement. In Badaxe, a sign of a full life and a good life was to be able to pass your farm to a son and move into a house in town. Luke had signed a contract with William, and he was taking over the farm on July 1. He was engaged to get married in the fall, so Agnes knew he would stay on the farm. They had made a similar arrangement with Mark two years before. He was single and free and when an opportunity came along for a better job, he'd left without notice.

William and Agnes were young to retire. William was only 56. He had worked hard to build the farm, and she had worked hard to raise and feed thirteen children. William had done very little on the farm for the past ten years, and it would be better for Luke not to have William around telling him what to do. If Luke needed help or advice, William would always be in town and Luke could ask. If they lived on the farm, William would not wait to be asked.

Agnes liked the new place located near the center of Badaxe. There was room for a garden. The house was only two blocks from Fred's Skelly station so William would spend a lot of time there, and Agnes could walk to church. Once her mother retired to town, she had gone to church every day, and Agnes wanted to do that now. She planned to go to mass every morning and to vespers on Wednesday and Stations of the Cross on Friday night. No longer would she be dependent on William giving her a ride. She'd just walk. William promised to plow half the yard into a garden. She'd go to mass, work in her garden and William would go to Jamboys' place. She looked forward to it.

The house needed work. There was no indoor plumbing. Old man Monti had plenty of money to put in indoor plumbing, but he was of the old way and thought it was sinful to waste money on an electric pump and a sewage system. So they had used an outhouse and Mrs. Monti pumped water by hand until the day she died.

The house hadn't been painted or wall papered in years—maybe not since the Monti's were in their fifties which was well over thirty years ago. The Monti children had left a lot of the old things they did not want in the house. So William, Agnes, Joshua, Gabriel and Leonardo had some work to do before they moved in. First they hauled truck load after truck load of junk to the dump. There was an old oak table, an oak ice box, a wood stove and a lot of smaller things that had to go. Only a few paintings advertising old-time beer and chewing tobacco were kept. William thought they might be worth something some day, so he stored them in the attic.

Agnes and Joshua began to steam off layers and layers of wallpaper. William and Gabriel divided a bathroom out of the master bedroom, dug a man size hole around the well and put an electric pump and a pressure tank in, dug a septic tank and ran sewage pipes from the kitchen and the bathroom to the tank. William hired old man Al Pemchi to melt and pour the lead into the pipe joints to hold the pipes together.

Weeks later, with the plumbing in, the wall paper removed, the walls painted and the woodwork cleaned and varnished, what was left of the Genotti family moved their belongings the one mile from the farm to the town of Badaxe. It did not seem so far, and all their friends would still be their friends. Yet it was a move from one way of life to a very different way of life. Over the summer, Luke was left to run the farm, Lucy moved to Prairie du Chien, Gabriel left to study at the seminary never to return home except to visit and Joshua worked a summer job away from home. When he came back for school he spent 100% of the day on the bus, in school and studying in his room—in other words he too had left.

In one month Agnes' family decreased from five children to one at the same time she left the only life she had known to live in the town of Badaxe—overnight she became a "city slicker" with one child instead of a farm woman with thirteen children. The sudden emptying of her home was offset for now as she still had Leonardo to raise, William to fight, Jesus to pray to and a garden to nurture. It should be enough, but it felt lacking after so many productive years. She looked to Jesus for her strength, but like so many of her generation, faith only sustained her for so long.

Zita Gets Married

"What! She can't marry him," William cried. He never said another word to Agnes or Zita about Zita's decision to marry Robert, a man twice her age. When Zita called to tell her mother she was getting married, Agnes' reaction was less than joyful, but she had been polite. She was disappointed, but she also knew by now not to interfere with her grown children's choices. When she hung up, William asked, "What'd she call for?" Agnes said she and Robert were going to get married. Then came the line that originated from so deep and burst so forcefully. Where did it come from? Robert was a nice guy. Zita wasn't pretty, smart or a lot of fun. She was nice and a great house cleaner, but quite frankly most people thought she was less than plain, and she was clearly mentally slow. Sure Robert was older and not a charmer himself and also not so bright. He was kind and a steady worker. Zita was lucky to get anyone and especially lucky to have Robert dote on her. They were comfortable with each other and both believed they were lucky to have each other. Robert was past forty and never had a woman before. Zita had never had a date in her twenty-two years. Later in the day Gabriel said to Agnes, "The old man should be tickled to death for Zita. How does he get off yelling with so much hatred, angst and fear?"

As the wedding approached, William said nothing. As plans were made to travel to Milwaukee, how to get there, where to stay, William was not part of the discussion and no plan involved him. He had opted to stay home while everyone else in the family went to celebrate the special occasion in the Genotti family. Agnes accepted for the first time she would go to one of her children's weddings without William at her side. She was not happy about this—but she became resigned to it.

Joshua asked his mother, "Why is Dad not coming to the wedding? Robert is a nice guy. He's not so old. Zita's lucky to get anyone. Robert works hard He's got a good job, he's making good money—hell, these are all the things the Old Man values. Doesn't he realize how he's making Zita feel?"

Agnes hesitated. Should I tell him? Will it be fair to William? To Zita? She can't, so she repeats what has now become the party line, "Dad doesn't feel good. The trip to Milwaukee would be too much for him." Joshua had been there when William got "sick" because Robert and Zita were going to get married. Agnes hoped Zita and Robert would buy the lie and Joshua and Gabriel would say nothing. Gabriel said, "Robert's sister believes Dad is sick—she must have heard from Robert that he was too sick to come. The son-of-a-bitch. The hypocrite. He can't go, but he can lie. Well, at least it saves Zita's feelings."

The wedding day came and Gabriel drove to Milwaukee with Agnes, Lucy and Leonardo in the car. Gabriel drove all the way across Wisconsin and even in Milwaukee. The four of them talked and joked and laughed. There would have been no talking, joking and certainly no laughing if William had been along. He'd have either yelled at Mother or listened to Paul Harvey and Jolly Rogers on the radio. More than once Gabriel said, "This is fun, I think I will drive more today than I have my whole life. If the Old Man had come, I'd be bored in the back seat." Other than that, no one mentioned William during the entire trip. Gabriel got more excited as they approached the city. It was the first time he would drive in a big city like Milwaukee. He'd been to Milwaukee before and he'd memorized the map Zita had sent on how to get to the wedding place, so he was confident he'd find the place. He wanted to look like an old pro—didn't want to show he'd never driven in a city so he wheeled the car like he'd been there many times. Leonardo, Joshua, Lucy and Agnes just kept talking like they expected him to take them to the right place. Gabriel pulled up to the wedding site, parked, jumped out and opened the door for his mother. He'd never done that before and everyone admired his gentlemanly act.

The wedding came off without a hitch. Things could work without William in control. Zita was radiant; Robert relieved. He'd not only found a woman that would marry him, but he found a woman he loved and who loved him. Gabriel was the best man and Carol, Robert's sister, was the bridesmaid. There was joy in the hall. Agnes realized if William had been there the joy would have been soured. So she forgot he was not there, and she hoped Zita and Robert would forget he was not there. Zita blushed with happiness; Robert smiled with contentment. Everyone was smiling and laughing and Agnes let herself join in the fun. She danced and laughed and talked and had a couple of drinks. Weddings were a great way to celebrate life and without William at her side she celebrated more openly.

Only later that night would she recall why William had objected so much to this marriage, and she wondered if she had done right to enjoy the day so much. When Zita was born,

Doctor Gallagher had said she should never have children. It would be best if she did not marry, for if she had children they would be disabled. William had never again spoken a word about it to Agnes or Zita. Even now he said not a word, but Agnes had to think that his deep set revulsion to Zita's marriage was related to the words of the doctor at Zita's birth. "The doctor could be wrong. They been wrong before," she had told William at the time. William had to agree because he was always saying, "doctors don't know shit from shinola". They never spoke about it again—Agnes thought that the doctor's words had somehow reached so deep into William that he could not talk about it. Still, she was surprised when his reaction to the wedding erupted after so many years of silence.

William Goes to the Hospital

William had been especially grumpy for the past few months. Not that Agnes noticed. He was less talkative than usual if that was possible. He walked a little slower and went to Jamboys' Garage less often. He'd kicked Joshua out of the house when he came home with an advanced case of adult mumps, and he'd refused to go to Zita's wedding. This was not so much out of the ordinary for William that Agnes took notice until after he woke on that June fourth morning and said. "I'm going to the doctor today. Will you come with me?" Agnes was glad to go. She figured after seeing the doctor, she'd persuade him to go shopping with her. She hadn't been to LaCrosse in two or three years and there were some things she wanted to buy that were not available in Badaxe or from Sears-Roebuck. William was very quiet on the trip in, and Agnes began to think about how he'd changed a little. William wasn't known to hide his pain. He'd seek sympathy for a scratch on his finger. He was also known not to complain if he was in real pain.

Maybe he was really sick. After all, he would not pay a doctor unless he was in a lot of pain or thought something was not right. Agnes asked what was wrong. She got a grunt. Her mind wandered back to the list of things she wanted to purchase in LaCrosse. She wondered how she had managed to get along without a new scissors and a replacement head for her sewing machine for so long. She also wanted to look for a new bra and a pair of panties. She tried to remember when she'd last bought a pair. Wouldn't it be nice to have a new blouse? Something to wear to Mass on Sunday.

She hoped they didn't have to wait at the doctor's too long. Sometimes Dr. Gunderson would be backed up two or three hours. There wouldn't be much time to shop if that were the case. Luckily, they only had to wait about twenty minutes for Dr. Gunderson. William went into the doctor's office alone. Agnes kept going over her list trying to memorize the things she wanted to buy. Suddenly she realized William had been in the office too long. I wonder what's happening. Dr. Gunderson came out with William. "Agnes, I'm going to hospitalize William. He's got something going on in his lower intestine and I think we better find out what it is." They checked William into the hospital, and he immediately went into a tailspin. Now that he admitted he was ill it seemed the illness was allowed to have its full effect. On the second day the doctor said, "It appears William has an inflammation in his lower intestine. I have scheduled the operation for tomorrow morning. We cannot wait." The doctor spoke with urgency. Agnes called Lucy, Pina and Leonardo to tell them and to ask them to call the rest of the children.

Gabriel, Luke, Lucy and Joshua showed up a couple hours before the surgery to comfort Agnes. They had been told all operations are serious, but there had not been a hint that William's surgery was so serious until one of the nuns came out to say things were not going well. William's intestines had been infected a long time, and the doctor was having a difficult time removing it all.

Agnes' heart stopped for a moment. What could the worst be? The worst would be if they cured William, and he lived in chronic pain and became an old crotchety man and Agnes lived to care for him until he was one hundred. Agnes had not thought about William dying. He was too mean to die, as they say. The thought of his death now entered her head followed quickly by the thought of life without William. Agnes had assumed she'd always live with William. For Agnes, divorce was out of the question, and the thought of William passing away before her had never entered her head until now. After all, most women in Badaxe died well before their husbands. Her grandpa, John Veneri, was twenty years older than his wife, but he still outlived her. The thought of no more shouting, no more fighting over every penny, no more knocks on the wall in the middle of the night felt good—for about fifteen seconds.

In a nanosecond, those thoughts lead to a flood of guilt inevitable for a woman of her upbringing. How dare she imagine William dead when he was in the operating room fighting for his life? The nurse, not sensing that she was getting a reaction to her statement, repeated "The surgery is not going well. You should prepare yourself for the worst."

Agnes popped out of her thoughts to hear the nun repeat her anxiety. She asked the sister what was happening. The nun explained in simple language that William had a major infection in his lower intestine and the doctor was removing a sizable section. The surgery was complicated by the fact that the infection was so wide spread and William's body had gotten so weak from the long neglect that he was not responding well. His life systems weren't giving the doctor much help to make the surgery work correctly. Agnes began to think that William wasn't fighting for life because she had wished him to die. She had dared to enjoy an imaginary moment of life without William and God would now punish her by taking away William's will to live.

A tear formed in her eye, but she stopped it before it became a drop. She must be brave. She must be ready to stand next to William when he came out of the operation and give him the hope that his life would go on. With so many cousins, uncles and aunts, friends and close relatives, she attended death several times every year of her life. It made death no less frightening. Her role was to provide hope for life to those who were dying. Death was frightening enough. To know one was dying would be too much and, at the least, would hasten death on.

The waiting room went to silence for a few minutes. Lucy reached out to touch her mother but didn't. Matthew finally said, "The Old Man's too tough to die. He'll be all right." This cut the air and the talk led from one thing to another until they were talking about the weather and the outlook for the crops this season.

The nurse returned and told the small conclave that William was in the post-op room. Agnes wanted to see him.

The sister told her he was unconscious. Agnes kept walking toward the nun to be taken to William. The nun recognized the determination and led her to the post-op room. William had tubes in his nose and down his throat. There was no other sign of life. She started mumbling the rosary and before she knew it she felt her hand coming to the end of the fifth decade of the beads. She looked at William and recognized death. "I'd better tell Matthew and Lucy to call all the children and William's brothers and sisters. Better let Fred Jamboys know, too. Got to call Father Schulte—William will need the Last Rites."

She took a deep breath. No reason to tell the children that it was over—just let them know it was indeed serious. William was unconscious. The children were in the next room. The nurse was with another patient. Agnes continued to cry for a moment and then pulled herself together to face her children.

Death Again

William hung on for over one week. The doctor and nurses thought he might make it. He got up enough energy to yell at Gabriel when he came to visit and told William that he stopped on his bakery route. "Why you driving so far to deliver bakery? No profit if you spend it all on gas."

Agnes knew he would not make it. She stayed with him twenty-four hours a day for the first week. Geno and Stella, Dom and Sara, Matthew, Luke, Mark and a lot more people came to visit. Usually William was unconscious so Agnes had to get up her energy and strength to talk to everyone. All the visitors cheered her up, but they also wore her down. She needed some real sleep. She woke William up and told him she was going to go home. He said "Good—get some sleep—see you tomorrow." She wanted to lean over the bed and kiss him on the cheek. She never knew why she didn't. That moment would haunt her for a decade.

Lucy came back to sit with her dad. After a half-hour, she dozed off. When she woke a couple hours later, she could hear that William had stopped breathing. She ran to him to check for a pulse and then ran out to find a nurse. The nurse came, called the doctor who confirmed the obvious. William had died—probably peacefully in his sleep—alone.

Lucy drove the eighteen miles to Badaxe to tell her mother that William had died. Agnes had gone to sleep seeing herself frozen about to kiss William good-bye. She had dreamed his death, saw Lucy curled up in the chair beside his bed and had seen William's soul wrench itself away from his body—had seen his eyes open—his face go to horror—his body twitch as the soul cut loose, and she watched his soul float through the wall with the devil and God pulling it in different directions.

When Lucy nudged her to wake her, she knew what Lucy had to say before she opened her eyes to see that it was still dark and to see death in Lucy's eyes. Agnes reached out and touched Lucy's hand to say I know—you don't have to tell me. At that moment, Lucy's tears flooded down her face and Agnes put her arm around her to comfort her. Lucy had found her father dead and had to be the carrier of bad news. She had to drive all that way in the middle of the night, come into the dark house and wake her mother with this awful news. Agnes hugged Lucy longer than she ever had since she was a baby. Then she walked to the telephone, and began to call each of her children. She felt nothing. No remorse, no relief, no sadness, no joy. Nor did she feel the coldness of the June night air.

She started with Pina and went down the line until she got to Gabriel. She did not have his phone number, so she called Matthew again to get his number. Matthew said Gabriel did not have a phone, so he'd go tell him. Agnes asked Lucy to call the uncles and aunts. Then she sat at the table and stared out the window that was still dark. She could hear Lucy saying "Dad died tonight" but she sat in denial feeling neither thought nor emotion.

The sun had risen and the water on the Mississippi sparkled in the morning sun. It did not seem right that the sun should shine or that the water should sparkle.

William's Funeral

Everyone in Badaxe came out for William's funeral. His body was on display at the Francini Funeral Home in LaCrosse. The place was packed at the wake and in fact half the people had to stand in the entryway and yard when Father Curti said prayers over William's body. They all said the rosary together and then retreated into the night.

The next morning, the mourners gathered again at the funeral home. Agnes greeted each one in a cruel ritual that was part of death in Badaxe. Mark, her second son whom she hadn't seen in three years, came with his wife and seven children. Agnes wondered where he'd been when William was so sick. Uncle Geno and Stella offered their condolences, and Sara hugged Agnes.

Orsola said, "It was a shame William passed away so young."

Young Larry Kelsey mumbled something as he walked with his head to the floor. Agnes heard, "sorry" and filled in the "I am."

Matthew just shook her hand while his wife said, "My condolences, Agnes" a bit too loudly. So it went for nearly an hour as William's sons and daughters, grandchildren, brothers and sisters, in-laws, uncles and aunts, cousins, friends and acquaintances filed by Agnes telling her that they were sorry and giving her their condolences. Following the awkward moment with Agnes, each mourner shuffled up to the open casket. Some knelt before William and said a prayer to God to take his soul quickly to heaven. Others genuflected quickly and some crossed themselves with the sign of the Cross. Stella and Sara kissed William on the forehead. It may have been the first time he was ever kissed in public. Mostly, though, people were in a hurry to meet their obligations and get away from the dead body. It wasn't because they were squeamish about death or dead bodies. Living in a small town of less than seven hundred people where everyone knew everyone, there were six to twelve deaths every year, and unless they were exceptionally busy in the fields, everyone went to everyone else's funeral. So the normal conduct was to give the closest relatives their condolences, say a quick prayer to God to be kind to the dead person, and to get to the visitors room to talk to your friends. There was always more time to pray at the pre-services in the funeral home, in the church where the priest would say Mass and take advantage of the death to make a point in a too-long sermon followed by a shorter sermon at the grave site. While William had no enemies in the crowd, he was close to no one except Fred Jamboys and his brothers Geno and Dom. So the procession of well-wishers and prayer-givers moved along at a steady pace.

Agnes noticed wrinkles in people's faces she'd never seen. While all were walking by her at regular funeral speed, each person seemed to spend an inordinately long time to offer her their best. She saw their mouths open, and then tongues begin to move before a word came out. She noticed the yellow, gray, and black in people's teeth. Nose hairs were enlarged. It was as if she were observing the entire event through a zoom lens.

After what seemed a week or two, everyone had come. Father Curti came and took Agnes' arm to lead her to the casket. The cue had been given, and the murmuring suddenly stopped, and all eyes went to Agnes. The heat of their eyes bore through her. She thought everyone didn't stop talking to show respect, but to see what she would do when she came to the casket. Would she cry? Would she kneel and stoically pray? Would she kiss William on the forehead? On his lips? Or would she spit in his face? The thought almost brought a smile to Agnes.

She had always bowed her head to provide a private moment for the closest of kin. She never sensed until this moment that her fellow parishioners all stared at the victim of death. Agnes approached the casket holding on to Father Curti's arm. She became aware that her legs were weak, and she felt like falling to the ground. "I mustn't." She must face this moment with strength the way Jesus found his own death with strength. She took a deep breath. She looked at William. He was so still. Almost like he was sleeping, but something was different. His head looked larger. Maybe the undertaker had inserted too much fluid and stretched his skin to the maximum.

For a moment he looked like a wax figure. Had the old bastard played a trick on her? He'd made a wax statue of himself and then ran out on her. She realized it could not be the case— William was too cheap to stage such an event even if he wanted to escape—plus he would not have thought of it.

Then, for a moment, she thought his eyelash moved. Maybe he wasn't dead. Agnes had heard of people declared dead, even buried, who were still alive. The doctors didn't always know. She caught her breath as she saw William get ready to pop up and bellow out "What the hell's happening! Who did this! God damn it, I'm not going to pay for this!" She'd heard of dead bodies springing up in coffins like ghosts from the night. Some kind of reflex action in death. Like the chickens flapping around after their heads were chopped off.

She blinked and stared again at William. He was stiff, and she guessed he hadn't moved. Or had he? Should she ask the doctor to check him? How horrible it would be to bury him alive. Everyone would just think she was being hysterical. Of course he was dead. The doctors and undertaker couldn't both be wrong. Besides, they drained the blood these days and put in some red fluid. She knew they did that because she'd heard it so many times.

She reached out to touch William's face. Maybe she could feel the warmth of the body. Maybe he'd move when she touched him. She'd find out he was still alive, and she'd call out for the doctor. They'd rush William to the hospital, put blood back into his veins, and he'd come back. It was possible. She touched his face with her hand. It was cold and too hard. She ran her hand over his face, touched his eyelids delicately praying they would respond. They were heavy with death. Her hand paused on his eyelids. For a moment, Agnes thought he was a stranger. Older than she had remembered him. Stronger and handsomer. She studied this man's features with whom she'd spent forty years. She leaned over and kissed William on the forehead with tenderness. She moved to kiss him on his lips—but stopped just short.

Nightmares

Agnes stood before William lying in the hospital about to die. She saw herself lean over the bed to kiss him on the cheek. She hesitated, and then they were in the funeral home, touching his eyelids, his head too big, and his look that of a wax figure. She kissed his forehead. He jerked up to look at her with eyes that stared, "Why do you kiss me now? Why didn't you kiss me then? Why did you let me die without a kiss? And now kiss me after I'm dead? What hypocrisy!"

Every night as she woke out of this dream, her gown was wet and perspiration had gathered on her forehead. She bolted up in the bed and stared into the darkness. The street light shining through the window created deep and long shadows in her tiny bedroom. She'd stare into this space and relive that moment she had not kissed William and that moment when she caressed his cold firm lips that could not respond. The motion picture of her mind clicked in, and she'd replay some part of her life with William. Sometimes she'd hear the knock on the wall, deny hearing it, but give in to the call, roll out of bed, work her way through the dark to William's bed, lie still as he would grab her breasts a little too hard. Now she observed her face. Nothing, just a blank stare into the ceiling. William was running his hands over her body. Agnes lies motionless. He touched her kneecaps; ran his hands up the inside of her thighs. Touched her private spot. Climbed on her entering her. She takes a deep breathe. Agnes watches herself lie with no emotion—touch William more like a mechanical being than a person.

"How could I be so cold?"

"He was a caring man. I never really gave him a chance."

Sometimes the movie of her mind replayed the funeral. The undertaker closed the casket and rolled it down the aisle of the funeral home. Agnes saw herself follow—get into the car with Gabriel, Leonardo and Joshua—her three youngest with her in this time of sorrow. It brought a half-smile to her face. Some nights she watched Matthew, Mark, Luke, Geno, Dominique and Fred Jamboys lift the casket into the hearse as everyone filed out and got in their cars.

The hearse started down West Avenue toward Highway 35. Gabriel started the family 1959 Chevrolet and followed the hearse. Agnes felt the other cars pull out behind them. The hearse pulled out on to highway 35 and picked up speed to about 40 mph. The caravan weaved down the Mississippi River road toward Badaxe Church. Agnes was startled as she came around a corner and peered over one of William's favorite spots to ice fish. He had often built a shanty on the bay and fished there for days at a time.

Agnes turned to look back to see who was following. She was surprised to see car after car. She looked back one mile until the cars disappeared around a bluff. Farther down the road she saw more cars. They stretched for miles. She imagined it was the largest caravan ever for a Badaxe funeral. There must have been five hundred cars all full of people.

The scene faded to inside the church with every pew and even the balcony full of people. Father Curti was blessing the casket and saying something in Latin. Agnes was surrounded by her thirteen children and their spouses. Father Curti went to the pulpit and started on one of his long sermons. Agnes loved his sermons, especially the ones he gave at weddings and funerals and on Good Friday. But she remembered nothing about this sermon. Now and then she'd hear "William" or "Agnes" or "children", but she had not heard anything else, and she could not recall his sermon. She saw her family sitting in the front pew, and she saw Lucy and Pina crying. She saw the tears trickle down Leonardo's and Gabriel's cheeks. William had been hard on Gabriel, calling him the black sheep; yet he was crying.

She wanted to cry. She wanted to let the hurt, pain and anger out. She wanted to let go of this man who had created so much love, happiness and terror for her. She knew that tears were necessary, but they did not and would not come.

The service was over. Father circled the open casket, said some final words in Latin, blessed the body with holy water, gave a benediction, and closed the casket to say, "This is William's final moment on earth. Now we must all let him go." He moved slowly, recognizing the importance of the ritual. The pallbearers rolled the closed casket to the church entrance. Agnes followed with her children, beginning with the youngest, Leonardo, following her. The pallbearers picked up the casket, carried it down the steps placing it in the back of the hearse.

Leonardo opened the car door for Agnes. She said, "No. I want to walk."

So the hearse drove up the gravel dirt road to the hillside overlooking the steeple, and Agnes and her children followed on foot. The rest of the parish followed the sign, and everyone trudged by foot through the muddy road the half mile to William's graveside. The casket was lowered into the grave, and Fr. Curti said one more goodbye; a goodbye for those that had not yet been able to say goodbye in person.

Agnes lingered by the graveside after the rest left. She stared at the casket, waiting for William's spirit to leave her as she had seen it leave his body. He hung on. She turned, looked down at the steeple and to the Mississippi River over the steeple. "William, life flows. The river runs. The steeple stands. Death comes. Sorrow ends. Please, leave me now. I have things to do." She felt him hang a bit harder to her soul. She lowered her head and walked down the hill. The grave digger, Cousin Josh Andretti, seeing how torn Agnes was, waited for her to get into her car in the church lot and be driven off before he threw the first shovel of dirt over the casket.

In Agnes' movie the grave stayed open forever. When she went to visit William and say some prayers to God to save him from purgatory, the casket lay shining at the bottom of the grave, and William reached up holding on to her with a strength and determination she never knew he had. Agnes had seen some television shows where the grave digger tossed a few shovels of dirt on the casket before the mourners dispersed. She always wondered if William would have let go if Josh had covered the grave in her presence.

Most nights Agnes tried to go back to sleep, but the image of William sitting up in the casket, his veins popping from too much blood—or was it too much anger—kept her awake.

Hoeing Tomatoes

About three months after William died, Luke found Agnes in her garden humming and gently hoeing her tomato patch. She was hoeing out one tomato plant after another. She had already cut all the peas and beans off. Luke knew full well what Agnes' garden meant to her. He'd been to visit his mother at least once a week since his dad died, and he'd seen her every Sunday in church. She'd seemed fine. In fact Luke thought she might be happier without Dad around. He remembered the day in July, Agnes and Gabriel had come back from a shopping spree in LaCrosse and Agnes had bought a new rug and a dining room set. She was bubbling with happiness like a little child set free. But now that he thought about it, he remembered how sometimes when he came to visit, Agnes was quiet. Maybe she'd say something about her garden or the weather and that was about all.

Something had snapped—she was hoeing out her tomato plants and leaving the weeds to take over. Luke walked toward Agnes and said, "Hello."

She did not respond.

"Nice day."

Nothing.

Luke approached Agnes slowly, touched her right arm, slid his other hand over the hoe and pulled it away from her to disarm her. He nudged on her arm asking her to come. She obeyed with no hesitation, and they edged toward the front door of the house.

Luke sat Agnes at the dining room table. He took several days' dishes off the table, starting with the knives and forks. He did not know if his mother was suicidal, but no use taking a chance. He threw the old and dried food in the garbage, stacked the dishes, and hauled everything to the kitchen. After wiping the table, he sat down to talk to Agnes. Maybe the heat had gotten to her. What he saw was vacant eyes gazing out the window. Only she was looking at the wall. She did not know Luke, herself, or where she was. Luke called Lucy to ask what she thought he should do. She said, "Better call Matthew. He'll know what to do."

Matthew suggested Luke take Agnes to her doctor right away. Maybe she had a stroke. He'd put her in the hospital. Luke packed a few things for his mother in a brown paper bag and put them in the trunk. He came back to the dining room where his mother hadn't moved a muscle since he had sat her down.

"Mom, I'm going to take you to see Dr. Gallagher."

No response, but when he touched her arm she got up and headed toward the car as if she understood. Dr. Gallagher asked, "How are you doing, Agnes?"

"I'm fine," Agnes said—her first words of the day.

"Luke seems to think you might have over-heated in the garden. Want to tell me what happened."

"I'm fine," Agnes said.

"Do you forget where you are sometimes?"

"I'm fine."

"Do you know who I am?"

"I'm fine."

Dr. Gallagher motioned for Luke to step out of the room. He followed Luke and said, "I think she'd better see Dr. Becker. He's a psychiatrist, and I think he'll know better how to treat her."

Luke said, "Okay" and Dr. Gallagher went back in to talk to Agnes.

His voice changed to that of a typecast kindergarten teacher as he spoke too loud and too slow. "Agnes, I'm going to have your son take you to see Dr. Becker. He's better trained to diagnose your condition. His office is just down the street. I think you can walk there."

Agnes got up and started toward the door. Luke took her arm, and they walked out the front door and down 6th Street to Dr. Becker's office.

St. Anne's Hospital

Agnes shot up with a scream. Her dream had returned. Her lips had touched William's cold lips. She had screamed herself back into the world.

She stared at the darkness and wondered why the street light wouldn't make shadows as a huge image of William appeared, condemning her. "We had a good table. It was good enough for your mother. It was good enough for me? It's not good enough for you? Who you think you are? How could you throw away my money on a stupid rug?" The face was bigger than the bedroom wall, and it screamed over and over, "How could you spend my money on that junk?"

Agnes clapped her hands over her ears, but the voice shouted louder. She closed her eyes, but the face got brighter. When she opened her eyes it was still there but William looked a little like Joseph Stalin. "Stop it! Stop it! Stop it!" she murmured, but the voice got louder and the face bigger. Agnes screamed at the top of her lungs. The voice stopped and the face faded. She screamed again to chase away this horror. The light blinded her eyes. Agnes jumped back in the bed and pulled the blanket over her head. Who broke into her house? Was it a murderer? Or a thief? Or just Lucy had heard her scream and come running down to see what was wrong? Agnes peaked out and saw a white figure in the brightness. She sighed a moment of relief as she thought it was the Angel of Afterlife coming to take her. She was about to run to her when she realized it was a nurse. "What is a nurse doing in my home?"

"You all right, Agnes?"

"How does she know my name is Agnes? It has to be the Angel of Death—she is just dressed like a nurse."

"Agnes, you all right? It's okay. You'll be all right. Do you know where you are? This is Saint Anne's. You've been here three months now. It's okay. We'll help you get better. Remember me? I'm Lucy. Remember? It's okay. We're going to make you better. There is nothing to be afraid of. Come on now. Let's lie back down and get some sleepy-bye. Okay. It's all right. Lucy will protect you. No problem. Just lie down and get some sleep. The bogey man wouldn't come. Now, now. There you go. I'll just pull these covers up and tuck them in. Just close your eyes and go back to sleep now. It's okay. I'll turn the lights out now. Beddie-bye. Sleep tight."

The white apparition was gone. Agnes opened her eyes—it was pitch dark. Where was the light from the street? Did someone close my shade? She reached over the left side of her bed and ran her hand across the wall toward the window, but there was only the wall. Who took out the window? Agnes noticed a bit of light coming from under the door. "Who had the light on in the kitchen?" she wondered.

It was all too much, so she lay back in the bed. The room began to spin out of control. Agnes closed her hands over her ears to block out the spirit, tried to go to sleep, but the room spun and spun and spun like a perpetual motion top. As it spun, it chased her back into unconsciousness.

Death Comes to America

It was the morning of June 12, 1963. Agnes was meeting later in the day with the head psychiatrist for an evaluation if she could be released. An early riser, Agnes went for a walk over to the hospital gardens where she hoped to see the sun rise. It was overcast and the air smelled like rain. "No sun, today," Agnes heard herself speak. "Geez, maybe I am crazy—that is what they say, isn't it? If you talk to yourself, you are probably crazy." She pursed her lips, so she could not say more words out loud while her thoughts continued, "I gotta show'em I ain't crazy—talking to myself not the right thing to do." She went over some questions they would ask. "What day is it?" "Wednesday." "What month is it?" "June." Who is the President?" "Jack Kennedy." "How old are you? "Sixty." "Where is your husband?" "He is dead." She stopped the monologue. "They wouldn't really ask me that, will they? That would be an uncaring question."

While the threat of rain was imminent, it had not started to rain when it was time for Agnes to head to the cafeteria for breakfast. She grabbed a tray and sat it on the tray slide bar and moved slowly down the bar looking at a vat of oatmeal, a dispenser with a choice of corn flakes, Wheaties, Rice Krispies or Sugar Frosted Flakes, and containers of bacon, scrambled eggs and French toast. None of it appeared edible, so Agnes settled on two pieces of toast, some jam and a cup of coffee. She picked up her tray, looked around to see who was eating. Seeing her friend MaryAnn, she walked toward her table and sat the tray down in front of the chair that was facing the window where she could watch the storm come. She was barely aware of the TV blasting behind her. She had purchased her first TV a few weeks before being admitted. She turned the TV on when she awoke and turned it off before she went to bed. It served as company though she rarely watched it. So the TV behind her sounded like it should be there, and should be ignored at the same time. Agnes looked at MaryAnn, "This food is so bad here I am just eating toast. On the farm, breakfast was always a big meal—sometimes we ate a bowl of cereal, two or three eggs and three or four pieces of toast with jam on them. I can no more eat that much of their slop than I can fly. Not sure how I can survive on just toast." MaryAnn nodded in agreement.

"We interrupt this program with breaking news" caught Agnes' attention as she had never heard those words coming from a TV. "Fifteen minutes past midnight Medgar Evers got out of his car beside his house in a Negro residential area. In a vacant lot a sniper shot a single shot from a high power rifle." Agnes turned her chair around, so she could see what was on the screen. She saw the driveway where Evers was shot, a policeman standing in the vacant lot, Evers addressing a crowd, and Martin Luther King speaking. She heard the mayor of Jackson, Mississippi offer a $5,000 reward for anyone who gave information that led to an arrest and conviction of the killer.

MaryAnn spoke first, "That is a joke—no jury in Jackson will find anyone guilty. It's not a joke—it is a crime, but it is true." Agnes was not sure what was going on. She had just purchased her first ever television six weeks before being admitted to St. Anne's and most nights she did not start watching TV until after the news had played. She asked MaryAnn who was the guy who got shot and why were they covering his murder—weren't there too many murders in America to cover them all. MaryAnn explained to Agnes that Medgar Evers had made some headway in calling attention to the plight of Negroes in America.

"I don't know much about that stuff. I always thought we preached that everyone was equal—I been hearing some about how some people think they are better than other people, and they are supposed to be Christian. I don't know much about it, but I always thought the Church said we were all brothers and sisters and should treat others like we wanted to be treated. Seems like we ought to do that. That man looks like a nice guy—why would anyone want to kill him?" The bible says thou shalt not kill. I think we are not so Christian anymore. Let's say a rosary for his wife and children and pray that God lets him in heaven—it sure looks like he deserves that."

Home Again

Luke came to take Agnes home. She was both anxious about going home and eager to get home. It was May, and Agnes knew that she had already missed some important planting dates for her garden. Luke had assured her that he had come into town with his tractor and had plowed and raked her garden; it was ready for planting.

Agnes was anxious because she'd been in the hospital since September. Luke and Lucy came to visit regularly. Gabriel came once in a while, but she hadn't seen anyone else in months. Gabriel told her that Stella, Sara, Cecelia, Jake, Liz and a lot of other people had come to visit when she was first in the hospital, but they had all stopped coming because Agnes often did not recognize them. He did not tell her that sometimes she'd say strange things, like "I'm going to have sex with Peter [another patient]. I never touched anybody but William and I want to find out what it's like." Sometimes she'd scratch her butt for a long time like no one was around.

Agnes did not remember any of this, and there was no reason to help her remember. Agnes couldn't remember coming to the hospital. She'd try to reach back as far as she could, but it was all blurry in her head. She sort of remembered a turkey and some pumpkin pie with Lucy sitting next to Grandpa. Sometimes she could see a Christmas tree in the corner of where she went to eat every day. The tree had a pumpkin and red hearts on it as well as twinkling lights. She wondered if it was more her dreams than her memories.

Sometimes she thought she might have been in the hospital forever, since she could not remember any beginning. On the other hand, she could remember before the hospital. She remembered washing Joshua's hair, William knocking on the wall, picking saffron, Leonardo's first Holy Communion. These memories were vivid so Agnes knew that there had to have been a life before the hospital.

She found herself strangely detached from these memories. While most memories were fondly recalled, they were not accompanied by other emotions. She felt no fear at the memory of her wedding, wonderment at the birth of Giuseppina, or sorrow at her father's funeral, anxiousness at buying her dad's farm, or love at Leonardo's graduation from high school at Holy Cross Seminary.

She wondered if these weren't dreams of someone else's life. She felt more observer than participant. This life before the hospital did not have the reality of life in the hospital. The memories of the fear before shock treatment, the joy of winning the bingo game, the taste of the meat loaf were shaded with concrete emotions and passed before her eyes with vivid detail. Agnes thought it might be possible that these other memories were from a movie or a book. Maybe from a previous life in another time.

She packed her things that morning with her heart noticeably racing inside her. She seemed to stand outside her body and watch herself pack. Sometimes she'd direct herself. "Now, Agnes, fold that a little neater. You don't want to have to iron it when you get home. That's it. Shake it out, now fold it in half and then quarters. Now fold it the other way. Okay, good. You know you'll have enough to do when you get home. The whole house will be dusty. You'll have to get things in to eat. The garden needs to be planted. You don't want to have to iron too because you're too nervous to fold your clothes right."

Agnes moved in slow motion. Folding everything up in too-small bundles. Placing them carefully in the suitcase as she might if going on a world tour rather than eighteen miles home. She was to be released after lunch which was served right at noon. Luke was to pick her up at 1:00. Agnes looked at the clock. It was only 8:15 a.m. She had started to pack at 8:00, and she thought with all the folding and refolding she had done that it must be past 10:00.

She took a last look around her room to make sure she had everything, opened and closed each drawer in the chest of drawers, bent over to look under the bed, opened the closet doors, and ran her hand over each shelf though she could easily see they were all empty. She took the blankets and sheets and shook each one separately to make sure nothing was caught between them. Just to be safe, she repeated the entire search. Satisfied that she had packed everything she closed the suitcase, carefully placed it near the door and sat in her arm chair and waited for Luke to come.

Adding Machine

Gabriel had gone to the University of LaCrosse. Agnes attended his graduation, and she had seen him walk across the stage in a black robe along with a thousand other people. Agnes had worried that Gabriel would lose his faith going to a public college and all, but he did get married in the church and still went to mass every Sunday. He hadn't become a priest, but now he'd graduated from college, married a nice woman, taken a teaching job and had a second child on the way. There was much to be thankful for, and she had prayed to Jesus to thank him for the way things were going.

Joshua, Gabriel's older brother, was now going to the University of LaCrosse. He came to visit Agnes once or twice a month. She made him risott, baked chicken and a pie. Agnes liked to make her children their favorite foods and Joshua let her know this is what he liked so it's what he got. Every time he visited. They did not talk so much for Joshua was quieter than the rest, and Agnes had always found it a little hard to talk to him. One Sunday he mentioned that he might not be able to come for a while because he'd been cast in a play, and he'd be busy. Agnes remembered that Gabriel had been in some plays, but she'd never gone to see him. Father Duffy had directed a couple of shows years ago and every Christmas the children would act out a skit at church. Agnes knew that being in a show meant getting on stage and saying some words in front of the audience. She'd been surprised when she found out Gabriel had done this because he was so shy. She had wanted to see him, but he'd always told her after he'd been in a show. Now Joshua was going to be in a show in six weeks. What a surprise. He was shyer than Gabriel. To go in front of a lot of people and say memorized lines. She wanted to see it. She'd go—why not?

"Joshua, I want to see the show. When is it? Maybe you could come and get me or Luke could drive me up."

"I think I could get you. You'd have to come early because we have to put makeup on."

October 15 came. Joshua had called the night before to check to make sure his mother was still planning to come to opening night. "Of course, what time should I be ready?"

"Five O'clock, I'll drive down to get you. I don't get out of class till four and I have to be back here before six, so be ready to go at five."

Agnes usually knew exactly what to wear, but this was different. Should she wear her best dress or would she be overdressed? Surely she should get dressed up; people didn't go the theater in their work clothes. She decided the best was to wear her second best dress that was very plan but still new enough to be considered a dress-up dress. By four-thirty she'd changed her dress and put on her Sunday shoes and some lipstick. She was ready to go. She sat in the rocking chair and waited. "Wonder what Joshua will be doing on stage. Wonder if he has a lot of lines. What was the name of that show again? Something about a machine. Can't remember. Wonder if it's a play about farmers. Let's see. The something Machine, that's it

The Adding Machine. Well, guess it's not about farmers. They never have enough to add, unless it's troubles and I guess you don't need a machine to add them up." She smiled at her clever diversion.

Try as hard as she could she couldn't imagine what she was going to see. It'd have to be different from the Christmas shows the children from St. Francis presented. Joshua was spending a lot of time for the past six weeks on this. Gabriel had worked very hard on the plays he was in and directed, and they both took it so seriously. They talked about it like it was harvest day and it was going to snow tomorrow and everything had to be gotten in today. If it was that important, what was it?

Maybe it was like TV. People saying all those things to each other with so much earnestness that you believed you were watching them in real life. "I suppose it takes some doing to get to the point where they can act them things out like they are really happening."

Joshua came and they headed up the Mississippi River road. Joshua appeared preoccupied. "I suppose he's running lines through his head," Agnes thought. "Best to leave him alone." She'd been up and down this road a few times in her life, but she still was amazed at the sheer beauty of the bluffs and coulees boarding the Mississippi River. The sun was beginning to set over the River and the leaves colored from the first frost tempted the eye with their majesty. Agnes recognized as much as she had always liked this ride, that she was seeing the entire splendor as if for the first time. She usually made this trip in time of stress; going to the doctor or to the funeral home. She always made the trip with someone else because Agnes could not drive. "I'm glad Joshua is so lost in his own thoughts. I can really look at what God has made here," she thought as she soaked in the exuberance of the evening.

Joshua took Agnes to the theater, showed her where the restrooms were, the front door to the theater and then took her to the box office where he got her a ticket. "This is my mother" he said to the girl behind the box office. He said "This is my Mother" with pride in his voice. Agnes liked it, and she liked that her son was so pleased to have her at his play.

"Mom, I got to go to the dressing room, get my makeup on and get ready for the show. At 7:30 they will open these doors and you can get in the theater. The seats are reserved; see here on the ticket you are in row E seat ten. There will be an usher, and she'll show you to your seat. You can wait here or go out for a walk. Maybe you want to get a coffee at the restaurant we passed down the block."

"Go ahead, I'll be okay, you go get ready for the play."

Agnes went down the street. When she saw the cafe she thought, "Yes, I'll go in and have a cup of coffee. She'd heard about people going into a restaurant and having a cup of coffee. It seemed like a funny thing to do, but why not, she had some time to waste, and she could use some coffee for the night was getting nippy. As she headed toward the door, fear took over her chest. She almost turned around but then thought "what am I afraid of? This place is here for people like me to come and have a cup of coffee." She opened the door and stepped in but the contraction in her chest grew. She looked around expecting everyone in the place to stare at her.

They did not. Agnes walked up to the counter and ordered coffee with cream and sugar. She pulled up her purse and dug out the exact change for the girl at the cash register. She spotted a table off by itself and headed toward it, set her coffee cup on the table and sat down. Agnes looked about the room where there were a dozen or so students all chatting and laughing between sips. She wondered if they came here often. She tried to remember when she last sat in a cafe and had a cup of coffee because she had nothing better to do. "It was at Woolworth's. Must'a been easy 20 years ago." She sees herself sitting on a stool in Woolworths with Lucy at her side. Lucy is eating an ice cream sundae and Agnes is chatting away with the waitress while her Woolworth's coffee gets cold. "I think I will drink this one while it is hot." Agnes kept her eye on the clock on the wall. She decided to stay put until 7:15. She wanted to get to the theater before 7:30, but not too much before.

About twenty people were waiting in the lobby. "I bet they are parents." As she approached a couple who were a little older than the rest, a chubby boy opened the doors to the theater and everyone moved toward the doors with determination. Agnes got in line near the end of the line. When asked her name, she said, "I am Joshua's mother."

"Joshua?" the girl sitting behind the table asked. What is your name? Agnes replied, "Agnes." The girl looked down at a list of names and said, "I don't see an Agnes here. What's your last name?

"Genotti"

"Oh, you're Josh's mother? I don't see a ticket here for you—are you sure Josh got you a ticket?

"Ya." Agnes reached into her purse and pulled out her ticket.

"Oh, this line is for people who do not have a ticket yet. Just give your ticket to John over there by the door, and he will tell you where to sit."

The girl then gave the ticket back to Agnes. Not sure what to do she studied the couple in front of her and saw that they gave their ticket to the chubby boy who tore it in two and gave half back to them. "I can do that." She handed her piece of paper to the chubby boy like she knew what she was doing. He looked at the ticket and said, "You are in Seat ten, Row E."

"What? My son said I was in Row E, seat ten."

"That's right—the usher will give you a program and show you to your seat." Agnes was glad she did not have to figure out where seat ten in Row E was. She took the program and sat in the seat the usher showed her. She opened the program but the print was too small. She took her reading glasses out and opened the program to the notes from the director. He sure wrote with a lot of big words. She paged forward, looking for some reference to her son. On the cast list she saw Zero....Josh Genotti. "How can you play zero? That's no name for a person."

I Never Liked Sex

It was some time after William died and Agnes' extraordinary forty years began to collapse into the inevitable decline of life, that she shared this secret.

"I never liked sex," she said quite spontaneously one day as she sat at the table with Gabriel and Leonardo. It was a statement that came from nowhere, then floated across the table and rested in the air before it exploded.

Gabriel thought, "I never once seen Dad and Mom touch. Never once kiss or embrace." Yet clearly they had kissed and they had had sex. "I never thought of them having or not having sex. I guess I'd figured they liked it if I had thought about it."

Agnes never liking sex while giving birth fourteen times and raising children with hefty sexual appetites? It was a thing to marvel. Now that Agnes had said it aloud, it had to be pursued. In thirty-six years of matrimony, Agnes must have had intercourse with William five thousand times. Maybe more, because William liked sex. To participate in an activity that often and never like it—that was an idea to explore.

"You mean not once. You never enjoyed making love to Dad even once?" Leonardo asked.

That caused a moment's reflection. Was she recalling each of the five thousand times?

"Never."

Leonardo hesitated, and then asked, "Did you ever have a climax?"

"No. Never."

"Then why?"

"It's what I was expected to do—I suppose. I don't know; I never liked it though."

Agnes had revealed more about herself than she knew how, and she was not about to discuss this further. She got up and went into the kitchen to make dinner and left Gabriel and Leonardo to their own thoughts.

"The idea of Dad never once raising Mom to a climax isn't so hard to accept. But to screw five—maybe six thousand times and never enjoy it once—not even on those nights of conception—or the first time after childbirth or on one of their anniversaries or New Year's Eve or the wedding night of one of her children?" Gabriel stopped at that thought. "Never once, not one time," she had said.

Leonardo asked, "Is it possible that he never in thirty-six years aroused her to a climax? Did she hold herself back for Jesus? Was she so duty bound in bed that she never gave herself to Dad in a way that might let her enjoy the act of procreation?"

Agnes walked in with a pot of steaming risott, placed it on the table with a thud that made it clear the discussion was over. No, she had never once enjoyed sex and that was that.

Spray Drift of Kindness

"What's a spray drift?" Agnes asked the first time she heard that there was a spray drift of kindness hovering over Veneri Valley where she had been raised, and that it extended into Badaxe City and beyond. Her younger brother, Frank, explained "It has a couple of meanings, but what people are talking about here is a nut theory that somewhere in our valley there is a "spring of kindness" shooting out a powerful invisible "spray" that carries "feelings" of contentment that results in those under its influence being kind. The idea is this energy drifts down the valley to Badaxe and depending on the winds floats up or down the river for a few miles."

"You think that is why people are so content here?" Agnes asked.

"Content? Or just lack ambition?" Frank laughed. Then in a serious tone, "I gotta admit once I moved up on the ridge I started to work harder. Maybe there is something to it." More laughter.

Many in the area claimed they felt the drift of kindness from the time they immigrated to Badaxe. There seemed to be a built in need to be generous to one's neighbors and that drive that brought them to America to get ahead was dampened. Cynics like Frank thought it was just a way to justify people's laziness. Others said, "I do not see that people in the drift work any less, it is just that they are more willing to share—more importantly they will not step on their neighbor to get ahead."

From her earliest memories, Agnes believed she should not only treat her neighbors as she treated herself, but just a little better. If asked, she would have told you it was because of her Church's teaching. She often told her children, "Jesus said 'Thou shalt love thy neighbor as thyself.' Seems to me it is better to love your neighbor a little more than yourself—treat your neighbor better than you want to be treated. No harm in being more generous than expected. The nuns told us this means to be kind to your neighbors; especially the ones less fortunate than you are."

Agnes clung to the belief that her impulse to be kind was ingrained in her and others of her parish because of the teachings of the church until she retired in town and became friends with more people who were not Catholic. When isolated on the farm, she rarely talked to anyone who was not part of the church. Nearly everyone in the town brought a house gift when she moved in town and often a neighbor would come by to pull weeds out of her garden when they saw Agnes in the garden. "Just stopped by to help." "It's nothing" was the common reply to Agnes when she said, "Thank you."

"Gee, I guess you do not have to be Catholic to be kind and generous," she thought. "People here are all so friendly—Catholic or not. Maybe there is something to that spray drift thing."

"Hey, Mom. What do you know about the spray drift that is supposed to be here?" asked Gabriel on one of his visits home. "Sounds pretty superstitious to me."

"Maybe it is and maybe it isn't. The theory is these bluffs around here ooze with a spray of kindness that floats over the area especially over the town and the valley I grew up in. The spray is a spray of contentment making everyone under its spell to be satisfied with what they have and who they are. Since everyone is content there is no need to be greedy or selfish. Some say that is why everyone here is so kind. I never believed the spray drift story even when Grandpa told me he first heard of the power the bluffs around here to create harmony, balance and tranquility from the Indians that used to live here. Grandpa said they told him the spray drift had made this valley the happiest place on earth where conflict and selfishness were not possible. I wanted to believe it was the Church that made everyone here so good, but lately I see a lot of non-Catholics are just as content, just as good and ever bit as kind. Might be some truth to that old Indian tale about a spray of contentment."

Gabriel said, "I don't think it's the church. I've met a lot of Catholics every place I have lived, and they are just as willing to step on you to get ahead as the rest. Here is the only place that is not true. Mom, you really think it is the spray drift?"

Waiting for Gordon

Gordon was fussing. Lucy handed her firstborn to Agnes and he immediately became quiet. Agnes, Lucy, her husband and Leonardo, who would be Gordon's godfather, walked up the Badaxe Church steps that had witnessed so much of Agnes' life. Leonardo opened the hand-carved church doors and the small party entered the vestibule. Father Cerletti, the new parish priest, was waiting for them. He greeted Agnes with a kiss on the cheek and congratulated Lucy on her good-looking baby. "Let's have a moment of silent prayer before we proceed."

Agnes prayed "Dear Jesus, take care of this child and all my children. Leonardo and Joshua are in college. Gabriel is a teacher. Hannah has a beautiful family in Canada. Mark is happily married and Matthew has reached his dream of making a lot of money. They all love you, Jesus. Look at little Gordon's mom—she's full of life. Her womb gave birth, her breasts are full—ready to feed this child, her cheeks are bursting with color; she is the new mother."

"I am mother of thirteen children. Grandmother to sixty-four and soon I'll be a great-grandmother. Jesus, I wanted to be a virgin for you. I wanted to sacrifice with a full life of obedience and poverty. I wanted to save souls poorer than me for you. I never became your bride; I never made it to the convent—I never went to China or Africa to help save poor pagan children for you."

Rev. Cerletti touched his hand into the Baptismal fount, scraped out a handful of water, poured it over Gordon and said, "I baptize thee in the name of the Father, Son and Holy Spirit."

Agnes looked at Lucy's first baby, and saw in his face her true calling. She was born to be a planter, a maker of things, and a mother. Not Mother Superior, but Mother Giver of Life. Her calling had been to give life, and she had done it well. She had filled these forty winters, springs, summers and falls with planting, cultivating and harvesting and giving birth. She gave more than she took; lived up to the vow she never spoke; and added a little to the spread and smack of the spray drift of kindness.

Epilogue

It is now a dozen years since Agnes died. Life goes on as it always had. The death of a cherub does not stop the flow. This year (1990) alone, Agnes gained one new grandchild, twelve great-grandchildren and seventeen great-great-grandchildren.[1]

The account of humanity is the story of Agnes; planting, cultivating and harvesting, in pursuit of truth, beauty and goodness, embodying spirituality, empathy and passion, committed to create, birth and nurture and to uphold parity, liberation and fairness. She was Mother who created more pumpkins than she needed, whose chickens laid more eggs than she could use, who had many children but fewer than she was able to care for.

---

[1] In 2019 the author of this novel poked around a bit and identified over three hundred and fifty living offspring of the corporeal Agnes that inspired the stories recorded in our epic tale of the mother of all mothers.

Coda (2021)

The story of humanity is not the tales of kings, ministers and warriors; it is not the history of nation-states, religion and weapons; it is not the accounts of legislatures, judges and police; it is not the chronicles of classists, sexists or racists; nor is it the fabrications of oppressors, oppressed and enablers.

Kings and all their surrogates, by definition, took more than they gave, leaving the earth a little more depleted than they found it; taking their ill-got goods to the grave with them thus robbing all in favor of gaining nothing. The story of legislatures, judges, and police are merely the stories of those who would give credence to the stories of kings, popes and generals. Certainly we can agree we would be immeasurably better off if there were no and never had been a racist, sexist or classist on earth. We must stop looking to the power builders, brokers and abusers (the "heroes" of the past) for guidance. They have nothing to offer. Their stories hold supreme over us because we validate their right to be by repeating, ad nauseam, their fabricated mendacities thereby crediting them with enhancing the development of humanity. Nothing could be farther from the truth. Damn their stories. They are of no importance as they are and were of no consequence. Their story is vacant. Let it go.

Humanity's evolution is rooted in the story of Lucy, Eve, Agnes, and your mother. It is their story of planting, cultivating and harvesting that gives meaning to our existence. It is our mothers' story that can inspire us to be fertile, to make more than we break; to offer more than we take; to love without reserve, fear or expectation.[2]

Agnes' pollination of all she touched stays past her time growing exponentially for all time enhancing our lives with both her action and her story. Her gift is the story of us all. Without Agnes and all the mothers she exemplifies, humanity would have become extinct millennia ago.

---

[2] Agnes was isolated from racism which so ate and continues to eat at the American psyche, so we cannot look to Agnes to inspire understanding here.

Book IX Essay

Note: Each volume of *The Story of Our Stories* includes one or more essays either related to the themes of the book, or were or might have been written by the main character(s). The "essay" for this volume is a letter exchange between Alexandra and Gabriel.

Put what back in Christmas?

December 10, 1989

Dear Gabe,

Merry Christmas.

Or should I say Merry Xmas. I was listening to Paul Harvey today and he was ranting about using X for Christ in Christmas and how we had to put Christ back in Christmas. Where does he get off? You know I love Paul Harvey and listen to him every day. But sometimes he is just wrong and this is one of them.

Christmas is a holiday for everyone and if calling it Xmas helps others feel like it is their holiday too, then let's call it Xmas. I know enough about my religion and early pagan religions to know that on or around December 25th many religions and kingdoms had a mid-winter holiday focusing on generosity for 100s of years before Jesus was born. I also know that Jesus was probably born in the springtime and that in early times his birthday was celebrated on the same day we celebrate your birthday.

I am glad we celebrate Jesus' birthday on this day because it was and is a holiday when people were and are expected to be cheerful and generous and come together as a community. That is what I believe Jesus stood for, so to celebrate his birth in the middle of the winter on a holiday that many peoples had celebrated by giving gifts, greeting each other and making festive events to overcome the doldrums of winter makes perfect sense.

To tell other people they cannot celebrate on a holiday that has existed for thousands of years is the opposite of what Jesus would want. Let's put the X back in Xmas. Let's open up the holiday to include all. There is absolutely no reason for anyone to shy away from the great mid-winter holiday. By calling the holiday Xmas everyone can make X mean what they want so they can feel personally invested and engaged. For me, X has always stood for Jesus as in the Chi-Rho sign. Xmas for me is Jesusmas or Christmas. For non-Christians it can mean whatever they want it to mean as long as it means sharing and loving. The important thing is for everyone to feel community and be generous and to greet everyone you see. Maybe we should greet everyone everyday —

but we don't —so let's make it so everyone wants to greet everyone on Xmas and stop being so stupid by isolating ourselves from everyone else. I think Jesus would want us to greet people of other religions and even people of no religion. It is what he preached.

Give Robert, Doug and Anne Marie a big kiss for me and tell them I wish then a Merry Xmas.

Love,

Sis

December 11, 1997

Dearest Alex,

I am finally answering your letter – more than a little late. Our Xmas letters crossed in the mail that year and that was that. I should have replied to your insightful letter – I am so sorry – but I will answer you today. I know you can't read it, but maybe my late reply will find its way to your memory.

Merry Xmas! I could not agree more with you. I am so glad you saw through Harvey's nonsense. You know I didn't like him at all because most of what he said was bull – I know you liked him and all. Anyway, glad to hear from you and to read about your insight on the winter solstice holiday.

Yes, humans have been celebrating Xmas for well over 4000 years. That is one of those statements that is both true and false. Humans have been celebrating the mid-winter holiday for over 4000 years but it was not until about 1650 years ago that the Bishop of Rome, Julius I, choose December 25th as the day to celebrate the birth of Christ and according to the Catholic Encyclopedia there is no evidence of the word Christmas being used until the eleventh century. Xmas was definitely in common use by the twelfth century and may have been used well before that.

Best I can tell you are right that Christians did not celebrate Jesus' "birthday" until around 100 years after the event and then celebrated it on April 17. April is the most likely month in which he was born. It was not until Julian I moved the birthday to December 25 was that considered the day to celebrate his birth. Julian's motivation was to get his members to stop celebrating the Pagan winter holiday by turning the holiday into a Christian Holiday. They could still celebrate the holiday, as they would no matter what, but now they would believe they were celebrating a Christian event.

There is strong evidence that many activities associated with the holiday that is currently called Christmas can be traced back to the Mesopotamians and the date of December 25 was selected by Julius I to co-opt the day the ancient sun-god Attis in Phrygia and the Persian sun-god, Mithras' birthdays were celebrated. Julius also wanted to take the thunder out of Saturnalia, a Roman festival dedicated to Saturn, the god of peace and plenty, that ran for a week and ended on December 24.

Isn't it funny that some of today's so-called Christian folks want to deny ownership to those who would celebrate this ancient festival, of which close to 100% of its meaning and rituals predated their religion by hundreds of years? Personally I have no problem with followers of Christ wanting to assign the birth of their scriptural God to the joyous mid-winter holiday. It makes perfect sense to have a reason to have a day that can outweigh the doldrums of winter – exactly the reason the Romans, Mesopotamians, Phrygian, Persian, Scandinavians, and many more cultures made festivities on or about the winter solstice. I suspect the whole gift giving ritual developed as a nice way to barter – if I had excess wheat, I'd give it to you and hope you would give me some of your excess olives of which I had few if any left and/or some wheat next year if my fields were fallow.

For at least a few decades, some American Christians have been trying to lay proprietary claim to a holiday that their religion had originally appropriated by yelling "Put Christ back in Christmas." Part of their objections seems to be around the holiday spirit of giving, singing and decorating – all the very reasons the holiday was invented in many cultures and why the Christians of the fourth century adopted it into their annual rituals. This is one of the few holidays where Christians can celebrate the goodness of God through the goodness of humanity who invented ways to defeat the loneliness and potential hazards of winter by sharing in stored goods, creating colorful displays, and singing to lift our spirits when nature is most barren. Isn't it ironic that the objections the few have about the "commercialization" and the universality of the holiday are exactly what the birth of Christ should mean to them – the beginning of a new life – new way of life – a more positive upbeat existence full of love and kindness.

I totally agree with you, "Let's put the X back in Xmas. Let's open up the holiday to include all. There is absolutely no reason for anyone to shy away from the great mid-winter holiday." The only reason anyone does not celebrate this great holiday is because they fear it may somehow mean they are paying tribute to Jesus. Quite the opposite, the Christians are, intentionally or not, paying tribute to paganism. They cannot "take Christmas back" because it was never theirs. Sure, because they dominated medieval Europe they were able to make the word Christmas stick to the holiday, but they did not invent the holiday, did not create its traditions and have no proprietary ownership. It is a holiday for all; a holiday where we come together across boundaries and ethnicity. The rest of us must claim back our holiday and make it so we can come together across religious and tribal beliefs. In pre-Christian times, countries that fought with each other enjoyed celebrating themed-winter holiday – celebrating the time the days began to get longer.

Just as the Christians should not only allow but encourage us to celebrate this most universal holiday, we should continue to welcome them to also celebrate our holiday. If they choose to spend some time being isolated so they can sing in their church; that is fine. If their idea of an interesting and uplifting decoration is a manger and its figurines, why not?

Let's get the "Christ" out of Christmas. The name has distorted the meaning of the holiday and encourages an intolerant view of the one truly universal holiday. Recently the name has encouraged the most religious to attempt to redefine the holiday season to their less than celebratory rituals. It is like having France claim that only Frenchman can compete in the Olympics. Wouldn't that defeat the purpose of the Olympics? Would you laugh especially hard if Olympic organizers dared to say Greece cannot compete? Is that any different than the Christians saying pagans cannot participate in celebrating the mid-winter holiday that they created and generously allowed the Christians to adapt as one of their holidays?

What's the solution? Like you wrote so elegantly so many years ago, put the X back in Xmas. It opens up the holiday for everyone to give generously and decorate lavishly. X, as in an equation, can mean whatever the celebrants want it to. The Christians can celebrate Jesus' birthday; the rest can celebrate giving, the winter solstice, or whatever they want to celebrate. In the end everyone is ahead. Even the hardiest atheist could not object to Merry Xmas on public grounds. And the Christians can take pride in knowing that everyone—possibly all over the world—is celebrating the birth of their founder, even if the celebrants did not know or admit it. It is a win-win-win solution.

Pre-Christians were generous at winter solstice in order to share their harvest with the less fortunate so everyone could make it through the winter—next year the rain might fall on your field and I will need you to share. Christians give because they believe it was on that day their founder gave up the glories of heaven to sacrifice himself for humans. Absolutely, Sis, let's put the X back in Xmas.

I miss you so much, especially all the wonderful conversations we had about poetry, life, religion and politics.

Love,

Gabriel

The Book Of Agnes

Appendix

The Story of Our Stories is inspired by a family of immigrants who came from Northern Italy and settled in Bad Ax, Wisconsin. In tribute to the ancestors, each volume traces the genealogy of one of the families. This volume includes the Ahnentafel chart tracing the family of Mary Caroline Nicolatti, the mother of the woman whom inspired our novel.

Mary Caroline Nicolatti

First Generation

1. Mary Caroline Nicolatti was born on 20 February 1880 in Trento, Tyrol, Austria. She was christened in Santa Maria Maggiore, Piazza Santa Maria Maggiore located between Via Rosimini and Via Cavour, Trento, Italy. She died on 18 September 1947 in Genoa, Wisconsin. She was buried in St. Charles Cemetery, Genoa, Wisconsin.

Mary was christened as Maria Carlotta Margareta Nichelatti in Santa Maria Maggiore in Trento, Italy. This is the church that held the third Council of Trent. It is not known why a second tt was added to her name as her ancestors names were recorded as Nichelati with one t. In America she wrote her name as Nicolatti.

Mary came to the US in 1881 per the 1900 census. She often said that she came to the US when she was 1 year old. She always had her garden where she raised much of her family's food. Just before her death she donated to St. Charles Church a stained glass window with a picture of the Blessed Virgin that is located over the main altar. For several years the window was covered over due to a remodeling. In 2010 the window was framed and now hangs above the altar.

Mary could whip out a lunch in no time at all. Jim Venner remembers his family stopping over unannounced as they went through town and Grandma would bring out something to eat at a moment's notice.

Mary married Bartholomew "Tom" Venner son of John Baptist "Giovanni" Venner and Mary Madeline Starlochi on 29 April 1902 in Genoa, Wisconsin. Bartholomew was born on 17 November 1873 in Genoa, Wisconsin. He died on 16 April 1946 in Genoa, Wisconsin. He was buried in St. Charles Cemetery, Genoa, Wisconsin.

Second Generation

2.   John M. Nichelatti was born on 6 April 1851 in Cognola, Trentino, Tyrol, Austria. He was christened in COGNOLA - SS Vito, Modesto e Crescenzia. He died on 17 August 1932 in LaCrosse, Wisconsin. He was buried on 20 August 1932 in St. Charles Cemetery, Genoa, Wisconsin. He married Margaret Gabriel on 6 February 1878 in Santa Maria Maggiore, Trento, Trentino, Tyrol, Austria [now Italy]. Few families used more variations in the spelling of their surname than the Nichelatti family. Versions of the name include Nicolatti and Nickelatti and others. The death certificates of John and Margaret were issued with their surname spelled differently. The family name in Italy was Nichelati. Reviewing similar names in use today in Italy the prevalent spelling is Nicoleti with very few use the spelling Nicolatti. The Nichelatti

family came to America in 1881. The Nichelattis settled in Norway, Michigan. In 1882 or 1883, they settled on a farm east of Genoa, now on County Trunk K in Section 22 and 23 of Genoa Township. The date of the first deed recorded to John Nichelatti is dated 18 July 1883; the deed shows he paid $800 dollars for 20 acres, purchasing the acreage from John Ott. The farm ownership to this day remains in the family. The census records for the year 1900 state they came from Austria. The 1910 census records state that both John and Margaret and their parents were born in Italy. However, with Austrian boundary changes that occurred after World War 1 the cities they came from are now part of Italy. He sometimes went by the name of Giovanni Nickelotti. According to the 1900 census records the family was naturalized in 1881 in Pennsylvania. Birth/Death Dates from his death certificate filed in Register 416A LaCrosse County, Wisconsin

3. Margaret Gabriel was born on 16 February 1855 in Levico, Trentino, Tyrol, Austria. She was christened in SS Redentore, Via Caproni, 16, 38056 Levico Terme (TN). She died on 23 July 1926 in Genoa, Wisconsin. She was buried on 25 July 1926 in St. Charles Cemetery, Genoa, Wisconsin. Margarita was born and raised in Levico Terme, Trento, Tyrol, Austria [Now Italy]. Her surname was Gabrielli. She started out studying to become a nun. However, she did not get along with the Mother Superior so she went to work for a rich family in Trento, Austria. That is where she met John. Does this all sound something like Maria of the Sound of Music? Margaret Gabriel Nichelatti's brother Joseph Gabriel's wife died in Genoa in 1884, leaving Joseph with no one to care for his three children. Joseph moved from Genoa to the state of Washington

to make a living, where he worked in the mining trade. He left his three children with John and Margaret, where they grew up with the twelve Nichelatti children. In the 1900 census an Anna Gabriel was identified as a 16 year old niece still living with the Nick family. The original Nick family home was small and very basic. How 16 children made it in that house is hard to imagine.

Third Generation

4. Michele Stefano Nichelati was born on 24 October 1813 in Povo, Trentino. He was christened in Santi Pietro e Andrea. He married Maria Antonia Chiogna on 31 December 1838 in Civezzano.

5. Maria Antonia Chiogna was born on 17 September 1818 in Civezzano, Trentino. She was christened in S. Maria Asunta.

6. Giovanni Battista Gabrielli was born on 11 Jun 1801 in Levico, Trentino. He was christened in SS Redentore, Via Caproni, 16, 38056 Levico Terme (TN). He married Orsola Epifannia Fruet on 15 July 1848.

7. Orsola Epifannia Fruet was born on 2 December 1817 in Levico, Trentino. She was christened in SS Redentore, Via Caproni, 16, 38056 Levico Terme (TN). She died in Italy.

Fourth Generation

8. Leonardo Andrea Gregorio Nichelati was born on 12 March 1781 in Povo, Trentino. He was christened in Santi Pietro e Andrea. He married Maddalena Martignoni.

9. Maddalena Martignoni.

10. Bortolo Chiogna was born on 11 January 1780 in Civezzano, Trentino, Tyrol, Austria. He married Lucia Bampi on 30 April 1810 in Civezzano, Trentino, Tyrol, Austria.

11. Lucia Bampi was born on 16 November 1779 in Civezzano, Trentino, Tyrol, Austria. She was christened in Santi Pietro e Andrea.

12. Michele Gabrielli was born on 26 February 1770 in Levico, Trentino. He was christened in SS Redentore, Via Caproni, 16, 38056 Levico Terme (TN). He married Anna Libardi.

13. Anna Libardi was born in Levico, Trentino. She was christened in SS Redentore, Via Caproni, 16, 38056 Levico Terme (TN).

14. Antonio Fruet married Anna Visintainer. Apparently not born in Levico

15. Anna Visintainer

Fifth Generation

16. Giacomo Nichelati was born on 2 December 1729 in Povo, Trentino. He was christened in Santi Pietro e Andrea. He married Barbara DeMarchi.

17. Barbara DeMarchi.

20. Pietro Chiogna was born on 30 August 1738 in Cognola, Trentino, Tyrol, Austria. He was christened on 30 August 1738 in Cognola, Trentino, Tyrol, Austria. He died Santi Vito. He married Caterina Pallaoro.

21. Caterina Pallaoro.

22. Ognibene Bampi was born on 8 March 1755 in Civezzano, Trentino, Tyrol, Austria. He married Maria Scartezzini.

23. Maria Scartezzini.

24. Michele Gabrielli was born on 3 November 1726 in Trentino. He married Barbara, surname unknown.

25. Barbara.

26. Bernardo Libardi was born in Levico.

28. Cristino Fruet.

30. Udalrico Visintainer.

Sixth Generation

32.	Leonardo Nichelati was born on 9 March 1687 in Povo, Trentino. He died on 26 July 1759 in Povo, Trentino. He married Anna, surname unknown, about 1715.

33.	Anna.

40.	Andrea Chiogna.

48.	Bartolomeo Gabrielli

Seventh Generation

64.	Pietro Nichelati was born on 6 January 1648 in Povo, Trentino. He married Leonarda Lutti on 1 March 1677.

65.	Leonarda Lutti.

Eighth Generation

128.	Giacomo Nichelati was born about 1605. He married Elisabetta Battisti on 3 November 1631.

129.	Elisabetta Battisti.

130.	Leonardo Lutti.

Ninth Generation

256.   Ororico Nichelati was born about 1580.

258.   Pietro Battisti.

Synopsis of *The Story of Our Stories*

The Story of Our Stories is the story of Maria Prima and Maria Therese, Peter and John, Adelaide and Stefano, Agnes and her children, and especially the individuals who peopled the Mount of San Bernardo and the Valley of Saint James the Lesser who turned the roughness of Bad Ax into the gentleness of Genoa, Wisconsin—but first and foremost it is our story, the story of you and me. Our story is written as an epic composed of twelve books, each with a supportive appendix. Each book covers a different measurement. Some cover the life of a typical family member of a specific generation, others reflect many people of a generation, another traces the entire story from beginning to now, and one looks into a future predicated by the behavior of our mothers. Each volume tells a critical part of the story, is an integral part of the whole, and plays into the unfolding of the epic. While arranged by number, each book can be read independent of the rest.

Book 1: *Time to Journey Home*—is a travelogue about my trip back to the homeland and how I was inspired to write *The Story of Our Stories*. The appendix includes a pre-1909 ahnentafel history of the author, autobiographies of select persons who researched the family's ancestry, a manifesto calling for a new epic, and the story of rough-and-tough Bad Ax evolving into Genoa, Wisconsin—the home of a spray drift of calm. The closing essay in this book reveals the great inequality perpetrated by the Social Security Act and offers a fail-safe solution to equalize and perpetuate Social Security ad infinitum.

Book 2: *The Veneid*—This epic poem tells of a journey into our past (similar to the Divine Comedy) where the poet meets many of our mothers, who celebrate woman and kindness (contrasting to the Aeneid's celebration of man and war). The appendix includes the Geno outline of the female linage going back to Eve, traces the ahnentafel of the mothers, provides a chronology of major events, includes an essay on the supremacy of stories, and offers selections from The Truly Short History of Man.

Book 3: *Begetters of Children*—This work of historical fiction shows how the branch of one family settled on San Bernardo Mountain in Lombardy, Italy; developed a village; farmed unfarmable land; avoided plagues, wars, and other human disasters; had many children; immigrated to Genoa, Wisconsin; developed the land; and populated half of America (I joke only a little here). The appendix includes an article on the role of epic literature in shaping human perspective, a history of the founding and development of the mountain town of San Bernardo, the ahnentafel story of Stefano Pedretti, and facsimiles of vital records of San Bernardo.

Book 4: *Lost Book of Valle di Santa Maria Prima Della Morte*—This novel is based on Giovanni Vener's revelations about the life and accomplishments of his grandmother Maria Prima Della Morte (1758–1817). The appendix includes the genealogical history for Giovanni Vener (born 13 March 1829), the story of Campodolcino and Val San Giacomo, primary documents showing vital information of Giovanni's ancestors, a short work clarifying the illogicality of classism, an essay on the failure of the second amendment to protect freedom, and an article catechizing the god story.

Book 5: *L'Ultima Preghiera*—Marie Teresa Cerletti-Pedretti speaks her last prayer aloud a day or two before her death on January 29, 1853, as she realizes that her Maker has called her too early, before she can raise her family and prevent her elder sons from abandoning their heritage to the dream of a better future. The appendix tells the stories of the major churches of worship where the baptisms, marriages, and funerals of our characters took place, presents Maria Teresa's ahnentafel, explores the transitional year 1848, and includes Maria Teresa's letter to her children on the beginning of life.

Book 6: *Lettere d'Amore*—Stefano Pedretti and Adelaide Lombardi wrote a score of letters while courting each other at great distances in 1853 and 1854. The last letter is written by Adelaide forty years after she tragically lost the love of her life to a freak lumber accident. The appendix includes the ahnentafel of Adelaide Lombardi, tracing her family back to Airolo, Switzerland; the story of Airolo; primary documents of Adelaide's ancestry; photographs of our main characters' gravestones; an essay identifying the three stages of love; and observations on the imminent failure of compromise to resolve anything.

Book 7: *Diary of Giovanni Vener: An Immigrant's Journey to the Heart of America*—selections from the diary of a pioneer written while incarcerated in the Vernon County Insane Asylum at the turn of the century. John Venner spent the last days of his life confined, and his diary fluctuates between manic and depressed days. Readers glimpse inside of the head of an immigrant reliving the high points and the low points of being an innovator on the frontier. Giovanni's story is supported with the second half of the story of Genoa, the town Giovanni called home and that he helped define. The book concludes with a manifesto by a great-grandchild of John calling for the end of famine, pestilence, and war—the trinity of premature death.

The appendix includes a score of facsimiles of Genoa postcards, the ahnentafel notations of Giovanni's wife, Mary Madeline Starlochi, and primary documents found during the research of Starlochi family.

Book 8: *Peter: A Profile* describes a transitional figure who dominates his community as the world leaves the age of horse and buggy for petrol-powered mass transportation. Peter Pedretti was the wisest man I ever met. He raised eleven children, mostly by himself as his wife died shortly after the birth of their youngest daughter. The appendix includes the story of Gofis, Austria, home of the Malins and Petlarnbrand; Tochov, Bohemia, home of Maggie's mother; photos of Peter's homes and farms; the ahnentafel of Peter's wife, Maggie Malin; an essay by Peter offering a path to making an ethical life; and selections from the multi-year Sunday-morning discussions between Peter, a progressive thinker, and his conservative brother Stephen, agreeing often on goals but separated on policy and implementation.

Book 9: *The Book of Agnes*—A novel based on one of Giovanni's granddaughters, Agnes. It is a tale of the extraordinary life of one woman's gentle manner, kindness, and fertility over forty summers and forty winters, when capitalists' greed undermined the economic stability of the world, a deranged ethnic population inspired by a maniac caused the death of fifty million people, and Soviet panic all but knocked out any remaining American sense and led to numerous wrongful wars. Walt Whitman had Agnes in mind when he eulogized the "numberless unknown heroes equal to the greatest heroes known."

Book 10: *Hoe-ers: Fifteen Stories by Thirteen Siblings*—The autobiographies of thirteen of Agnes' fifteen children are accompanied by the imagined dairies of two others. You will often read about the same events told from different perspectives. The appendix will include the story of the forty double cousins—the grandchildren Peter & Adelaide Pedretti and Tom & Mary Venner—along with the Geno story, tracing their paternal roots back to Northern Europe, the Middle East, Africa, and ultimately to Mitochondrial Adam. The concluding essay in this book will demonstrate that our worship of work—"get a job"—is nothing more than the continuation of the entitled keeping indentured serfs at service to their avarice, complemented by a tract calling for a maximum (as opposed to minimum) wage. A special section will include the creative writings of select "hoe-ers."

Book 11: *Mick: Planter of Seeds*—Selections from the author's memoirs show a farm boy becoming a college professor and going on to become an international arts festival impresario, renovator of abandoned homes, poet, and writer of this epic series. The appendix will include the ahnentafel of our author covering upwards of 480 ancestors, a photo essay telling with pictures and words the story of the immigrants who played the central role of turning this story into an epic, and select primary documents from the international theater festivals made by the author. The main essay will present the revolutionary view that life on earth is made up of trinities and not of dualities or singularities.

Book 12: *Il Lavoro di Artisti*—Book 12 presents a collection of artwork created by members of the family born into the fifth generation (the grandchildren of Agnes). Their work exemplifies that this family makes art instead of going to war to express their creative energy. The appendix will include the story of the children of Peter Pedretti and Bartholomew "Tom" Venner, including some fun facts about the families, a short thesis suggesting a radical reordering of representation in the US House of Representatives, and an essay demonstrating that the arts provide the exemplary methodology of education. The main piece is a manifesto by a great-grandchild of Giovanni Venner and Stefano Pedretti calling for the end of nation-states, monotheism, and weapons of destruction—the primary architects of war for the past three thousand years.

Note: The contents of these books are subject to change.

Other Books by Michael Pedretti
Begetters of Children
Time to Journey Home
Diary of Giovanni Vener: An Immigrant's Journey to the Heart of America
the dog and i: twenty-seven poems

Works in Progress
The Story of Our Stories [12 volumes]
Delighting the Senses [2 volumes]
Pinkie Rang the Bell: Poems from 2020
The Trinity and Other Essays

Experience "a New World epic of hope, change and freedom."
Discover your past though this " amazing series of characters and events."
Delight in "the exploration of life, creativity, growing things."

Made in the USA
Middletown, DE
10 July 2022